Julia,

THE ESCAPADE
CONTINUES.

Bill

# MISSING

Also by Bill Noel

*Folly*

*The Pier*

*Washout*

*The Edge*

*The Marsh*

*Ghosts*

# MISSING

*A Folly Beach Mystery*

## BILL NOEL

iUniverse, Inc.
Bloomington

# Missing
## A Folly Beach Mystery

*iUniverse books may be ordered through booksellers or by contacting:*

*iUniverse*
*1663 Liberty Drive*
*Bloomington, IN 47403*
*www.iuniverse.com*
*1-800-Authors (1-800-288-4677)*

*Because of the dynamic nature of the Internet, any web addresses or links contained in this book may have changed since publication and may no longer be valid. The views expressed in this work are solely those of the author and do not necessarily reflect the views of the publisher, and the publisher hereby disclaims any responsibility for them.*

*Any people depicted in stock imagery provided by Thinkstock are models, and such images are being used for illustrative purposes only.*

*Certain stock imagery © Thinkstock.*

*ISBN: 978-1-4759-5667-2 (sc)*
*ISBN: 978-1-4759-5668-9 (e)*
*ISBN: 978-1-4759-5669-6 (dj)*

*Library of Congress Control Number: 2012919387*

*Printed in the United States of America*

*iUniverse rev. date: 11/13/2012*

*Cover photo by Bill Noel.*
*Author photo by Susan Noel.*

# CHAPTER 1

Hotter summers had vacationed on Folly Beach before, or so they said. This was the worst I'd experienced in my six years there. A cheery television meteorologist had shared that the thermometer was pushing triple digits, and with the skyrocketing humidity, it felt much hotter. I had just left my photo gallery, where the ancient, undersized air conditioner had failed miserably to bring comfort to the few-and-far-between customers and the slightly overweight, aging proprietor. If anyone had stopped to offer me an Alaskan cruise, I'd have been packing.

A cruise wasn't in the offing, so rushing was unnecessary. I was in my early sixties and retired, and with the exception of Landrum Gallery, which had been named after yours truly in a moment of egotistical delight, my obligations were few. These included staying healthy, avoiding sunburns, keeping out of the way of the hyper vacationers on my small South Carolina island, and living out my remaining years enjoying the place. And there was much to enjoy—the sights and sounds of the majestic Atlantic Ocean, nearby beautiful and historic Charleston, and more friends than I'd ever had. Not to mention the thanks I gave for still being able to get around. Despite those pluses, the heat still sucked.

My cottage was only a few blocks from the gallery on Center Street, the literal and retail center of the island, so I could have walked home. I told myself that with the heat, it was safer to drive. That was my rationalization for driving when it was hot. I had other rationalizations for driving at different times of year. Walking was a close cousin to one of my allergies—exercise

I pulled my SUV into the side yard beside my house. I had learned years ago that on the quirky island, yards often served as driveways. I didn't want to be different.

I was occasionally greeted on my porch by a curious rabbit or a small lizard. But today I was surprised to see Samuel Perkins on my front step, fanning his face with a menu from a local pizza restaurant. It was late afternoon and the step was shaded by the house, but it was still skillet hot.

"Afternoon, Mr. Landrum," said the ever-polite, perspiring young man. It was strange being referred to that way since I preferred being called by my first name, Chris.

Samuel had turned fifteen a couple of months ago, but I'd first met him on my inaugural visit to Folly Beach. I'd been walking around the island photographing sights that I thought were unusual at the time, though I was later to learn that they were the rule rather than the exception, when Samuel startled me as I photographed a bottle tree in his neighbor's yard. The fifteen-year-old Samuel bore little resemblance to the towheaded youngster I had first met, other than his wide-eyed smile that revealed a youthful curiosity. He now stood five foot ten and looked me directly in the eyes. He was still trim, but muscles puffing out the sleeves of his black golf shirt told me that he'd spent more time working out than on a computer. The hem of his bright-red shorts fell far below his knees, and his black tennis shoes had covered more miles than many newer-model cars.

"Hot enough for you?" I asked, being the consummate conversationalist.

He nodded and gave me an exasperated look that was not uncommon coming from teens to the "elderly."

I wiped away a trickle of sweat that had rolled down my cheek. "What brings you here?" I asked.

Samuel turned his head to the left; his long brown hair flopped toward the door. It looked like it had been cut by a lawnmower with a dull blade. I translated the move as his wanting to get out of the heat. He got no argument from me.

He followed me into the small living room. "Something to drink?" I asked. "Got Coke, bottled water?" The refrigerator was also stocked with double bottles of white wine and a six-pack of Coors Light, but I wasn't going there with my young friend.

"Coke would be nice," he said. He watched as I walked to the kitchen.

He started to follow but turned and walked back into the living room instead. I grabbed two Cokes and returned to the room where he was staring out the window. He then walked to the other side of the room. He reminded me of a caged animal not knowing where, or whether, there was an escape route.

I pointed my Coke can toward the old, upholstered chair beside the front door. "Have a seat."

"Thanks," he said. "I think I'll stand." His left hand held the drink. His right hand went from his shorts pocket to his head and then back to his pocket.

I didn't know whether to stand or sit, so I walked to the thermostat and tried to force more cold air out of the vents. It wouldn't work, but it gave me something to do while Samuel relaxed enough to tell me what had brought him to my stoop.

"Mr. Landrum," he began, "I feel sort of funny coming here. You've always treated me nice. You sort of listened to me when other grown-ups ignored me."

I gave him my full attention. We were still standing.

He finally spoke. "Last night, a little after sunset—must have been around eight thirty—I was sort of walking past the Oceanfront Villas over on West Arctic." He paused and then smiled. "There's a girl there on vacation. I met her on the beach yesterday. Hoped to run into her at her condo. I didn't. Never mind." His smile turned to a frown. "I was up by where the road bends and goes back toward Ashley."

"Near the public walkway?" I asked.

"Exactly," he said. He walked toward the door to the kitchen. "Then I saw it. I know I saw it." He walked to the chair I had offered earlier and flopped down, almost dropping his drink.

I had no idea what was going on and lowered myself into the only other chair in the room. "What'd you see?"

"She was sort of walking toward the street from the beach," he said. He then stared at the Coke can like it was the most fascinating thing he'd ever seen. "She was walking down the ramp to the parking area. Then it happened."

He stared at the can.

"What happened, Samuel?"

"This man sort of grabbed her—"

"The girl from the condo?" I interrupted.

"No, another girl," he said, and then he paused.

"Sorry," I said. "Go on."

"Okay, he grabbed her and dragged her to a car, pushed her inside. His hand was over her mouth. She couldn't scream. I think she sort of kicked, but ... I don't know what. Mr. Landrum, she was kidnapped."

Festival and actually remembered my name. That meant a lot to a little kid."

I smiled and told him that I remembered.

"Then you caught some killers when the police couldn't. I remember one where the cops said it was a suicide and you figured out it wasn't."

"Just luck," I said.

"Don't think so," said Samuel. "Not according to the paper. That big story back in the winter said you had sort of baffled the cops with how you figured out the killer in Tennessee."

*And got someone dear to me killed in the process*, I thought.

I shook that dreadful memory and looked at Samuel. "What's that have to do with what you told me?" I asked.

"Mr. Landrum, I didn't tell the cops." He shook his head. "You've always treated me like I had some sense. I think if I went to the cops with my story, they'd laugh me right out of the station house. I know you'd know what to do, so here I am." He sighed like a weight had been lifted off his broad shoulders.

"Let me think about it."

"I sort of hoped you'd say that."

*What have I sort of gotten myself into now?* I wondered.

# CHAPTER 3

Karen Lawson was a detective in the Charleston County sheriff's office. Folly Beach is located in Charleston County, although many of its bohemian residents would like to deny it, and the sheriff's office investigates the more serious crimes on the barrier island. Through no fault of mine—well, maybe a little—I had become familiar with a handful of murder investigations that had taken place on Folly Beach over the past few years, along with several of the detectives.

Detective Lawson was in her midforties, had chestnut brown hair, was runner-trim, and had been my girlfriend, for the lack of a better term, for the last year. To confound my leisurely life of retirement, her father was Brian Newman, who for the past eighteen years had been Folly's director of public safety—"police chief" or "top cop" to the less-formal citizenry. We had become friends before his daughter and I had started dating.

Karen's work schedule was often dictated by inconsiderate killers who didn't limit their indiscretions to the traditional workweek. My schedule was more structured since I opened the gallery each Thursday through Sunday.

The day after I spoke to Samuel, Karen and I watched a matinee at the Terrace Theater, one of Charleston's better movie theaters, located off Folly Road near Karen's house. She liked it because it showed a wide range of movies, from first-run to *The Sound of Music* or *Psycho*. I liked it because Karen liked it and because it sold beer, wine, and champagne. Sunday had been one of the busier days at the gallery, and I used that as my excuse to nearly fall asleep during the tedious, how-many-facial-expressions-can-the-star-make chick flick. Karen, who wasn't as traumatized as I was by watching a romance, agreed that the film, whose title I'd already forgotten, didn't have enough action.

It wasn't as hot as it had been the last couple of weeks, so she suggested that we drive to the Battery and walk some of the flower-laden streets, ogling the mansions facing the Charleston harbor. After the initial shock from stepping out of the freezing theater into the eighties-plus, humid South Carolina afternoon, I decided it wasn't such a bad idea. It might wake me up. It took two trips around the block to find a parking space on East Bay Street. I parallel parked as the distinctive white-with-red-trim Carnival cruise ship slowly pulled out of the harbor on its way to exotic locations.

The temperature was more tolerable than in recent days, but after we walked up East Bay Street and a couple of blocks over Tradd Street, we agreed that the shade-covered benches in White Point Gardens looked inviting. We strolled hand in hand down Meeting Street and grabbed one of the traditional wood benches in the historic gardens that overlooked the bay. I had made the walk countless times but was still taken by the beauty, majesty, and history of the area.

I had debated whether to tell Karen about my conversation with Samuel, and the more I thought about it, the more I knew I couldn't keep it to myself. Besides, her experience could shed light on his story.

I caught my breath and took off my fedora-style, canvas Tilley hat and waved it in front of my face. It wasn't a blast of cold air, but it helped. We both wore shorts, and I could see drops of perspiration rolling down Karen's well-toned legs. I gave her a summary of Samuel's tale.

"Can you trust him?" asked Karen when I finished.

"I'm not certain. I've known him casually for years. He's a good kid, friendly and intelligent." I put the hat on the bench beside me and leaned back. "But truthfully, I don't know what he saw."

She reached across my lap, grabbed my Tilley, and began fanning her face with it. "I'm no expert on teenagers," she said. "Lord knows it's been years since I was one, and I'm not around them enough to know much. I know they have vivid imaginations."

I had spent some time a couple of years before with Jason, Amber's son, so I'd spent a modicum of time observing the mind of the young adult. "My experience is limited too," I said. "But Samuel came across as truthful and was sincerely upset by the mysterious event."

"Even if he thinks he saw what you described," said Karen, "you know eyewitness descriptions are unreliable."

I nodded.

"It could've been lovers having fun," said Karen. "Playing games, pretending, horsing around."

I nodded again and remained silent.

"Okay," she said. "What is it?"

"What if he's right?" I asked. I looked toward the bay and then back at Karen. "I'd feel terrible if someone was nabbed right off the walk to the beach and something horrible happens."

Karen smiled. "What's your gut tell you?"

"Samuel saw what he thought he saw."

She smiled again. "I can't do much about it from my end, but since you and Chief Newman are close, I bet he'd run it through his databases and see if anyone is missing who fits the description." She gave me a big grin. "Don't tell him I suggested it."

I said I'd get with the chief tomorrow. She said "good" and told me that all this detective work had given her an appetite. She wanted to know where I was going to feed her—or, more accurately, which air-conditioned restaurant we were driving to.

Fortunately, Karen was a cheap date, and we settled on McDonald's.

# CHAPTER 4

Karen gobbled a handful of fries to replenish the energy lost during the walk, took a sip of her drink, and then said, "I hear the mayor's trying to force the chief out."

The restaurant was packed, but no one paid attention to our conversation. Kids screaming about getting to the pool took priority over a balding gentleman and the attractive, twenty-years-younger off-duty cop who was his lady friend.

Mayor Joshua Lally had been elected in April and had used his landslide victory to hit the ground running. It seemed that his goal was to overturn everything the former mayor had worked for years to put in place.

"Doesn't surprise me," I said. "I've heard he's a puppet for that bunch they're calling the interlopers."

"You're right if you mean the new rich who are moving to the island and trying to sanitize it so it's like Isle of Palms or Daniel Island," she said, slamming her drink on the table and glaring out the large window at the traffic on Folly Road.

I'd struck a nerve. Over the last decade there had been skirmishes, some minor and some coming nearly to blows, between two groups. There were those who wanted to, as they put it, "keep Folly, Folly." The laid-back bohemian atmosphere and the dearth of hotels, major condo complexes, and upscale shopping so prevalent in up-and-coming beach communities were points of pride for most old-timers and newcomers who wanted the simpler lifestyle. And then there was the growing legion of recent arrivals who had money and wanted to use it to insulate themselves in McMansions, who abhorred the casual way of life and people, and who thought vacationers were as undesirable at "their beach" as sand fleas and tiger sharks.

Folly's mayor and six-member city council were elected to represent their constituents regardless of how diverse and divisive their interests may be. Each election brought the opportunity to change some of the cast of characters and the direction in which the majority led.

"Has the mayor or any council members told the chief they want him out?" I asked.

"Not directly," said Karen. "The chief isn't in a position to ask, of course. He's only heard rumors, unless there's something he hasn't told me."

Karen referred to her dad as "the chief" other than during the most intimate family conversations. For several years, many residents didn't know their true relationship and speculated—a kinder way of saying "sowed rumors"—that she was his young lover.

"Has the mayor said anything to him about his performance?"

"Yeah," she said and then made a noise between a laugh and humph. "Said he was too soft on criminals."

She shook her head. "The man's been Folly's chief for eighteen years. He came right out of the army, where he was an MP and Special Services before that. He's tough as titanium. Too *soft*? Bull!"

I had seen the chief at work and knew he was good at balancing strict law enforcement with doses of common sense. If an inebriated citizen walked home and was thirty feet from his front yard, the chief would help him make it home safely. He knew his islanders, knew if they were a danger to themselves or others, knew when trouble was around the corner, and understood that tourism was a major industry on Folly Beach.

I wasn't certain where our peaceful, calm conversation about the alleged crime that Samuel had reported had gone astray. Karen was livid. I reached across the small table and put my hand on hers. Her fist was balled up, but she didn't pull away. "What can I do?" I asked.

"It's unfair," she said as she looked at our hands on the table. "He's given a good part of his life to that community. He almost died three years ago doing his job and now this." Her gaze moved to my face.

"There's nothing you can do." She gave a strained smile. "Thanks for listening."

"Let me think about it," I said. "And I'll get with him tomorrow about Samuel."

*Let me think about it*, I thought. What did that mean?

*   *   *

I was cautious about the political dynamics and atmosphere at the police station, so I called Brian at home. He lived just off-island in a condo complex across Folly Road from the Piggly Wiggly, where he was close enough to respond to emergencies yet out of the fray of the beach life.

Brian sounded out of breath, and it scared me. He was in his late sixties, trim, and generally in excellent health but had had two heart attacks three years ago and almost died. I was relieved when he said he had jogged three miles on his treadmill and feigned being insulted when I said I was worried.

"Since it's not yet eight o'clock," he said and took a deep breath, "I assume this isn't a social call."

No wonder he was chief. "Got a favor to ask," I said. I gave him an abbreviated version of my conversation with Samuel and asked if he could check if there were any missing persons reports that would match the extremely skimpy description of the woman Samuel saw abducted.

"Saw allegedly abducted, you mean." Brian sighed. "Are you meddling in police business again?"

I huffed. "Of course not," I said. "I'm simply doing my civic duty and reporting a suspicious incident to the local authorities."

I had butted heads with the chief on a couple of occasions. Of course, it wasn't my fault that I had stumbled on a murder or two, and of course it wasn't my fault that I, along with a few, shall I say, *strange* friends had managed to catch the killers using techniques that were not found in any police procedures manual. I never could tell if the chief was more perturbed that a bunch of amateurs had achieved something that law enforcement had failed to do or that I nearly got some of his innocent citizens killed in the process. Regardless, over time he and I had become close friends. He knew that I was prone to butt in where

I shouldn't and I knew that he would grouse, grumble, and yell at me for doing it.

"Civic duty, right," he said.

"So," I said, "will you check?"

"Will you drop it if I don't?"

"Umm, well—"

"That's what I thought," he interrupted.

After a couple more back-and-forth digs, Brian agreed to check on missing persons and I agreed not to do anything about it until I heard back from him. I had no trouble agreeing to that since I didn't know what I could have done. He said he didn't have more time to waste on wild-goose chases and had to take a shower and get back to real police work. I said that I was sure that I had something important to do as well. I didn't know what it might be.

I hung up and walked to the aging Mr. Coffee machine. I had pressed the on button before I called the chief, but apparently the machine didn't get the message. After a long illness, Mr. Coffee had passed away. I stared at the deceased near-antique and reflected on the chief's statement about me meddling in police business.

Samuel had come to me because he trusted that I would take him seriously. No, I wouldn't stop.

Would that be a decision that I would live to regret?

# CHAPTER 5

It had taken me nearly six years of retirement—more accurately, semiretirement, since I opened the photo gallery four days a week—before I'd gotten the hang of cramming fifteen minutes of worthwhile activity into a twenty-four hour day. I got off the phone with the chief and walked next door to Bert's Market, Folly's iconic grocery, to take advantage of its free coffee and buy a replacement for my Mr. Coffee machine. I had often told anyone who asked that Bert's, in addition to never closing, sold everything from beer to bait. I quickly realized that a replacement for my coffeemaker didn't fall within that range, so I decided to take a road trip to America's answer to the total shopping experience—Walmart.

I wasn't a connoisseur of coffee and was befuddled by the thirteen different coffeemakers on the shelf. I thought all they had to do was to slosh hot water over ground coffee and drop it into a pot. So, I took the retiree's solution and picked the cheapest machine. Besides, Bert's made some of the best coffee on the island, and I was its neighbor. I couldn't think of a reason to buy a contraption that made frappes, tea, and hot chocolate, ground the coffee beans, and, I wouldn't have been surprised to learn, received 137 cable channels plus HBO.

"You escaped the island," came a voice from behind me. I tucked the seventeen-dollar purchase under my left arm and turned to see the smiling face of city council member Marc Salmon. He had a plastic Walmart bag in each hand.

"I see you're on a major shopping expedition," I replied.

I had known Marc for most of my time on Folly. He and a fellow council member, Houston, held court daily at the Lost Dog Café and spread gossip and occasional facts. He had been reelected several times and understood the compromises—waffling, according to cynical residents—needed to hold the job.

We shared comments about the hot temperatures, about the great deal he had gotten on laundry detergent, and about the herd of vacationers who had invaded the island before I broached the subject of Chief Newman. He'd made comments before that were supportive of the chief, so I felt comfortable raising the subject.

"I hear Chief Newman's head's on the block," I said.

"Hmm," said Marc. He set the two bags on the floor and leaned against an end cap in the pharmacy aisle. "Our new 'yuck, there's a vacationer' mayor's doing everything he can without calling out the National Guard to get Newman gone."

That answered any question I may have had about Marc's loyalty to the new mayor. "Going to succeed?" I asked.

Marc looked around. "Wouldn't be surprised. Don't think the majority of the council members are on Lally's side—yet. But he's doing everything he can to stack the deck." He looked me in the eyes. "Maybe Newman'll resign. He doesn't have to put up with that crap."

Marc knew that I was close to the chief, and perhaps he was hinting that I should carry that suggestion to him. If so, he clearly didn't know Chief Brian Newman. There's no way he would resign.

"Let me know if you hear anything," I said. Marc loved to talk, so he'd take that as a personal invitation to nose around.

With a new coffeemaker in hand and an ally on the council nosing around, I had already exceeded my fifteen minutes of worthwhile activities. I headed home to my air-conditioned cocoon to plan tomorrow's worthwhile activity—planning that would prove to be worthless.

accumulate in a womanless home. Jacob moved a pillow off the couch and waved for me to sit. He offered me a drink. I declined.

"Samuel's in Charleston with friends. A friend's mother took three of them to the market. She had to pick up some gifts to send to a cousin, and the boys wanted to tag along." He laughed. "Think Samuel just wanted to get away on my day off."

Fleetwood Mac played in the background, and the large window air conditioner roared through its efforts to cool the house. It failed.

"Samuel had come to me about an incident a few days ago," I said. I wasn't comfortable telling Jacob about it, but I had to tell him something.

"I know, I know," said Jacob. "He told me. Sorry he burdened you."

"No burden at all," I said. "I wanted to let him know what I'd found—actually, how little I had found."

"Mind if I get a beer?" said Jacob. "Sure you don't want one?"

I said no to both questions as he headed to the back of the house. I looked around. The room didn't have any personal items or mementos sitting around except for one silver-framed photo on the small table by the door. It showed a much younger Jacob with his arm around a petite, attractive, curly-haired blonde whose arms were on the shoulders of a young boy, perhaps four or five years old, standing in front of her.

Jacob returned to the room and caught me looking at the photo.

"Happier days," he said. "That's Patricia, my wife, and Samuel ten years ago." He looked down on his bottle of Coors and then slowly back at me. "It was taken six months before we lost her."

"I'm so sorry."

His gaze had fallen back on the beer bottle. "She went in the hospital for routine surgery on a torn ligament in her leg—waterskiing accident. She got MRSA, a staph infection. Dead three days later."

"I'm sorry," I repeated. What else could I say?

"Yeah," he said and slowly shook his head. "Samuel took it hard—as you could imagine."

"He seems like a great kid," I said. A bead of sweat rolled down my left cheek, and I wiped it away.

"Sorry about the heat," said Jacob. "The air conditioner's busted, I think."

"Not a good time for that," I said and smiled.

He shook his head and continued, "Yeah, my boy's a good kid." He paused and then smiled. "Most of the time. It's been hard on him. I've tried to be a good dad, but bringing him up alone, I haven't been here for him much."

"I can't imagine," I said—a feeble response, at best.

"To make ends meet, I've had to spend whatever hours they can give me at the Pig, and for a few years, I had to take a second job washing cars." He paused and took another swig. "Ate up most of the hours in the day—hardly ever saw the boy."

Jacob worked in the meat department at the Pig and was there nearly every time I was in the store. I was also surprised that Samuel had never mentioned his mother.

"I guess I'd better be going," I said.

Jacob motioned for me to stay seated. He looked at the floor and at the photo of the family's happier days. "I'm not saying that Samuel didn't see what he told you, I'm really not. But—" He paused and turned toward me. "Umm, let me tell you something. This isn't the first time that Samuel has come up with a story that's—let's say a stretch."

"A stretch?"

"The boy has a powerful imagination," said Jacob. He paused again and looked at the ceiling like he was trying to remember something. "A couple of years back, he read in a history book that in World War II a German submarine was spotted off the coast near here. Don't think it was ever confirmed, but that was the story."

"I remember hearing about it," I said.

"In March, the boy and a schoolmate, Ron, came home from the beach down by the Tides and swore they saw the conning tower of a sub popping up out of the water in the direction of Kiawah."

"Anyone else see it?" I asked.

Jacob shook his head. "Samuel told the story twice, and I looked at Ron. He slowly shook his head, so I asked him if he'd seen the sub."

"I'm guessing he didn't," I said.

"He told me that that Samuel saw it and by the time he could show Ron where it was, it had submerged." He shrugged.

I didn't say anything.

"Sure you don't want a beer?" asked Jacob.

He had apparently given himself a promotion while away from my struggling photo gallery. Before answering the call from Cal, Charles was my unpaid sales manager, and now the gallery was only open four days a week. I learned the first two years that I could lose as much money being open every day as I could lose only being open four days. And, after all, I was supposed to be retired, so four sounded better than seven.

Truth be known, I had missed his quirky habits and the nonsensical conversations and good times we had had together before he went to Cal's aid. "Sounds good," I said. "Then I won't put you on the payroll starting Friday."

"Seems that's a little low on the pay scale for someone with my talents," he said and glanced sideways at me.

The two seagulls squawked at the boat they were circling like they expected the two fishermen to throw them some lunch. A young girl squealed from glee as her dad yanked a small shark onto the deck of the pier. And my newly rehired sales manager—correction, executive sales manager complained about his nonsalary. All was abnormally normal on Folly Beach.

\*     \*     \*

Charles arrived a half hour before I normally opened the gallery. Another one of his quirky habits was alternating among what seemed like a limitless supply of college and university T-shirts or sweatshirts— long-sleeved regardless of the temperature. His first day back was no exception. A black bear's head zooming off somewhere with the words "Michigan Tech" in gold under it adorned the gold, long-sleeved shirt that covered the chest of my "executive" sales manager as he entered the front door with a cheerful smile. His cane tapped the well-worn floor.

He waved the cane around the room. "Are we going to sell a herd of these photos today?" he said in a singsong voice.

We had never sold anywhere near a herd of photos since the gallery opened—although I'm not certain how many that would have been. Fortunately, I did not have to count on the profits from the gallery to survive. If I did, there wouldn't be a gallery. The financially draining business cost me considerably more than I took in, but as a result of an early retirement buyout from my boring job as a bureaucrat in middle

America, two lucky real estate ventures, and an inheritance from an acquaintance on Folly, I could still lose some on my expensive hobby while keeping the doors open.

"Hope so," I said, optimistically. "We have a herd of them available, and with an executive sales manager now on staff, I expect miracles."

"Then I've come to the rescue," said Charles. "Speaking of rescue, a little bird told me that you're trying to find a missing person."

Charles had always amazed me with his sources, but this one threw me. I hadn't told anyone other than Karen and the chief. Neither of them would have said anything to him.

"Little bird have a name?" I said.

"Yep," said Charles, who then took his cane to the office in back and threw his hat on the table that served as a dining area, work area, argument area, and, most days after six, bar at Landrum Gallery.

I followed. "Could you tell me who it is?"

He grinned. "Yep."

Charles and I were extraordinarily unlikely best friends. This was one of the moments I wondered why.

"Who was it?" I asked, as directly as possible.

"Dude," said Charles.

"Where did he hear it?" I said, choosing my words carefully. Jim "Dude" Sloan was the owner of the surf shop, an aging hippy who came to the beach more than a quarter of a century ago, and, as he said, "forgot to leave."

Charles went to the small refrigerator in the corner, took out two Diet Pepsi's, and handed me one. "Got to tell you everything, don't I?"

"Yep," I said and smiled.

"Dude said he was in the Pig 'fetchin' a butt roast and talkin' a spell' with Jacob Perkins."

"And Jacob told Dude that I told him that Samuel told me about a kidnapping," I said.

"Yep," said Charles.

"Why would Jacob tell Dude?" I asked and pulled the tab on the Pepsi.

"Dude strikes folks like a cute puppy," said Charles. "They take one look at his scrawny bod and his Arlo Guthrie look-alike hairdo and want to rub his scraggly, beardy chin and tell him things. Go figure."

Telling Dude things beat waiting for him to say anything that was longer than a half-dozen words. He seldom got out a complete sentence. He fit in on Folly like lawyers at a car wreck.

"Did he say anything else?" I said.

"Forget what Dude may have tried to say," said Charles. "What's up with the missing person? Found her yet?"

I proceeded to tell Charles about my conversation with Samuel and then what his dad had to say about his son's stories.

"Believe Samuel or his dad?" he asked.

"Not sure," I said and leaned back in the wobbly, wooden chair. "I don't know what Samuel saw, but I know whatever it was scared him. He wasn't making it up."

"It still could have been exaggerated a tad. If his dad's right, it wouldn't be the first time."

I agreed with Charles but still couldn't get past Samuel's fear.

# CHAPTER 9

I was having lunch in the Lost Dog Café while Charles performed his executive sales manager duties at the gallery.

"Remember Constance Garvin, the missing grad student from Columbia?" said Chief Brian Newman without preamble. He towered over me as he stood at the table.

"Sure," I said. "Was it her?"

He reached for the notebook in his breast pocket of his blue, flowery Hawaiian shirt but pulled his hand away. "No, sorry." He looked at the seat on the opposite side of my favorite table. "Join you?"

"Sure."

Amber set a Mason jar of tea in front of the chief before he noticed her. She was in her midforties and as attractive as she had been the first time I'd seen her in the Dog six years ago. Her auburn hair was pulled back and held in place with a rubber band. She and the dog in the restaurant's logo on her T-shirt smiled at Brian. He ordered a Folly mahi salad and gave my half-eaten hot dog piled with cheese and onions a nasty look. I wasn't nearly as concerned about my diet as both Amber and Brian were about what I ate.

"What's the story?" I said.

"It appears that little Miss Garvin took off a couple of days after her spat with her boyfriend and ended up in Destin, Florida. She pouted, felt sorry for herself, frequented the area bars for a week, got a sunburn on parts of her body that shouldn't have seen the light of day, and then called her parents."

"So we're back to zero on missing persons," I said.

"Afraid so," said Brian, "I checked before coming over. There's only one new report, and it's a guy."

"So that's all we can do?" I said.

He rubbed his chin, stirred a packet of real sugar into his tea, took a sip, and then said, "There are a few scattered missing person databases in surrounding states, but I don't have access. Unless something comes up, all we have is the word of a teenager who saw something in the dark."

*   *   *

The bleak economy, my bleak outlook, and knowing that Charles would take care of the rare customer who wandered in contributed to my overall lack of enthusiasm for opening the gallery. Business had never been good. Before moving to my island heaven, I had sold my photos at art shows across middle America. Owning a gallery had been my dream, so when I retired early, I needed to find out if I could make it work. For reasons I will never understand, Charles had latched on to me and cheerfully thrown himself into the project. Income had never approached expenses, but the first two years were manageable. Then the economy tanked, and, as hard as it was to believe, vacationers didn't put wall art on the same level as food and shelter. Go figure.

If it hadn't been for an unexpected inheritance from a near stranger, I would have closed Landrum Gallery two years ago. I now kept it open more for something to do than the belief that I would ever sell enough to cover expenses. Since the death of my ex six months ago, the distractions of the gallery and a few close friends were all that kept me sane.

Saturdays were the only days where enthusiasm overcame my apathy for opening. Occasionally, an influx of photo buyers required me to help Charles. I popped out of bed earlier than usual and looked forward to picking up a cup of coffee from Bert's and walking the few blocks to the gallery before the sweltering August heat enveloped the island. I opened the front door and came within inches of stepping on Samuel's left hand. He was sitting on the step and leaning back; both hands rested on the ledge near the screen door.

"Oh, hi, Mr. Landrum," he said and jumped up. He brushed off the seat of his plaid shorts and moved away from the door so I could get out.

I smiled at the awkward teen. "Selling encyclopedias?" I asked.

"Huh?"

I realized that my reference was lost on Samuel. If he knew what an encyclopedia was, he would be referring to an online version. To think that someone would actually go door-to-door selling a multivolume, heavy set of books would have been a totally foreign concept to the youth of America.

"Never mind," I said. "What brings you out this early?" I pointed toward Bert's. "I'm going over for coffee and then to the gallery. Want to tag along?"

"Umm, okay, part of the way," he said and walked in step with me across the yard to the grocery's property.

"How long were you there?"

"About an hour," he said as if his actions were normal. "It was early, and I didn't want to bother you. Didn't want to wake you up. I sort of figured you'd come out sometime."

We reached the double-door entry to Bert's. I was greeted by Eric, one of the long-term employees and typical characters who either worked at or frequented the grocery. Eric was behind the counter and holding a dog treat for one of the island's many canine residents. Samuel and I walked past the counter to the coffee urn along the side wall.

Samuel moved closer and whispered, "Dad told me that you two talked about me. Said you talked about what I saw."

I nodded.

"He told you that I just thought I saw the lady being taken—abducted or kidnapped, or whatever, or ..." He paused and looked toward the ceiling like he was trying to come up with another word to describe what he saw. "I might have sort of only thought I saw some other things in the past, like a submarine. Dad thinks I make stuff up."

No use pretending otherwise. "He did say something like that."

"I had to tell you that I really did see, you know, the lady getting taken. I ... I'm grateful about how you treat me ... like an adult. I know what Dad thinks." He nodded. "He may be right about some of it."

I nodded again and filled my coffee cup.

"Dad's wrong this time, Mr. Landrum. I don't know what else to say."

"Samuel," I said. "I do believe you saw something happen. I don't think you made it up."

"Thanks, Mr. Landrum." Samuel looked over at Eric and down at the second dog that led its owner through the store on a leash. He kept his eyes on the dog but said, "What can we do about it?"

*Good question*, I thought.

"I don't know. I really don't," I said. "Let me think about it."

He looked at me. His eyes were sadder than the basset hound's that had just entered with one of the cooks from Planet Follywood. He was counting on me to do what?

"So," I said hoping to change the subject, "seen that girl again? The one you were looking for at the Oceanfront Villas?"

He looked at the dog and then back to me. "You do remember stuff, don't you?"

I shrugged.

He smiled. "Yeah, saw her yesterday by the pool at her condo. I was outside the fence and pretended like I was looking for a friend at the pool. Stood there for ten minutes before she saw me."

"Did you sweep her off her feet?"

Samuel blushed and looked at the concrete floor. "You're funny, Mr. Landrum. She did say hi and walked over. I told her I was looking for Jason. She said she hoped I found him and that she was going to be here another week and maybe we'd see each other again. Then her pesky younger brother came over and pulled her arm and said she needed to get back in the pool with him."

"Don't guess Jason was at the pool?" I said and smiled.

"You're funny," said Samuel. He gave me a big grin.

I had succeeded with getting his mind off whatever he saw—or thought he saw. Now, how could I get my mind off it?

# CHAPTER 10

The distance from Bert's to the gallery was fewer than a handful of blocks, but I was in no hurry to get there. My thoughts kept going back to how positive Samuel was about witnessing a crime and the trouble he had gone to this morning to walk to my house and sit on the steps for more than an hour so he wouldn't wake me, all to convince me that he was telling the truth. I looked across Center Street at city hall. It not only was the seat of government for the tiny community but also served as the police and fire station. I had taken Samuel's story to the chief; what else could I do?

"About time you got here," said Charles before I'd closed the door to the gallery. He looked at his bare wrist, the spot where most people wore a watch. Charles, being Charles, didn't own a timepiece, but the gesture wasn't lost on me. Timeliness in his world was either next to godliness or slightly above it.

"Able to handle all the customers?" I asked. It was fifteen minutes before the gallery's usual ten o'clock opening.

He wore a white, long-sleeved T-shirt with what appeared to be the head of a bulldog in front of the letter T. I was not going to ask him about the shirt.

He exhaled like he had been snowed under working the cash register. "Barely," he said.

"Glad I made it in time to save you," I said as I looked around the customer-less gallery. "Who do you want me to help next?"

"Funny," he said, the second person this morning to make that astute observation. "Truman State University." He pointed to the creature on his chest.

I ignored him and walked to the back to see if he'd already started the coffee. He said something about bulldogs and Missouri, but I kept walking. He followed me and, fortunately, changed the topic.

"Remember Aunt Melinda?" he asked.

I poured out the lukewarm coffee from Bert's and filled the cup from the old, but still operational, coffeemaker.

"Who?"

He sighed. "My aunt, Melinda. Remember? I told you about her."

I didn't remember. "When?"

"You know, back when we met?"

"Oh," I said. Did I need to remind him that was several years ago? "Guess I forgot?"

"I keep forgetting about you old people's memory." He moved to the table and sat in the chair where he could see if anyone entered the gallery.

I also chose not to remind him that he was only three years younger—presenile, he would say.

"Aunt Melinda's my mom's sister. She was my role model when I was a pup."

I did remember that Charles was raised by his grandmother. His parents had died when he was younger than Samuel.

Charles smiled. "I remember how she taught me to avoid work."

"Good teacher," I said.

"Yeah," said Charles, who thought it was a compliment. "She also taught me to cuss. That was big since I was growing up in a home with my nunnish, librarian grandmother who refused to check books out to anyone under the age of thirty if there was a cuss word between the covers."

Charles gazed at the door to the gallery but his mind was back in Detroit and in his youth. "Aunt Melinda also taught me to drink." He shook his head. "Unfortunately, she was too good at that. Grandma said that Aunt M. was an alcoholic. I didn't know what that meant then, but I guess it was true."

"Did something happen to her?"

He shook his head. "I called her when I landed on Folly." He looked at the ceiling. "Then she called me, oh, it must have been fifteen years back to see if I was still here."

Charles reached in his pocket, pulled out a wrinkled envelope, and handed it to me.

It was addressed in shaky, block letters to:

Charles Fowler, Somewhere on Folly Beach
Post Office, FIND HIM!!
Folly Beach, South Carolina

In the upper left corner, the return address read:

Aunt Melinda
Don't You Dare Send This Back. Find Charles!

I looked up at Charles and said that I was impressed with the United States Postal Service for getting the envelope to him. He leaned back in the chair and said, "They didn't want to get on her bad side. That's my Aunt Melinda."

I was almost afraid to open the envelope, but I did anyway. Inside was a baby blue sheet of paper the size of a note card. It had a border on two sides that looked like a climbing rosebush and in the middle in the same shaky block lettering that was on the envelope:

Greyhound Station, North Charleston, wherever that is
Sunday, August 18, 2:05 Afternoon
Coming from Asheville
See ya. You'll recognize me—I'll be the chick getting off a big ole bus.
Aunt M.

I looked back at the envelope. It was postmarked in Detroit three days ago.

I double-checked the date. "That's tomorrow," I said.

"Think I don't know it?" said Charles. He picked up his cane from the table and waved it toward the door to the gallery. "What am I going to do?"

I pointed the envelope at him. "This is the first you've heard from her in fifteen years?"

He nodded.

"Guess we're going to the Greyhound station tomorrow afternoon," I said.

"No," he said and shook his head. "You don't have to go. You've got a gallery to run." He shook his head again. "Why's she coming? What am I going to say? Hells bells, what are we going to do? How long will she be here?"

I said exactly what Charles would have said if the tables had been turned. "What time are we leaving for the station?"

He glared at me and started to say something. Then he hesitated and said, "One."

The bell over the front door rang before we could talk about his other excellent questions.

"Yoo-hoo, Chris. Yoo-hoo, Chuckster. Anybody here?"

The unmistakable voice of Heather Lee was followed by her peeking around the corner into our hangout. Heather was in her late forties, wholesomely attractive, with curly brown hair and, in Charles's words, a cute-as-a-button freckled nose. She was also his girlfriend. "Made for each other," was the phrase most people who knew both of them resorted with when describing their relationship. Heather prided herself in two things. She thought that she was a good country music singer and a psychic. Her psychic powers had never been completely refuted, but there was absolutely no disputing her ability to carry a tune, country or otherwise. She couldn't—period.

What everyone did agree on was her persistence. Every week, come hell or hurricane, she participated in open-mike night at Cal's Country Bar and Burgers and was permitted to sing, using the term loosely, two songs. Cal, in a display of great wisdom, scheduled her performance for later in the night to allow his patrons to imbibe enough adult beverages not to care what the alleged singer warbled from the bandstand.

Despite her vocal shortcomings, Heather had brought happiness, companionship, and a sense of control to Charles since they started dating three years ago. For that, I had become one of her biggest fans.

Charles jumped up to greet his main squeeze. She was in work clothes, an off-white outfit that looked like a cross between medical scrubs and a karate uniform. Heather was a freelance massage therapist but worked primarily at Millie's Salon, Folly's premiere salon located in an old house less than a block off Center Street. Luckily for Heather's economic outlook, she was a much better massage therapist than singer or psychic.

Heather said that she had an appointment with a client in a half hour, figured we would be in the gallery, and wanted to say hi. The gallery was between Millie's and her small apartment in Mariner's Breeze, a run-down former bed-and-breakfast that had been converted to a dilapidated boarding house.

She eyed the refrigerator, so I asked if she wanted something to drink. Another thing that Heather and Charles had in common was a lack of motorized transportation. August was a brutal time to do much walking in the Low Country. She quickly said, "Something cold would be nice."

I told her to grab whatever she wanted. She picked a Diet Pepsi and joined us at the table. "Hear you're on missing person patrol," she said and then took a large sip—more accurately, a gulp.

"Where'd you hear that?" I asked.

Charles leaned forward and tapped the table. "She's psychic."

Heather took another sip. "Not this time, Chucky," she said. "Remember, I work in a beauty salon. Everybody there knows everything about everyone." She nodded. "Don't need no psychic talents to hear stuff."

I thought I'd try one more time before simply assuming that everyone on Folly knew about my alleged quest. "So who told you?"

"Let me think." She put her forefinger under her chin and closed her eyes. "I think it was Helen, who said she heard it from her mother Mable; I think Mable heard it from Roxanne, who heard it at the meat counter at the Pig." She paused and looked at Charles and then back at me. "Or maybe Roxanne heard it from somebody else who heard it at the Pig."

"Never mind," I said. By now it didn't matter.

Charles picked his cane off the floor and pointed it at me. "If you ask me—and I know you will, eventually—you're heading on a wild flounder chase. Let me tell you, when I was Samuel's age I was at my peak imagining things. I knew that Martians had invaded the next street over from my house. I knew I saw two of the little green men out behind the neighbor's garage."

"What were they doing?" asked Heather.

"Charles," she said and wiped the perspiration from her forehead. "God gave you many talents, but when he got to *P* in the alphabet, he plum skipped over *patience*." She turned and waved bye to the Greyhound bus and then back to her nephew. "Why, you're my only living relative and it's been a few weeks since I've seen you. Why shouldn't I come a-callin'?"

"Now, Aunt M., a few weeks?" said Charles. He had turned in the seat and was facing the visitor. "If my memory's close to right, it's been fifteen years since I heard from you. At fifty-two weeks a year, that's about … about fifty-two times fifteen … about … well, about a whole bunch more than a few weeks."

She reached to the front seat and patted Charles on the top of his thinning hair. "You always were a stickler for detail." She grinned. "Remember how I always told you not to learn so much, how it'd clutter up your brain so it couldn't think about good stuff?"

Charles took her hand from his head and squeezed it. "I do remember. You also taught me that work was something to be avoided at all cost. And that a good cuss word communicated more than any dozen words that were in a first-grade schoolbook."

"Ah, the good old days," said Melinda. She pulled her hand out of Charles's, patted him on the head again, and then sat back in the seat and adjusted her shoulder harness. "Charles, even when you were a small kid, you were my favorite relative. Now you're my only relative—well, the only living one." She looked out the window as we pulled on the ramp to I-26 heading toward Charleston and Folly Beach. "I'm not counting hubby number *quarto*. Think he's still alive—shouldn't be, that old buzzard."

Charles had told me that he'd known about three husbands, so there must have been at least one more since he'd escaped Detroit. He asked her what had happened with the fourth husband, and she reminded him about her advice not to clutter his brain and that her fourth—"and last, God is my witness"—husband wasn't worth a single brain cell so she wouldn't mention him again. Charles said something like, "guess it wasn't an amicable parting," and Melinda pounded her fist on Charles's head. I was glad I hadn't commented on her latest spouse.

Charles then asked Melinda how long she planned to stay.

That's when things got interesting.

# CHAPTER 12

"Oh," she said after Charles asked her how long she was staying. "Maybe a few weeks, months. Could be a year. Depends?"

"On what?" said Charles.

"When I kick the proverbial bucket," said Melinda as casually as if she was telling us how she enjoyed the bus ride.

I gripped the steering wheel more tightly and glanced over at Charles. He took the highly unusual approach of not saying anything. But his head swiveled toward the backseat. He smiled, but it was strained. "So, you're moving here?" he said. "Umm, that's great."

She laughed. "You sound excited. Wondered how you'd take the news. Your reaction was so Charles-like."

"No," said Charles. "I am excited. You surprised me."

I was still confused about "few weeks, months. Could be a year." Fortunately, Charles never feared to tread where no man dared to go. "So, what's that about a few weeks then?"

"Didn't want to spring it on you so soon, seeing that we haven't laid eyes on each other in decades. But you did ask." She reached out and put her arm on his shoulder. "It appears that I already have a big toe on the wormy side of the sod."

"Huh?" said Charles. He spoke for both of us.

"Seems that I have a terminal case of the big *C*. The docs don't think I'll be seeing the Easter bunny hopping around in the spring."

Charles's right foot nervously tapped the floorboard, and he reached around with his right hand and placed it on Melinda's. I stared at the here and Samuel was already fidgeting, so I refrained and politely asked Samuel to tell the officer what he had seen.

Samuel looked at me and then turned to O'Hara. He sat up even straighter in his chair. "I saw a lady kidnapped, or as Mr. Landrum here likes to say, abducted," said Samuel.

For the first time, O'Hara focused on Samuel. He leaned close to the table and was no farther than three feet from my friend's face. "When? Where?"

Samuel took a deep breath and then told his story, nearly word for word the same as he'd shared with me. He described what she was wearing and what kind of car the abductor drove. He left out the part about being at the Oceanfront Villas to see a girl, but there wasn't any need to clutter the story with that excellent teenager reason for being there.

O'Hara began taking notes once he figured that Samuel might actually have seen something. Samuel had left out when he had seen the alleged abduction, and when O'Hara asked again, Samuel shared that it was last Wednesday.

"Are you sure?" asked O'Hara. He looked up from his notepad and tapped his pen on the table.

Samuel said he was. Officer O'Hara wrote the date down and underlined it twice. He seemed relieved and asked Samuel two more times if he could recognize either person if he saw them again. Samuel said that he didn't know. At this point, O'Hara looked bored, and didn't hide his efforts to dismiss us. He said he was glad we came in and that he would tell the chief. I'd wager that he had no intention of telling anyone. I didn't share that the chief and I were friends and that I'd be reporting my meeting with one of the chief's public servants, using the term rather loosely. Brian wouldn't be pleased.

Samuel and I left the cool but unwelcoming police station and stepped out into the heat of the day.

"That guy's got that puny-guy disease, don't he?"

I laughed. Samuel meant small-man syndrome, and he had hit the short nail on the head. "He thinks a bit too much about himself," I said, trying to be as polite as possible. "He's just doing his job."

"Not very good," said Samuel.

*Not very good, indeed*, I thought and nodded.

"Think he believed me?" asked Samuel. "He sort of wrote the stuff down, but didn't care about anything other than if I was sure when I saw the kidna ... the abduction."

"He may not have been polite," I said, "but he got all the details. He also said he'd tell the chief."

We walked side by side down Center Street toward the ocean until we reached the island's sole traffic light. At the corner I told him that I was heading home, and he said that he would go the opposite direction and walk by the Oceanfront Villas a few times. He didn't say it, but I knew that meant he was hoping to see the vacationer of his dreams. He also started to say something else but couldn't quite get it out.

"What?" I asked as we stood in the shade of the nearby restaurant.

"I know a lady was taken. She didn't want to go. They weren't horsing around," he said and then turned in the direction of the alleged abduction. "What can we do, Mr. Landrum?"

I wasn't pleased with the brush-off we had received at the police station but wanted to shelter Samuel as much as possible.

"There's nothing else you can or should do," I said. "You took your story to the police, and they got what information you had. They know where to reach you if they want to talk again or show you pictures of either the lady or the man."

Samuel jerked back like I'd slapped his face. "You don't think they're going to show me pictures of the puffy, chopped-up lady from the park, do you?"

"I doubt it."

"I'd sort of throw up if they did." He hesitated and shook his head. He reminded me of a dog shaking water off its fur. "It really is her. I know it is." He stared me in the eyes. "It really is her."

My naive wish for a nap was long gone, so the second thing I did when I got to the air-conditioned comfort of my cottage was to call Charles. The first thing was to take off my sweat-soaked golf shirt and hang it on a kitchen chair. Charles had talked recently about buying a cell phone, but despite his significant inheritance, he hadn't taken that major leap into the current century. An answering machine was another piece of electronic gadgetry that he had stubbornly resisted. After five rings, I knew that I wouldn't be getting an update on what he was doing with Aunt Melinda and turned my attention to which gourmet delicacy

I would prepare for supper. Bologna won out over peanut butter, and I had a quiet meal. I tried to put Samuel's situation out of my mind.

I failed.

# CHAPTER 14

"How was your room?" I asked.

"Fit for a queen," said Melinda. "Weren't any queens there, so they let me stay." She laughed like it was the funniest thing she'd ever said. I hoped it wasn't.

Charles, Melinda, and I were sitting at my favorite booth at the Dog. Charles had called and asked if I wanted to pick him up, gather Melinda from the hotel, and then take them to a late breakfast. Charles was generous like that. Since I was curious about how they were getting along and especially interested in what her plans were, I agreed to play chauffeur.

Melinda wore a bright red blouse that was so wrinkled it looked more like linen than polyester. The second button was missing, and her white shorts had a purple stain on the right leg. Her bird-thin legs, somewhere between light gray and the hue of milk, reflected life in the north. Her eyes had lost the bloodshot look that greeted us when she walked off the bus yesterday. She looked refreshed.

Amber was quick to the table with menus, Ball jars full of water, and unconstrained curiosity. Charles introduced Melinda to Amber and shared that Amber was the greatest, kindest, sweetest, and most attractive waitress south of Barrow, Alaska. He told Amber that Melinda was by far his most favorite relative and that even if they hadn't been related, she'd be his most favorite old person, next to "old Chris here."

I smiled and hoped Amber had other tables to wait on. She did, and she said she'd give Melinda a chance to look over the menu.

Melinda selected the breakfast burrito and then looked around the restaurant and scratched her left arm. "Think I'm getting fleas."

Charles looked around. Each wall was covered with photos of dogs: dogs of customers, dogs as customers, dogs of the world, and dogs of every shape, size, and socioeconomic strata. He smiled. "Now, Aunt M., they're only photos. There aren't any fleas in here."

She reached over, scratched Charles's left arm, and then smiled. "Bet there's a picture of a flea." She paused and looked around the room again. "Glad it's not named the Cobra Café."

More evidence that Charles and Melinda were related. As fascinating as the discussion was, I wondered what plans they had made about her stay. Charles's apartment was too small to accommodate her. Even though her room at the Tides was fit for a queen, neither Charles nor, I suspected, Melinda had the resources to afford a stay of *months, could be a year.*

"Did you decide where Melinda will be hanging her hat?" I asked.

"Don't know about my hat," she said and continued to look around at the canine images, "but Charles said he knew the perfect place to park my wig." She looked at Charles and patted his arm instead of scratching it again. "I've never mistaken my nephew for perfect, so I took his suggestion with a grain of sea salt."

"Now, Aunt M., I said I'd take care of you." Charles squeezed her hand and turned toward me. "I thought Mariner's Breeze would be nice. What do you think?"

I thought, *thanks for putting me on the spot* but said, "Sounds great."

Mariner's Breeze had seen great times, a thriving bed-and-breakfast business, and popularity that had spanned several states. Unfortunately, that had been some thirty years ago. It was now a large two-story building with paint peeling in chunks from its formerly white exterior. Occasionally, an unsuspecting vacationer would find an old brochure that touted the bed-and-breakfast and be politely told that yes, rooms could be rented for the night, but the breakfast part of B&B was served off-site, which was hospitality-speak for "find breakfast wherever you want to eat, just not here." After the new, attractive, upscale Water's Edge Inn bed-and-breakfast opened a few years ago, most of Mariner's Breeze's rooms and suites were converted to long-term, low-cost rentals.

Despite its shortcomings, and there were many, Mariner's Breeze was located on premium real estate. It backed up to the marsh and the Folly River and had a fantastic sunset view. "Perfect" would not have been a word I would have used to describe Charles's choice of lodging, but the rooms were clean, it was less than a half block from Charles's apartment, and Heather, his main squeeze, lived there.

"Good," said Melinda. She looked around again. "Got to go to the pups' powder room." She pointed her finger in the direction of the kitchen, and then the outside patio, and then behind our booth.

Charles told her that the restroom, the one for people, was around the corner in front of the T-shirt display. She slowly pushed herself from the table and headed in that direction.

I leaned closer to Charles. "Can she afford Mariner's Breeze?" I whispered.

"She's got money," said Charles. "Maybe a lot. I asked her if she needed help with the rent. She held her chin up high and said, 'I've got a few dollars, thank you.'"

Charles looked at the next table and commented on the weather to a young couple having a peaceful breakfast. They smiled, mumbled something about it being hot, and then returned to their food.

I patiently waited for him to turn his attention back to our table. "Learn more about her health?" I asked.

Charles started to answer but looked over my right shoulder and smiled. "Welcome back, Aunt M."

"There're even dogs in there," she said, shook her head, and pointed toward the restroom.

"Hmm," said Charles, clearly not interested in any further discussion about four-legged creatures.

Amber returned with our food, and Melinda told her that they needed to get together sometime. Melinda said she wanted to catch up on the gossip about her favorite relative and that good-looking other gentleman sitting at the table. She looked at me and said, "The one who seems to like Charles for no apparent reason." Amber told her she doubted that Melinda had enough time to hear everything.

Charles cringed when Amber said it. So did Melinda. She patted Charles on the arm again, looked up at Amber, and said that she would make time. I exhaled and felt sorry for Amber, who didn't know about Melinda's death sentence.

Melinda picked at her burrito and then took a small bite. She said, "Yum" and then turned to me. "Charles tells me that the two of you are professional amateur detectives. Something about you getting into trouble and then him having to come to the rescue and pull your bacon out of the fire—time after time."

Charles leaned back on the booth and smiled. I looked over at him and then at Melinda. "I wouldn't say—"

She waved her fork in my face. "No need to finish whatever you were going to say. I knew Charles before he could ride a bike and long before he inflicted himself on you." She looked over at him and waved her fork in his direction. "He's a sweetie, but occasionally he gets his stories a bit lopsided and upside down."

"Nooo," I said.

"Didn't think that'd shock you," she said and gave one of her laughs. "Now I'm going to sit here and keep eating while you give me your version of the pickles the two of you have dived into."

"Okay, Aunt M.," said Charles before I could set my coffee cup down, "Let me tell you about the first time I saved him after he came a-vacationing here and stubbed his big toe on a dead body. Chris seriously irritated a killer. And I had to—"

She gave a move with her fork that would be the envy of any orchestra conductor. Charles sat back as the fork nearly clipped his nose. "Let's hear your friend's version, shall we?"

*Note to self: Don't mess with anyone's elderly aunt brandishing a fork.* I nodded to Melinda, smirked at Charles, and proceeded to share a few stories about how Charles and I had stumbled, bumbled, and even made a few correct decisions that helped the police catch some really bad guys. Each time I mentioned something that Charles contributed to the solution, Melinda patted him on the arm. He tried to interrupt twice, but the flying fork and a dirty look from his only living relative stopped him. I thought about starting to carry a fork around with me but doubted that it would have the same effect.

Melinda was a good listener and always gave an appropriate "ooh," "wow," or "cool" at the right spot in the stories.

I wasn't going to tell her about Samuel and the alleged abduction, but Charles got in enough about it that Melinda asked what he was talking about. I gave her a capsule version of Samuel's story and our trip to the police station. Charles said that I certainly was working hard to solve a mystery that didn't exist.

Melinda proved once again that she was related to Charles when she waved her fork at him, a move that I was getting used to. "My favorite nephew," she said, "despite your many shortcomings, picking friends doesn't appear to be one of them. You have chosen Chris here as your best friend, so he must be good, able to be trusted, and usually right." I wanted to interrupt and ask about his many shortcomings, but I sat silent and wondered where she was going with her wisdom. "So, if he says that someone he trusts—that youngster named, what was it again?"

"Samuel," I said.

"Yeah, Samuel," she continued. "If Chris trusts Samuel and Samuel said someone was swiped right off the walk, then probably she was, God help her soul."

"Aunt M.—"

There went the fork again. "Y'all need to figure it out now. And I'll help."

I hadn't looked at my watch and was surprised when I looked around the room and saw that most of the lunch crowd had departed, either for the beach or an air-conditioned condo. Melinda was still attentive, but I noticed her head nodding. I suggested that we should get her checked into Mariner's Breeze. She nodded. Her fork hand was exhausted.

# CHAPTER 15

"Christer," said Dude. He flailed his arms and pointed to the empty space beside me on the bench. "Parking space available?"

My translation of Dude-speak was that he was asking to join me. I had ignored the heat and walked to the end of the pier to watch the sun set over the island. I was exhausted after helping Charles get Melinda settled in a three-room "suite," as Charles kept referring to the tiny bedroom with a kitchenette, living room about the size of a medium-sized doghouse, and bathroom that wasn't large enough for a tub, just a half-sized shower tucked in the corner. She had joked that it would do since it was larger than her subsoil home would be. Charles and I had smiled, but I didn't see the humor. My exhaustion was more emotional from dealing with the terminally ill, sweet lady, rather than physical. The walk had felt good.

"I'd be honored," I said—although it was a slight exaggeration—and removed my Tilley from the bench. Dude was attired in his ever-present tie-dyed shirt and cargo shorts. His long white-and-gray hair flowed to the beat of a different hairdresser.

"Missin' chick be found?" he said.

Dude had the uncanny ability to underwhelm anyone who met him for the first time—several times in some cases. He had never met a sentence that he couldn't screw up. He apparently thought that he only had a limited supply of words to speak in his lifetime, and he didn't want to run out before he met the great surf maker in the sky. He was also proof that looks, and even words, could be deceiving. It had taken a while, but I had learned to appreciate his humor and innate intellect. He said that he had never completed high school but was world-wise and extraordinarily knowledgeable about astronomy, and despite having just turned sixty, he could still surf with the "baddest" surfers on the island.

"Maybe," I said. Dude could also bring out the brevity in those who spoke with him.

"Bloated bod be her?" he asked.

"Good possibility," I said and then told Dude about Samuel and my trip to the police station.

"Cutie-face O'Hara be poser," said Dude.

Charles was usually around to translate Dude-speak for me, but now I was on my own. "That's bad, right?"

"Well, yeah. Bad be bad; not good bad," said Dude.

I actually understood—I'd been on Folly too long. I agreed with Dude after only one exposure to Officer O'Hara, but I wanted to hear his reasons. "Why?"

"Cute-face cop be on surfer patrol. Chills cop car at Washout fishing for trouble." Dude shook his head in disgust.

The Washout was a popular surfing area on the east end of the island. Surfers have had a decades-long love-hate relationship with Folly Beach. The local government was often caught in the middle between the free-spirited surfers and the business and full-time resident community who were often at odds with them. Dude had made a surprisingly good living catering to the surfer crowd. He knew most of them by face and almost as many by name. He had a reputation with the surfers as a stand-up guy, someone who would know about the occasional violation of law or social standards by his customers but was also a good representative for them in the more established, conservative crowd. In other words, he wasn't a snitch.

I shared that I was going to talk to Chief Newman about how Officer O'Hara had treated Samuel and me.

Dude grinned and looked over my shoulder. "You be future-seer," he said.

"Thought I saw you out here," came the distinct voice of Chief Brian Newman from behind me.

"Park a spell," said Dude as he moved over to make room for Brian.

"Just for a minute," said Brian. He had on a blue-and-white striped shirt and gray dress slacks. "Got a meeting at city hall—fun, fun, fun."

"Chris got words for you," said Dude. He looked at me and grinned.

I frowned at Dude and then turned to Brian. "I'll tell you later."

"Good," said Brian. "I wanted to tell you that the woman who drowned wasn't the person Samuel thought he saw."

"Bummer," said Dude.

"You sure?" I asked.

Brian took his small notebook out of his shirt pocket and flipped through a few pages. "Yeah. According to the coroner, she had been dead for at least three weeks. That's a week before Samuel saw whatever he saw. He also said she's African American."

"No Gidget be missin'," said Dude.

"Female surfer?" I asked. Dude would have had the inside track if any surfers had been missing.

"Duh, yeah," he said.

I turned back to Brian. "Who was she? What killed her?"

He looked back at the notebook. "Not certain, but she generally fits the description of a missing person from Georgia, Nicole Sallee, age twenty-five. About the same height, five foot six, trim." He shook his head. "She had a master's degree from Valdosta State University and was a part-time model. She'd won a bunch of beauty pageants when she was in her teens. She had told her friends she needed to get out of Georgia and figure out her life. She was married but had left her husband."

"When will you know for sure?" I asked.

"A few days."

"Dead how?" asked Dude.

"Nothing obvious," said Brian. "Could have been accidental drowning. Don't even know if she was ever on Folly. She could have floated over from Kiawah or have fallen off a boat anywhere out there." He waved toward the Atlantic and looked at his watch. "Got to go; just wanted to let you know it wasn't who Samuel saw."

Brian headed toward the street to his fun-filled meeting at city hall.

Dude looked in the direction the chief had headed. "Be two missin' peeps now."

"Actually," I said, "there's only one missing. It appears that Ms. Sallee has been found."

Dude looked at the ceiling and then back at me. "Bod not missin', story be nowhere to be found."

*Excellent point, my sentence-challenged friend*, I thought. Excellent point.

# CHAPTER 17

Charles returned with Chief Newman in tow. Brian teased that he had made the mistake of walking past Taco Boy and gotten caught. He had known Charles for several more years than I had and was familiar with my friend's quirks. They weren't close—in fact, they were opposite in many ways—but for some strange reason, they respected and liked each other.

Charles pointed to the empty seat beside me and nodded for Brian to join us. "You weren't running, so I figured you weren't chasing a bank robber or a speeding poodle," said Charles in response to Brian's quip. "Anyway, I wanted to introduce you to my favorite relative, Aunt Melinda Beale. She's come down from Detroit."

"Only relative," interrupted Melinda. "Don't let him fool you into thinking he chose me over anyone else. The rest are planted under tombstones."

Brian gave her his best Chamber of Commerce smile. "Any relative of Charles is more than welcome here."

Melinda grinned and turned to her only above-ground relative. "Well, ain't he a charmer?"

Charles shook his head and gave a look of disbelief at the same time.

"How long will you be visiting?" asked Brian. He didn't know what he'd stepped in.

"Until I croak," said Melinda with a mischievous smile.

Brian started to speak, shut his mouth, and glanced at Charles, who found the napkin beside his plate quite fascinating. Brian then started to push up from the table. "Well, then I hope you're here for many years." He grinned at Melinda and then turned to Charles. "Gotta go," he said. "Nice meeting you, Ms. Beale."

Melinda grinned again. "And you as well."

Brian stood beside the table. I didn't recall ever seeing him as uncomfortable. It was if he wanted to either interrogate the sweet lady who had made a fatalistic comment or run.

He didn't have to choose. Officer Cindy LaMond pushed her way through a group of college students who had gathered near the entrance. She looked around, spotted her boss standing at our table, and headed our way.

Cindy LaMond had been Cindy Ash until a couple of years ago, when Larry, the owner of Folly's only hardware store and a retired cat burglar, swept her off her feet and proposed holy matrimony. She was also a friend and had helped me out of potentially disastrous jams more than once.

She moved beside Brian and looked around to see who could hear. The closest table was occupied by a couple with three kids under the age of two. The parents had their hands full and paid no attention to us. The chief leaned in Cindy's direction, but Charles had already stood and moved between the two of them to introduce Melinda to Cindy. The new arrival smiled in the direction of Melinda and said she was glad to meet her. I hoped she wouldn't ask how long Melinda would be staying. She didn't; Cindy clearly wasn't at the table on a social call. She moved closer to Brian and began to whisper.

Charles, surprisingly, took the hint and returned to his seat. Cindy said something. The chief asked her a question, and she responded. I couldn't hear everything but caught, "body … coast guard station … freaked-out beach bum …"

Brian turned to Melinda, reiterated that it was nice to meet her, and said that he had to go. He put his arm on Cindy's shoulder and turned her toward the door, and they both headed for the exit. When they got to the door, Cindy turned and wiggled her hand by her ear to signal that she would call me. The chief was already on the sidewalk headed toward the police station.

Melinda asked Charles to order her another Mexican cocktail. Then she leaned across the table and whispered, "Did that mean they found another body?"

Before I answered, she added, "Where's a coast guard station around here? I don't remember seeing any cute boys in those adorable uniforms, especially those tight, white dress uniform jackets."

Melinda may have things wrong with her, but her hearing and eyesight were better than mine.

The question involved trivia, so Charles jumped in and explained that there was no longer a coast guard outpost on Folly but that there had been a thriving station on the east end of the island. My mind wandered to what Cindy had said, and I wasn't paying attention to Charles's explanation of which years the coast guard station was operational, how many men had been stationed there, and why it was shut down.

My ears perked up when he began telling her that the far end of the property was where I had found the body of the Charleston developer whom he had told her about. Charles loved telling the story, particularly since he took full credit for saving my life, catching the killer, and curing the common cold. Time had clouded reality. I occasionally think about the incident and shutter at the thought of how close I had come to being killed simply because I had taken an early-morning walk on the beach to photograph the historic Morris Island Lighthouse.

Now, if I accurately caught the gist of Cindy's muted words, the deserted military station had been the site of another death. My mind then skipped from my ancient history at the desolate property to the possibility that the new victim might be Samuel's abducted woman.

Charles tapped me on the arm with his cane. "Again, isn't that right?" he asked.

I didn't know what he'd said, but I figured if he asked me if something was right, it must be so. I said, "Yep."

He smiled and turned to Melinda. "I told you so."

I refocused on the conversation and was able to enjoy more of the back and forth between Charles and his long-lost relative. Only five times in the next half hour did I wonder when Cindy would call.

# Chapter 18

"What took you so long to call?" said Larry.

I hated caller ID. "Huh?" I said.

"Cindy got home a half hour ago and told me she saw you, Charles, and his aunt, Mable." I heard Cindy say something in the background. "Sorry, Melinda. She told you she'd call about the body," said Larry. "I knew you wouldn't be able to wait until we finished a wonderful pizza my loving wife brought home and enjoyed a refreshing beer. You're as impatient as Charles." He laughed, and I heard the phone clink down on a table.

"You had to prove him right, didn't you?" said Cindy. She sounded exasperated, but a giggle gave away her mood. That must have been quite a pizza.

"Sorry to interrupt supper," I said. "Want to call me later?"

"We're actually done. Larry enjoys giving you a hard time."

"So what happened?" I said.

"Don't know a lot," she said. She mumbled something to Larry, and I heard her say, "Hush" and then giggle again. There was a pause, and then she said, "There, I'm in the living room while my macho hubby wipes off two plates and throws the pizza box in the trash—he's so talented. Where was I?"

"You made it to *don't know a lot*," I said.

She cleared her throat. "About eleven hundred this morning, Stanley Learner, one of our homeless beachcombers, was out on the east end of the old coast guard property waving his metal detector around like he actually expected to find buried treasure. He was by the dunes line. Instead of a treasure chest full of gold, frankincense, and myrrh—whatever the hell that is—old Stanley used his army surplus folding shovel and dug down about a foot and found himself a left hand with bright red fingernail polish. Unfortunately for Stanley, it was still attached to an arm and the rest of a body. Old Stanley let out a scream that probably could have been heard in downtown Charleston. It was heard by a vacationing firefighter from Mississippi who had the misfortune of being near Stanley. The vacationer took one look at the exposed arm and knew CPR would have been a waste. He threw up and then called the cops."

"Did she wash up on shore?" I asked.

"No way," said Cindy. "It was past the high tide line, and most of her body was buried under a foot of sand. She was fully clothed. Her shirt had metal buttons; that's what got Stanley's metal detector all excited. She wasn't supposed to be found."

"How long had she been there?" I asked.

"Won't know for a few days," said Cindy. "The coroner said that it hadn't been too long. Said it was probably not over a couple of weeks."

That would fit with when Samuel's story. "Anything else? Race? Hair color?"

"Just a minute, Larry," she said. "Maybe he can't handle the two plates after all. Where was I?"

"Details," I said.

"Caucasian, dark hair, no tats, good figure I guess, trim ... that's about it."

"Age?"

"I'd guess under thirty—maybe twenty-five or so."

"Cause of death?"

"There was blood in her hair, but they couldn't tell. I'll call if I learn anything."

I poured a glass of Chardonnay and moved to the living room. My first thought was that Cindy and Larry's pizza sounded good, but I was too lazy to go get one and felt guilty about ordering a delivery for one person. Oreos, raisins, and wine surely cover all the food groups and were within a few feet of my chair. With supper plans taken care of, my second thought was to call Samuel and tell him about the body. But school had started, so I didn't want to disturb him. Besides, I didn't know anything more than I had earlier other than the latest body fit the general description he had given.

I flicked on the television and flipped through five channels. Each had a game show on—low on my watch list—so I turned it off. I refilled my glass, grabbed the box of Oreos and a small box of raisins, and returned to the chair. I was sitting in my paid-for cottage two blocks from the Atlantic Ocean, was blessed with a handful of close friends, was retired, and was putting my feet on the ottoman ready to kick back and enjoy the rest of my days on this earth. So why did my mind keep drifting back to dead bodies, the last conversation I had with my ex-wife before her tragic death, and Samuel's real, or imagined, sighting? I couldn't turn the clock back to what might have been with Joan, but what could I do to help Samuel get answers that were making his young life miserable?

It's not an everyday occurrence that a body drifts up on the beach, but it does happen, especially during the summer when more people migrate to the beaches than can comfortably be watched. Finding the corpse of the late Ms. Nicole Sallee on the beach was not that terribly strange. It was horrible, but it wasn't strange.

The discovery of two bodies in such a short period—the latest clearly not an accidental death—pushed the limits of coincidence. They were relatively young, both had dark hair, and both were trim. Does that connect the two? On the other hand, they were found on opposite ends of the island, one was African American, and one had most likely been murdered while the other one could have drowned accidentally.

I didn't know more than what Samuel had said, but I knew that he was convinced that what he had seen was serious. I had learned to put faith and trust in my friends. They could be quirky, odd, a bit idiosyncratic, and in Dude's case, possibly not from planet earth. I barely knew Samuel, but he trusted me. He had turned to me in his time of fear and confusion, wanting to do the right thing.

One thing was certain after a third glass of Chardonnay, a half box of Oreos, and the second box of raisins—Samuel considered me someone he could turn to. I couldn't let him down.

# CHAPTER 19

A cold wave swept through the Low Country overnight and brought the temperatures down to the mideighties, the seasonal average. Where the weather gurus came up with the phrase "cold front" was beyond me. It wouldn't bake cookies on the sidewalk, but I didn't know anyone who considered eighty-five degrees cold. Regardless, it felt better, and I took advantage of it. The island was bordered on one side by the Folly River and the ever-changing marsh and on the other side by the Atlantic. There had been some mansion-creep over the last decade, but much of the peaceful island was still covered by vegetation. A small combined food mart, gas station, and Subway was the only retail chain presence.

I spent much of the day walking around some of the lesser-travelled streets photographing the details that give Folly Beach an abundant amount of its charm. Yard art ranging from the traditional bottle tree to creative ways of hanging computer monitors in large oaks kept my camera busy and my mind off the two bodies. Charles usually accompanied me on these photo safaris, but he was spending the morning with Melinda. They needed time together, so I didn't tell him what I was doing.

I found myself in front of the Oceanfront Villas and smiled as I thought of Samuel hanging around hoping to see the girl of his dreams. I walked a block farther on Arctic Avenue to where it took a ninety-degree turn away from the beach. I stood in the curve of the lightly travelled road and gazed at the public beach access walkway where Samuel said he had seen the abduction. There were only two lights on the small restroom building, but they were enough to provide some illumination. I was surprised to see a row of vegetation between me and the walk from the beach, and the building blocked most of the parking area. I needed to return at the time of day that Samuel was here to see what it looked like. I tried to think of anything else I could learn by standing here. Little came to mind. The phone rang, and Karen distracted me from my futile efforts.

She was off duty, a rare occurrence in the summer. She once told me that scientists had determined that violent crimes occurred more frequently in the summer. It was partially because people were out more but was also related to the temperature, which peaked during the hot months. Around seven in the evening was the most crime-ridden hour because that was when the human body was at its highest temperature. Charles would have savored that nugget of trivia.

She asked if I had plans for the evening. I said no, and she said that she meant all evening. I asked if that meant tomorrow morning as well. She said that I was catching on. If I'd had plans to dine with the pope, I would have cancelled them. I didn't have to make that call, though, and readily agreed that I was ready, willing, and able. She giggled and said she would be over for supper.

Karen's unmarked, black Crown Vic pulled in my drive at six. I had been watching for her and walked out to meet her.

"So, where are we going to eat?" she said before even a hello. "I'm starved."

She wore light blue shorts and a blue-and-white striped polo shirt and carried a small red and white travel bag.

I took the bag from her hand and kissed her cheek. "Enough mush," she said. "Supper, food, where?"

I admired her athletic build but resented her ability to eat like a hungry sumo wrestler without gaining an ounce. I suggested Loggerhead's Beach Grill. She said that if they were quick with the food, she was all for it. I had chosen Loggerheads because the food was good and service quick but also because it was directly across the street from the Oceanfront Villas and a block from where Samuel had seen the alleged abduction.

We walked hand in hand five blocks to the popular restaurant. Several locals were already taking advantage of the "cold front" and sipping beer on the elevated deck that overlooked the Villas, and if a patron cocked his head just right, the Atlantic. We agreed that it was cooler than recent days but still hot, so we chose a booth inside. It was a wise choice; all the outdoor seating on the large wooden deck was full, and there were three couples waiting for tables.

Fortunately for Karen, and especially me, service was quick, and Karen was already eating conch fritters by the time the couples waiting on the patio had been seated. A half-empty bottle of Budweiser sat in front of her, and a glass of Chardonnay was in my right hand. Karen playfully slapped my left hand as I reached for one of the fritters. "Get your own food," she said.

I gave a macho whimper, and she grinned and generously shared one fritter. Her stomach was beginning to feel hope and she changed her focus from food to a less appetizing subject. "Saw the prelim from the coroner this afternoon." She plopped another fritter in her mouth.

"Oh," I said. I wanted to grab another fritter, but better judgment and the knowledge that our entrees would soon appear stopped me.

"Cause of death was blunt force trauma to the back of the head."

"That's no surprise," I said. "Cindy said there was blood in her hair."

"There was no evidence of a sexual assault," continued Karen. "And from what you told me about your young friend's sighting, it could be the same person. Time of death was two to three days after he saw the abduction. Interestingly, her clothes appeared new; a price tag was still on her blouse."

"Think the abductor had her change out of the bikini?" I asked.

"Yeah, or changed them himself after her death."

Her plate was empty, and she looked around for the waitress.

A scene was averted when Karen's scallops and my fried flounder arrived before she could remind the waitress that she was starved and armed.

"Any idea who she was?"

"Afraid not. No ID on the body, and no one with that description has been reported missing. They were able to get good dental imprints, but unless there's something to compare them to, they're worthless."

"Did the price tag say where the blouse came from?"

"Good question," said Karen. "But no, it was generic, with only the price on it."

"Then all you can do is wait until someone turns up missing?"

"That's about it," she said. "And speaking of missing, they confirmed that the body of the floater was Nicole Sallee."

"Did she drown?"

Karen took a bite of coleslaw and slowly nodded. "Yes. There was water in her lungs, but there was also a gash on the back of her head. That may or not mean anything. It could have happened after she was in the water."

"But it could be the same as the second girl?"

"Probably."

"So they were murdered the same way?"

"Not necessarily," said Karen. "Ms. Sallee's death still could have been accidental. She could have fallen on a boat, hit her head, and then slipped into the water."

"How likely is that?" I asked.

"Not very," said Karen. "If it were accidental, there probably would have been someone else around to see what happened or at least know that she was missing and report it."

"Sounds like two murders—two similar murders," I said as she finished her beer. "Who's working the cases?"

When I had first met Karen, she was the lead detective on suspicious deaths that occurred on Folly Beach. She had the respect of local law enforcement, and even though not many people had known that her dad was the chief, she would use his contacts when local knowledge was needed. When Chief Newman had a near-fatal heart attack three years ago, an acting chief was named, politics reared its ugly head, and battle lines were drawn between the Charleston County sheriff's office and Folly Beach, both in the local government and the local police force. After that, Karen was brusquely told that it would be better if she didn't work any of the beach murders. She wasn't told why and was a good enough officer not to ask. That didn't mean she liked it.

She grinned. "Your fave, Detective Burton."

I didn't return her grin. "Oh great," I said and shook my head.

Detective Brad Burton and I had met my first week on Folly. He was Karen's partner at the time, and for some reason, he disliked me at first sight. He was now near retirement, a slovenly dresser, and just as slovenly at his job. If anyone could get to the bottom of what was going on, it wouldn't be Detective Brad Burton.

"Have you talked with him about the deaths?" I asked.

"Yeah, sort of," she said and took a sip of the fresh brew. "He already has a full plate of murders, five active cases." She shook her head. "One of them is that front-page story about the jewelry store owner who shot the guy who was stealing the pendant to give to his dying mother. Half the citizens are crying for the head of the store owner for shooting the poor, loving son who was simply trying to do something nice for his mother. And then the other half are wanting to put the store owner on a pedestal and make him the NRA's man of the year."

"That's not Burton's problem, is it?" I asked. "They have the guy who killed the thief."

Karen looked out toward the ocean and took a bite of fish. "Sounds simple, and it should be, but with all the attention, he had to make sure all the details are covered and nothing is left to chance. The last thing we need is to miss something that blows up in the face of the prosecution, and in the paper, and on television." She looked around. "To be honest, Burton is not big on doing scut work. The sheriff's on his back about it."

"In other words, he's not going to be putting much energy in whatever's happening here," I said.

"Unless something different slaps him in the head," said Karen, "Ms. Sallee is an accidental drowning, and the latest victim is *probably* a murder, but without knowing who she is and no witnesses to whatever happened, she's a low priority. He told me that if I was trying to tie the two together, then I had a solution looking for a problem." She rolled her eyes. "The jerk. You didn't hear me say that."

"Say what?" I said and then smiled. "And you can't stick your nose in it."

She grinned. "Not officially."

That grin I returned. "Then unofficially, how about taking a walk after we leave here—a walk to where Samuel saw whatever he saw?"

"That sounds so romantic," she said. She took the last sip of beer and then raised her hand, got the waitress's attention, pointed to her empty bottle, and asked for one more.

* * *

We left Loggerheads a little after sunset and walked west to where Samuel had reported seeing the abduction. The sun had set on the marsh side of the island, but a golden sunset still glowed off the high clouds over the ocean. I didn't know what the weather was like when the woman was taken, but it was the same time of day. It could have been lighter or, if there was a heavy cloud cover, much darker. We could still get an idea of the visibility from Samuel's vantage point.

"Walk me through it," said Karen in her detective's interrogation voice. She was focused.

We stood at the bend of the road, approximately where Samuel said he had been. The long wooden walkway to the beach was clearly visible, but it was blocked by shrubbery closer to the restroom buildings beside the sand-covered parking area. I told her that according to what Samuel had said, the girl was grabbed on the handicap ramp to the parking area. A couple of palmetto trees partially blocked the view of much of the ramp, and Karen commented on how little he could have seen if he had been standing where we were. The trees, other low vegetation, and the building combined to make it impossible to see the parking lot.

"He saw the man force her into a car?"

"Yeah," I said. I wasn't able to see vehicles in the lot.

"And he saw the man put his hand over her mouth?"

"Yeah."

She stared at the wooden walk. "Are you certain this is where he was?"

"He said he was where the road took the right turn," I said. "Don't see anywhere else that could have been."

Karen turned and faced me. "Doesn't seem likely that he saw what he said, does it?"

"No," I conceded. "That's what I thought the first time I was here, but I wanted to get your take."

"He couldn't have seen it unless he was somewhere else." She pointed in the direction of where the street intersects Ashley Avenue.

She followed me to the intersection, where there was a clear line of sight to the entrance of the parking lot. "If he had been here," I said, "he would have been able to see some of the lot. If the car was parked near the entrance, he would've had a clear view."

"How certain was he when he said he was back at the bend of the road?"

"He told me twice and told Officer O'Hara the same thing," I said, trying to think back to when he first told me what had allegedly happened. "He never hesitated when telling where he was. He was nervous when talking with O'Hara, but his story was consistent."

"And he said it was a dark Crown Vic?" she said.

"Said it was like your dad's unmarked car. But he wasn't sure of the color."

Karen looked back to where Samuel said he was standing and then turned to Ashley Avenue. "He could have seen the car after it left the lot and headed toward town. Not before."

"True," I said.

"His dad said he had a vivid imagination?" she said.

"Yes, even gave a couple of examples." I shared the two stories that his father had told me.

"Yet you believe him?"

I nodded and looked back at the gravel lot. "Yes."

She was staring at me when I looked up. "Why?" she asked.

Sweat rolled down my breastbone, and the back of my shirt was soaked. I heard a clap of thunder in the distance. I looked back at the parking area and the walk to the beach and then motioned up Ashley Avenue in the direction of the house. We started walking along the side of the road.

"Charles once said that if you can't trust your friends, you can't trust anyone," I said. It sounded like a cliché and a horrible reason when I said it. "Samuel's a friend. Besides, my gut says he saw, or knows, something terrible happened."

Karen reached out for my hand. "That's good enough for me." She squeezed my hand and glanced over at me. "You may want to ask him again."

*I may indeed*, I thought.

Karen rubbed the sweat from her forehead and pulled her hair up from her neck. Sweat was running down my bare legs and into my Crocs. We were at the corner of Center Street and Ashley Avenue when God apparently noticed our overheated plight and dumped buckets of rain on us. The term "scattered shower" took on added meaning when I noticed that the ground a block away at the Tides was dry.

"You sure know how to entertain a girl," said Karen. She laughed and started jogging the last two blocks to the house.

I was pleased that she saw humor in what could have been an awkward moment, but I still had trouble keeping up with her. She had run track in high school and was in better physical condition than I had ever been. The screen door to my porch was open, so she hurried under cover of the porch roof while I was still a half block from home.

I asked if she wanted to take a shower and she said that she thought she just had. She then looked at the floor where water had puddled after dripping from her body and agreed that a controlled, non-Mother Nature–provided shower might be wise. She showed a much higher degree of wisdom when she invited me to join her.

I did.

# CHAPTER 20

Karen had slipped out early for work, so I walked to the Dog. Charles and Melinda were seated at a table in the middle of the room. The restaurant was half-empty, so I was surprised Charles had chosen the center table. He normally preferred the booth along the back wall or a table outside the stream of traffic.

"Hear you and Karen the Cop were doing a rain dance in the middle of the street last night," said Charles.

"Where'd you hear something like that?" I said as if it were wildly inaccurate.

"His honey called," piped in Melinda. "One of her customers at Millie's called her with the rain dance story. Then honeybunch called Charles, and then he told me as soon as he got to my place before we walked over here. I didn't have anybody to tell." She stopped and held her arms out to her side. "God, I love this place. All the excitement. All the gossip. I should've moved here eons ago."

Charles put his hand on Melinda's left arm. "Now, Aunt M., let's let Chief Rain Dance tell us all about it."

I started telling him that Karen and I simply got caught in a shower while we were on our way to the house. He grabbed his cane from the floor and pointed it at me. "Enough, enough," he said. "Don't ruin the story with a bunch of factie things."

"God, I love it," repeated Melinda. "Oh yeah, Charles told me more about his private detective agency. Never thought he had it in him, but guess he proved me wrong."

Charles's private detective agency was housed in his warped imagination. We had luckily solved a few crimes over the years. Each time, Charles talked about opening a detective agency, but it never got past the talking stage once he learned that there were bureaucratic hoops he would have to jump through. The state of South Carolina even had the audacity to say that Charles would have to work for a "real" agency for several years before he could hang out a shingle. He was convinced that he had learned all he needed to know from reading crime novels and watching television.

I never thought he had it in him either, but I didn't say so. "Yes, he's amazed me," I said.

She patted him on the arm again. "It was sweet of you, Chris, to help him out on some of his tough jobs. It was good that you helped, even if he did have to save your life more than once."

Melinda and Charles had already had their breakfast, and I had to wave for Amber to take my order. I thought that would be safer than strangling my friend in front of his aunt. Amber had no sooner left the table than Charles pushed his chair back and headed to the front door.

I couldn't turn to see who had entered, but I heard Charles say, "Good to see you … join us … meet my favorite aunt."

Charles returned with his arm on Chester Carr's shoulder and herded him to the empty seat to my right. I had seen Mr. Carr several times during my early years on Folly. He had worked part time at Bert's. I got to know him better in the winter when he shared some stories about living here years ago. He had introduced me to a ghost story that played a key role in an adventure that I had barely lived through. Chester Carr was in his late eighties and chunkily built, was mostly bald, and stood about five foot six.

Melinda stood before Charles could say anything else. She straightened the front of her new, bright green Walmart blouse and extended her right hand to Chester. He took her hand and planted a kiss on the back of it.

Melinda smiled and said, "You are a spittin' image of—what's his name?"

Chester reciprocated with an even larger smile. "Clark Gable?" he said.

"Hee, hee," said Melinda in a voice that sounded like a ten-year-old's rather than an age with nearly seventy years added to that.

"Robert Redford," said Chester.

Melinda laughed again and then snapped her fingers. "Mr. Magoo," she said.

The table wasn't large enough for both Charles and me to climb under, so we remained in our chairs and stared at the flatware.

Chester looked at Melinda through his bottle glasses, turned to Charles and then slowly to me, and then returned to Melinda and smiled. "My wife, Rosie, God rest her soul, used to say that. She always pinched my cheek when she said it."

Melinda reached over and pinched Chester's left cheek. It turned red from the pinch. His right cheek turned red on its own accord. "I always loved Mr. Magoo," said Melinda. "I also love your glasses."

Chester self-consciously adjusted his large, black-framed eyewear. "Thank you."

Charles saw that Chester not only wasn't insulted but seemed to be enjoying his brief conversation with Melinda. "As President Lincoln said, 'Everybody likes a compliment.'"

Melinda reached over and wiggled Chester's glasses. "It takes a real man to wear such masculine eyewear. All those new, puny glasses people wear are terrible. Heavens to Betsy, they can't even see out of them half the time." She pointed to a lady at the next table who was looking at the menu. "Bet she can't read a syllable. And look at all those fake jewels on the side. They shine like a diamond up a goat's butt."

Charles and I returned to staring at the flatware. Chester laughed and patted Melinda's arm. "How long will you be visiting?" he asked.

"Planning on moving here for good," she said and touched his glasses again.

After the first couple of times I heard her answer that question, I knew anything was possible. That one surprised me.

"It'll be mighty nice have another mature, attractive lady around," said Chester. "All the nice ladies with a little experience on them either have kicked the bucket or are warehoused in senior citizen storage buildings in Charleston."

"Why thank you, sir," said Melinda. "How old are you, anyway?"

Chester looked at me as if to say, "Is she supposed to ask that?" I simply grinned, so he turned back to Melinda. "Why I'm, umm, seventy-nine."

Apparently he forgot a decade somewhere in his calculations. Charles took a sip of water to keep from laughing. I leaned close to Charles and whispered, "Did you know Chester would be here?"

Charles got one of his mock-serious looks and said, "Who, me?"

"That's what I thought," I said. Now I knew why we were in the center of the room.

"I'd like to stay longer," said Chester as he slowly pushed himself up from the table. "I've got to get my hair cut."

"Where do you get your hair done?" said Melinda. "It looks so handsome."

I thought it looked like he forgot to comb his remaining locks after getting out of bed.

"Folly Curls," said Chester.

"Sounds like a chick place to me," said Melinda.

"I have mine styled by a coiffeur."

Melinda leaned back and looked at Charles. "Is that legal here?"

Charles turned to Chester, smiled, and then turned back to Melinda. "Think that's snooty talk for barber."

Chester ignored Charles and gave another large grin to Melinda; about half of his teeth were the color of coffee, but the intent to charm wasn't muted. "Dear lady," he said in a foreign accent, a poor foreign accent, "*oui*, it's French for a man who is a hairdresser."

"Just what I said," blurted Charles.

Melinda ignored Charles. "Might I assume that Folly Curls does women's hair too?" she asked.

Chester said that of course they did and told her where it was located. Then Melinda said she might need to check it out.

Charles reminded her that Heather worked at Millie's and they did women's hair. Melinda pointed out that Millie's might be a fine salon, but she would have some trouble making the extra three-block walk, especially since her nephew didn't have a car and she wouldn't be caught dead riding behind him on his bicycle.

Chester, who seemed to have forgotten that he was leaving, chimed in and said that he would escort Melinda to Folly Curls whenever she wanted him to.

Melinda patted the side of her wig. "Tomorrow might be a good time," she said.

Chester said he could work it into his busy schedule, and they set a time for him to be at her "quaint residence by the marsh." He then remembered that he was leaving, and the three of us watched as he slowly headed to the exit.

"That's one sexy gent," she said to no one in particular.

Charles nodded, and I remained neutral. I had described Chester to several people, but it had never entered my mind to use the word "sexy."

Melinda nodded to the left and then to the right. "I'm not exactly sure that he told the entire truth about how old he is." She turned to Charles. "Think I could hire your detective agency to investigate his age? While you're at it, see if he's been convicted of murder or not returning a book to the library? Can't be too careful, you know."

Charles told her that he would have to check his calendar to see if he would have time between ongoing cases to check on the potential age-stretcher, murderer, or book thief.

"While you're looking for open time slots," she said, pointing at me, "why don't you help your friend here solve his missing person's crime that no one thinks is a crime. Sounds right up your alley."

She knew her nephew well. But she couldn't have known what she was getting him into.

# CHAPTER 21

Saturday mornings in Landrum Gallery were fairly predictable. I'd arrive around ten. Charles would have already been there for a half hour and then complain about me being late. I'd ask him how business was; he'd say that no one had been in. I'd then ask him what I was late for. He'd mumble something about early birds catching worms. And then I'd smile and know the world was still spinning on its axis.

I should have known that the day would not be typical when I arrived at my regular time and the door was locked. I vaguely remembered Charles saying he'd be doing something in Melinda's apartment and possibly not being in this morning. To be honest, I was still recuperating from Melinda and Chester's teenager-like encounter and didn't pay much attention to what Charles said he was doing today.

A middle-aged couple hauling two grandchildren constituted my total business for the first two hours. They were ready to buy a large, framed photo of a sunrise over the pier until the younger of the grandchildren started yelling, "Beach, Grandma!" The dear child then plopped down on the well-worn floor and yelled, "Now! Now! Now!"

Grandma's face alternated between anger and embarrassment, and the grandfather cut our negotiating short and told me that they might be back to get the photo. Seldom was I happy to miss a sale, but this had rapidly become one of those times. The five-year-old successfully manipulated the mature, fifty-year-old couple, and they made an awkward beeline toward the sand, surf, and happiness for the kid. Where was Charles when I needed him?

Just before noon, the bell over the door alerted me to another potential customer. I was in back writing a grocery list to restock the refrigerator; actually, "grocery list" may have been a bit of a misnomer. All the items could be bought at a liquor store.

I left the list on the table and walked into the gallery to greet the latest arrival. I was met by a tall, maybe six foot two, and stocky gentleman in his midforties who looked totally out of place in the beach community. He reminded me of the overpaid vice presidents at my former employer. He wore a lightweight, dark gray, two-piece wool suit, a bright yellow tie with small, geometric squares, and a crisp white shirt with a button-down collar. He looked like he had stepped out of a Ben Silver catalog rather than out of city hall. It was Joshua Lally, Folly's new mayor.

He looked around the gallery and briefly took in the framed photos on the wall. To my knowledge, this was his first time in. He then turned to me. "Good day, Mr. Landrum," he said with a slight grin. "I'm Mayor Lally."

His photo had been in the local paper nearly every issue since his election in April, so I obviously recognized him. In most of the photos he had been dressed nearly identically to how he looked today. Only the tie seemed to change.

He had taken two steps into the gallery and appeared to be comfortable there. I walked over and extended my hand. He wiped some imaginary dust off his sleeve and made no effort to shake. "Welcome to the gallery, Mr. Mayor," I said.

Apparently he had reached his limit of small talk. "I would like to buy you lunch," he said and looked around the room. "Is this a good time?"

I had heard that he was all business, and none of my friends had more than a *hello* relationship with him. According to the articles in the paper, Lally had made boatloads of money when he sold his company, which had developed groundbreaking off-track betting software. He had sold the company to an international conglomerate and walked away with millions. The articles were vague about how he had landed on Folly Beach.

It wasn't the best time to leave, since Charles wasn't around to handle the throngs of customers, but I was curious about what had inspired the luncheon invitation and agreed. He walked to the sidewalk and turned toward the beach without saying anything. I locked the door and followed. It was already in the upper eighties, and I wondered why sweat was not rolling down his arms, out his monogrammed shirtsleeve, and past his gold cufflinks to his manicured nails. I felt totally underdressed but drastically more beach appropriate in my khakis and green polo shirt as we silently walked across Arctic Avenue and up the steps to the Folly Pier. Locklear's Low Country Grill was the only restaurant at the pier, so I assumed that was our destination.

There were several people milling around Locklear's since it overlooked the beach, but the restaurant still had empty tables.

"Good afternoon, Mayor Lally," said the smiling, twenty-something, sunburned hostess. "May I help—"

"Table for two. Private," he interrupted.

She nodded, looked around the dining area, and walked us to a table as far from the entry as possible. The table was beside a large window that overlooked the ocean. She still had a smile on her face, but it wasn't nearly as sincere.

A college-aged waiter was at the table as soon as we were seated. He set two glasses of water in front of us and asked if he could get us anything else to drink.

Lally glanced at the menu and without looking up said, "Iced tea, two slices of lemon, and three packets of Equal, not Splenda, not Sweet 'n' Low, not too much ice."

I said that water was fine.

No one was seated at the tables nearest us, but Lally looked around and took a deep breath. I had the impression that he would have had the management shoo out any patrons in proximity. "I'm not one to beat around the bush," he said.

*You can say that again*, I thought and nodded.

"Officer O'Hara told me that you dragged one of our teenage citizens into the police station and made him share some cockamamie story about an abduction."

I cocked my head. "Yes, I—"

He abruptly raised his right hand and shoved it, palm first, toward me. "Let me finish," he barked.

"Officer O'Hara said, and I completely concur, that the story was simply a teenage fantasy. Your young friend has seen too many dramas. His imagination has run wild, and you encouraged him to cause trouble."

The waiter returned, and Lally looked at the tea put in front of him. "I said two slices of lemon. There's only one. Can't you count?"

The waiter quickly apologized and scurried away to get more lemon.

Lally shook his head. "I can't stand incompetence."

*His career in politics will be quite interesting, then,* I thought and then shrugged.

"Forcing a teenager to go to the police is not my reason for this talk," he continued. "But it is a symptom." He glared at me. "Since you arrived on Folly, what, six years ago?"

He didn't wait for an answer or even give me time to shake my head again.

"You have done nothing but butt into the affairs of law enforcement. You've agitated our, how shall I say this, more bohemian citizens, irritated upstanding residents, and gone out of your way to embarrass the government."

The waiter returned to the table with a new glass of tea with the appropriate number of lemon slices and asked if we were ready to order. The mayor waved him away.

"If you mean helping the police catch—"

He raised his hand again. "What I mean, and hear this clearly, is that I will not tolerate your meddling, agitating, and officious behavior." He lowered his hand and took a sip of his two-lemon-slices tea. "Is that clear?"

I nodded.

"Another thing, Mr. Landrum. I understand that you are friends with our current director of public safety."

"Yes," I said. "Chief Newman and I have—"

"When I owned my company, I gave each of my employees one mistake. After all—" He grinned. "We are human and make mistakes." The grin faded. "One chance never became two. Termination was the only alternative. Do I make myself clear?"

"Perfectly," I said. "But do you think that will work with city government?" I hesitated and wondered what to say next; after all, this was the first chance he'd given me to finish a thought. "Government is a people business, and people make varying degrees of mistakes. Take your police department. Each officer makes hundreds of subjective decisions each day—do I stop a car for going one mile per hour over the limit, two miles, three, when? Most everyone leaving Cal's bar has been drinking; how much is too much? All subjective judgments."

"Good points, Mr. Landrum. Perhaps I'll consider them. But let me make one more point." He looked around the room; no one was near. "I do not like Chief Newman. I believe he has been on the job too long. He is way too tolerant of misbehavior. He is not tough enough on those who disturb the peace of our hardworking, respectable citizens. If he didn't have substantial support on the council, he would have been gone the day I took office."

The waiter returned to the table and again asked if we were ready to order. Lally said that we would let him know when we were ready and turned back to me. "Four years ago my mother died. I took over the family home on the west end of Folly. I lived in Raleigh where my company was and decided to remodel the house and use it as a vacation home. Then I had the opportunity to sell the company, so I decided to tear down the antiquated structure and build a permanent house and move my family here. Several million dollars later, I had built a house. I thought it would be peaceful and private." He hesitated and took a deep breath. The happy sounds of families eating lunch at such a scenic location reverberated around the restaurant, but all I could focus on were the harsh, unemotional words coming from the mayor.

"I was wrong," he continued. "Cars and loud trucks sped past it like the road was a drag strip. Kids actually walked through the yard to the beach. And the neighbor next door parked a thirty-foot-long fishing boat in his side yard. You know what the idiots at city hall said?"

I know what I would have liked to have said, but I merely shook my head.

"They said, and this is a direct quote, 'That's Folly.'" He gave a sinister laugh. "I'd invested millions of dollars in this island to be told, basically, there was nothing to do about the problems."

There had been an on-and-off battle over the years about what Folly was or what it should be. In dumbed-down terms, it was a classic battle of those who wanted to leave Folly alone versus those trying to make it more like Daniel Island or Kiawah—enclaves for the well-heeled, private estates. If anyone would let them, the second group would add a toll booth. One iconoclastic local had suggested issuing passports to the "country of Folly." Mayor Lally fell hard on the metamorphic side of the continuum. And it was obvious that he thought that the kinder and gentler approach of law enforcement encouraged by Chief Newman caused irreparable damage to what the new mayor thought Folly should be. The mayor's unofficial campaign slogan had been, "Let's take the folly out of Folly." He promoted tourism, but he meant tourism by the wealthy; he wanted more expensive condos and possibly a second luxury hotel. He wanted upscale shopping and even hinted that two four-star restaurants had committed to him that if he was elected they would move here.

I was as big a fan of politics as I was of colonoscopies, so I hadn't followed the election closely, but Marc Salmon had told me that the only reason that Lally got elected was because the previous mayor had taken to drinking his breakfast, lunch, and midafternoon snack. Salmon said, "Even Folly could take only so much alcoholic imbibery." The straw that broke the mayor's reelection was when, under the influence everyone assumed, he had asked the council to resign so he could appoint Flipper and Alvin and the Chipmunks to replace them. He did garner a couple of hundred votes in the election from those who thought the new council would have been an improvement.

Lally straightened his tie, wiped nothing off his mouth with the napkin, neatly folded it, and placed it on the table. "Mr. Landrum, I will do whatever necessary to see that your chief is replaced. Further, I will not tolerate any rogue citizen interfering in police business. If anyone does—" He pointed his index finger at me. "I will make his or her life a living hell. Believe me, I can do that." He nodded. "They tell me that you are bright, so I know you understand what I am saying. I shall not repeat it. That is clear, isn't it?"

"Perfectly," I said to the back of his head. He was already on his way out of the restaurant, but he stopped at a table near the door and shook the hand of the gentlemen seated with a small boy. He patted the youngster on the head and laughed.

His message was clear—way too clear.

# Chapter 22

Not only had the mayor not-so-subtly threatened me to butt out of almost everything except running my gallery and assured me that he would get rid of my friend as police chief, he had also taken me to a lunch at which I never got any food and he stuck me with the tab for his tea, two slices of lemon, and Equal, not Splenda, not Sweet 'n' Low.

I wasn't sure my legs were stable enough to walk, so I remained at the table and looked out to the patio tables and the beach. Two iridescent blue Grackles were fighting over a fry that a young girl had dropped on the deck. Another bird with scary, bright golden eyes had a monarch butterfly trapped against the fine, mesh screening that protected diners from other less-appetizing bird by-products and was ready to have it for lunch. I felt like the butterfly.

I was too shaken to return to the gallery. I wanted to take a walk, but it was too hot to go far. Instead, I walked to the end of the fishing pier; a place where I had often gone to think. There was a brisk sea breeze near the far end, and a group of optimistic fishermen watched their poles and hoped that the straight fiberglass rods would bend toward the water. I found a vacant wooden bench under the second level of pier and in the shade. I sat facing the beach and rehashed what the mayor had said and wondered why he felt the need to come after me. True, I had been involved in a few terrible situations, but I had never intentionally stood in the way of law enforcement investigating the murders. True, I had gone with Samuel to report what he had seen. What was so wrong with that?

And then there's Samuel's story. I looked left past the Tides and the Oceanfront Villas to the public walkway where Samuel had witnessed whatever. He had told me, and repeated to Officer O'Hara, a convincing story of seeing an abduction. Yet when Karen and I had stood at the spot Samuel claimed he was standing when he saw the incident, we had agreed that it would have been impossible for him to have seen what he described. If he had been thirty yards closer to Ashley Avenue, he could have witnessed the abduction, or at least, some of it. But he had been asked more than once where he was, and he hadn't wavered in his description.

The smart thing to do would be to write off Samuel's story the way that Officer O'Hara and Mayor Lally had apparently done. Samuel had a history of letting his imagination run amok. His version didn't appear feasible. And if he did see something, it could easily be explained as horseplay.

But hadn't a body been discovered that fit the woman's description? Hadn't she been murdered in a timeline consistent with his story? And wasn't the detective from the sheriff's office assigned to the case someone who I doubted could find a murderer in Sing Sing?

Charles had once pointed out that most smart thoughts left the brain when one left the congruous forty-eight states and crossed over the Folly River. I smiled to myself and said, *why not.* It was time to find Samuel and confront him with what Karen and I had seen. My young friend might be at home, since it was Saturday. I took a chance and walked to his house.

"Hi, Mr. Landrum," he said as he answered the door. If Samuel was surprised to see me, it didn't show. He said that his dad was at work and he was getting ready to walk to Roasted, the coffee shop in Tides, to get some ice cream and "check out" the ocean.

He asked if I wanted to walk with him. My back was already soaked with sweat, and the only thing that had kept my forehead from burning was the brim of my Tilley. No, I didn't want to walk six more blocks back to nearly where I had left minutes earlier, but I said, "Sounds good." I figured that after he got his treat at the hotel, we would be a couple of blocks from where he said he had seen the crime. I envisioned a show-and-tell in the near future.

"The air conditioner's broken," he said as he closed the door behind him. "Dad says it's on the fritz, whatever that means. All I know is it's making a lot of noise and blowing out air, but it's all hot."

Samuel's pace was much quicker than mine, and I slowed him down more than once. Roasted overlooked the hotel's pool and the beach. The pool was packed, and the beach looked like a solid mass of skin, flimsy swimsuits, and children scampering in and out of the water in time with the waves that slapped the shore.

On the way, Samuel talked about the first few days of school, shared that two of his friends from last school year had moved out of state, and commented on how crowded the sidewalk was. He didn't ask why I had appeared at his door or mention the abduction. We got our treats, moved to the lobby, and sat in two comfortable chairs that faced the beach.

He glanced up from his ice cream. "Did you come to tell me, umm, to tell about the girl? Was she the one they found the other day?"

It had been on his mind since I had arrived at his house, but he had patiently waited for me to bring it up. He couldn't wait any longer.

"I don't know," I said. "But I'd like for us to walk over to where you saw it happen. Is that okay?"

"I guess so, sure. Now?"

"Good time as any."

He took the last bite of ice cream, wiped his hands on his cargo shorts, which almost reached the top of his tennis shoes, and then popped out of the chair. We left by the side door and walked through the hotel's parking lot to the sidewalk along Arctic Avenue. The block-long, four-story Oceanfront Villas was on our left, and I asked Samuel if he had seen the girl of his dreams again.

He sighed. "Nah, I think her school started. I haven't seen her since last weekend." He smiled and waved toward the condo. "Her loss."

I laughed.

We walked a hundred yards or so farther to the spot where the road took an abrupt right angle and turned away from the ocean. Several hurricanes and years of erosion ago, Arctic Avenue had continued parallel to the ocean for several more blocks. Today, that was just a memory for island old-timers.

"Show me exactly where you were when you saw it," I said. We stood off the edge of the road and looked at the sand dune that rose approximately six feet above the berm. It was covered with sea oats and the slatted wooden fence placed to protect the dunes.

At a forty-five degree angle to our right were the elevated public restrooms, the ramp down to the parking lot, and a row of trash containers. We were within ten feet of where Karen and I had stood.

Samuel twisted his tennis shoe in the sand, glanced at the dune in front of him, and then looked at me. He didn't make eye contact. "Pretty sure I was right here," he mumbled.

"And where was the girl when you first saw her?"

He turned toward the walk. The view was blocked in front of us, and he twisted his head more toward the ocean end of the trail. He pointed to where the steps from the beach rose to the wooden walk. He didn't say anything.

"How about where the guy grabbed her?" I asked. I looked where he had pointed and then scanned the path of the walk.

"I think it was right at the corner where the restroom building begins?"

"You think or you're sure?" I asked. Two large shrubs blocked the view to that part of walkway.

He looked down at his feet. "Pretty sure," he said.

He was clearly uncomfortable. "It was almost dark," I said. "It would've been hard to see everything, wouldn't it?" I nodded my head and paused to give him a chance to collect his thoughts.

"Yeah ... umm, maybe I sort of didn't see everything as clear as I thought," he said in a low voice.

I put my arm around his shoulder. "Let's go over it again," I said. "Perhaps you'll remember things better now that we're here. I know I have a hard time describing something when I'm not looking at it."

He looked up from his shoes. "Umm, okay."

"You definitely saw the girl, right?" I said. "You remembered the bikini." I smiled.

Samuel smiled. "Yeah, a red one."

"Didn't think you'd forget that," I said.

He blushed. "She had long, brown hair too. It was wet like she'd been in the ocean. She was walking up the stairs by the beach." He pointed at the steps.

"And you noticed a guy over by the restrooms?"

"Barely. I wasn't paying much attention. He was sort of thin, wasn't too tall, and had long dark hair."

Now the moment of truth. "Did you see him grab her?"

He turned toward me but avoided eye contact. He then turned toward the restroom building. "Guess I didn't," he mumbled.

"That's okay," I said and again put my arm around his shoulder. "It would have been hard to see anything at the building and the parking lot from here. What did you see?"

He looked back down at his shoes. "I'm not sure I saw anything, Mr. Landrum." He hesitated. "I'm sorry. I knew if I said what happened no one would think anything of it. I know something bad happened."

"It's okay." I tried again. "What exactly did you see?"

"I couldn't see the girl after she got behind those bushes," he said and pointed to the shrubs beside the walk. "I turned to walk back by the Villas." He hesitated. "Then I heard a scream. It sort of sounded like it came from behind the building, but I couldn't tell for sure. She only screamed once." He hesitated. "I didn't know what to do."

He started up the road toward Ashley Avenue. I followed.

He stopped in the middle of the road and pointed ahead. "Then I saw the big car I told you about."

"The one that looked like an unmarked police car?"

"Yeah," he said. "It flew past heading toward town. I hadn't seen anyone else near the walk, restrooms, or parking lot, so I figured it had to be the long-haired guy. The girl was gone, so I figured she was with him." He turned and finally made eye contact. "She screamed, Mr. Landrum. She wasn't playing. They weren't horsing around. He took her."

# CHAPTER 23

Charles and I were at the Lost Dog Café. It was Monday morning, and we had arrived after the first wave of diners. I would have preferred to have been an hour earlier, but Charles wanted to walk Melinda to Folly Curls so she could have them do *whatever* to her hair—or, more accurately, to her wig.

"He lied about seeing an abduction," said Charles. "What makes you think you can believe him?"

"A gut reaction," I said.

This was the first time I had seen Charles since my unpleasant conversation with the mayor and my discussion with Samuel about the night of the alleged abduction. Charles had asked about Samuel, so I had started with that story. Besides, I wasn't sure how much of the mayor's conversation I wanted to share. Charles wasn't a fan of Lally, and I was afraid that if I told him everything he might go after the mayor with his cane flying.

He took a bite of eggs, set his fork on the side of the plate, and held up his index finger. "First, Samuel lied to you—and, oh yeah, to the police." Now he added his middle finger to the index finger. "Second, he has a history of imagining things. Third," he said but didn't add another finger, "he's a teenager. Reality ain't part of their reality."

"I can't argue with any of that," I said. "There are good reasons not to believe him."

"Correction," said Charles, who now picked up the fork and pointed it at me. "Those are three things that *you* would have thrown at me if I had said I believed the fifteen-year-old."

Now I was confused. "What're you saying?"

"I'm saying that if I was saying what you were saying, you would have said he imagined it. You would tell me to drop it."

I followed most of that. "And then what would you have done?" I asked.

"I would have said you didn't know what you were talking about. I would have believed Samuel and waded right in to finding out what happened. That would result in a big mess. You would have to save me from myself. Then I would have to save you from some bad person, and then ... hell, I don't know what then."

And he thought Samuel had an inflated imagination.

Before Charles could further confuse both of us, we were interrupted by Brian Newman. I don't know how much he had heard, but he towered over our table shaking his head. Charles asked if he wanted to join us. Normally he would have said no, so I was surprised when he motioned for Charles to slide over to make room.

The chief was in his usual uniform, a Tommy Bahama light blue camp shirt and light gray dress slacks. He apparently had as many of the loose, straight-cut, short-sleeved shirts as Charles had college logo T-shirts.

Kim, a new waitress, was quick to the table and took Brian's order. She headed to the kitchen, and he turned to me. "Got some news you'll be interested in."

I leaned closer to the table.

"Got a positive ID on the second victim," he continued.

"How?" I said. "Who is she?"

"I'd like to say it was good police work," said Brian. "But it was pure luck." He took the small, well-worn notebook out of his shirt pocket and flipped through a few pages. "Name's Kendra Corman-Eades—Caucasian, age twenty-eight, five foot three, from Athens, Georgia."

"Luck?" said Charles.

Brian sipped his water and then turned to Charles. "Her sister's birthday was four days ago, and she called us the day before yesterday. It seemed that Kendra called her every year on her birthday. She never failed—until this year. Her sister knew something was wrong, terribly wrong. If it hadn't been for the birthday, no one would have thought anything about not hearing from her."

"Why?" I asked.

"She'd never been married. She had several relationships with guys, but, and this is according to her sister, she'd begun to question her sexual orientation. She had a history of disappearing for weeks and even months. No one would've been concerned if they didn't hear from her."

"How did her sister know to call here?"

"Didn't," said the chief. "Kendra told the sister that she was going to get away and 'figure things out.' All she said was that she was going to the beach near Charleston. We were the third beach community she called. Pure luck."

"Are you sure it's her?" I asked.

"Yeah, her body was in fairly good condition, and her sister gave the ID." He looked around the room and then took another sip of water. "It was so sad. Her sister brought a photo album. Kendra was a lovely young lady. She had a degree from Athens Technical College and had won several beauty contests. Her sister said she would have made a career of contests if she could have. She loved nice clothes and working on her appearance; she barely ate to keep her trim figure. Sad."

"Any idea where she stayed?" I asked.

"Not sure she did. I'm having my guys ask around to see if anyone saw her. Her sister had a better photo, but it was still a couple of years old, and her hair was different."

"Could I get a copy of it?" asked Charles.

I didn't like the sound of that but remained silent.

Brian's eyes narrowed as he looked at Charles. "Don't think so."

That wouldn't stop Charles, but I remained silent.

Kim arrived with Brian's fruit parfait and refilled my coffee. The aroma of freshly brewed coffee was much more soothing than the conversation. I had a captive audience and decided to tell the chief about how Samuel and I were treated by one of his officers. I shared how Officer O'Hara had been dismissive and condescending and acted like he was doing us a favor by listening to Samuel's story.

Brian shook his head. "Wish that was the first time I'd heard that about O'Hara."

"Going to fire his ass?" asked Charles.

Subtlety is not Charles's strong suit.

Brian smiled and then looked around the room. "Guess who thinks Officer O'Hara is the best cop in South Carolina?"

"Association of Rude Police Officers?" offered Charles.

"Mayor Lally," I said.

Brian frowned and wiped his mouth with a napkin. "How'd you know?"

He had almost twisted my arm, so I proceeded to recount my unlunch with the new mayor. Charles stopped short of emitting steam from his ears. He pounded the table so hard that two customers at the next table stopped and looked our way. Charles looked at them and said, "Darn gnat. I got it."

Brian handled it more professionally, but he was peeved. He asked a few clarifying questions and then asked me to repeat the parts that could be construed as threatening.

Charles wanted to know if the mayor had actually called me a "rogue citizen" and said if I was a rogue, he couldn't imagine what that made him. I couldn't tell whether I was being complimented or insulted.

Brian finished eating and neatly folded his napkin and placed it on the plate. "This isn't your battle," he said. "Sorry he chose to drag you into it. I'll take care of it."

Charles's hands shook. "It most certainly is our battle," said Charles. "If the mayor wants to take you on, he'll have us to deal with us. Exclamation point."

Brian had known Charles for many years and knew the less said to him the better. He wouldn't be dissuaded by words alone. "Let's get back to what Samuel saw. Tell me about it."

The original police report was now worthless, so I told Brian the revised version of Samuel's story. He asked if I believed Samuel. I said that I wasn't certain but that the youngster was convinced.

Charles, said, "You bet we believe him. I think the girl he saw was Ms. Corman-Eades."

Brian pushed away from the table and started to the exit. He paused and then returned. "You fellows sure can make a parfait interesting." He looked down at Charles. "I'm wasting words, but try to stay out of trouble."

"Of course, Chief," said Charles, his best angelic look affixed on his weathered face.

Brian had almost made it to the exit when Charles reached for my cell phone, scrolled through the saved numbers, and punched call.

"Hi, Cindy. No, it's not Chris; your caller ID fibbed. Yep, it's his handsome and much younger friend, Charles ... What's so funny? Whatever." He glanced at me. "Listen, your boss—yeah, Chief Newman—was just here ... oh, the Dog ... he said you had a photo of the woman who was buried in the sand ... Yes, that's her. Anyway, he said I could borrow it for Chris to make a copy ... Okay, that'd be great. We'll be here."

He punched *end call* and set the phone back on my side of the table.

"Did I miss something in the conversation with Brian?" I asked. "Something about you not getting the photo?"

"Guess so," said Charles with a straight face.

# CHAPTER 24

Officer LaMond said she would bring the photo to the Dog, but it would be a few minutes before she could make it. Charles then asked Kim to clear the table and bring us two fresh jars of water. She smiled and said something about Charles being a big spender. He winked at her.

She left to rustle up our big order, and Charles stared at a photo of two basset hounds on the wall beside our table. "I've got a question," he said.

I assumed he was talking to me and not the dogs. "And it is?"

"Do you find it interesting that no one knew where the girls were going or where they were staying?"

I looked at the photo of the two dogs and then at Charles. "Could be a coincidence. Neither was married. Both headed this way to 'find themselves.' A lot of unattached people in their age group are here all the time."

"They're usually not dead, though," he said. "Didn't the chief say that Kendra had been in beauty pageants?"

"Yeah," I said, wondering where he was going with this.

"Didn't Cindy say that the first girl, Nicole something, had also been in some pageants? Do you think that's another coincidence?"

"Nicole Sallee," I said. "Don't know. I assume you're trying to say that there are similarities between the two."

Charles nodded. "Yep."

"There were differences too," I said. "One was white, the other black. One was murdered and—whoa, here's a big difference. There's no indication that Nicole was murdered."

"She was," said Charles with a degree of confidence usually reserved for statements like "the sun will come up tomorrow."

Cindy LaMond walked in before I asked why he was certain. I moved over to make room in the booth. She smiled at Kim, asked for a glass of tea, and then slid in beside me. She had a sheet of paper in her right hand and placed it face down on the table.

Cindy focused her attention on Charles. "Tell me again how the chief wanted me to give you the photo."

Charles waited until the waitress delivered Cindy's tea. "I'm not certain I remember the exact words," he began. I rubbed my eyes and didn't look at Cindy or Charles. "I'm getting old, you know; I might not have this exactly right."

Cindy took a sip of her drink, frowned in the direction of Charles, nodded, and then smiled. "Do your best, gramps."

"He said something about you having a copy of the photo and I, being a good, concerned citizen, asked if I could get a copy. Might jar something in my memory that could help the police." He stopped and then gave a big nod.

"And then the chief thanked you for your burning desire to help the police," she said, looking toward the ceiling and then back at Charles. "He said he would be glad to supply you with the photo and to call me to get the copy."

Charles glanced at me, and I started staring at the photo of the dog. "Something like that," he said.

Surely he meant to say "nothing like that," but I didn't correct him. By now, I wanted to see the picture.

She slid the paper to Charles's side of the table. "I left my crapometer in the car," she said. "So I'm *sure* that's what the chief said. And I'm sure that if I ask him, he'll confirm your story—right?"

"Umm, of course," said Charles.

I sat back in the booth and smiled. Cindy wouldn't ask the chief, but she would let Charles know that she didn't believe a word that came out of his mouth.

"Learned anything new about her death?" I asked.

"Nothing other than it was dumb luck that she was identified. Her prints were not on file anywhere, and if one of our resident bums hadn't been searching for doubloons, gold nuggets, mint julep cups, or whatever in hell he was using his magic metal finder for, there wouldn't have been a body to not be able to identify."

"What about Nicole what's-her-name?" asked Charles. "Any news about how she was murdered?"

Cindy grinned at Charles. "Don't know she was murdered. You know something we don't, or are you fishing again?"

"You'll let us know when you find out how she was killed, won't you?" said Charles as he ignored her questions.

"You know it," she said. "Keeping you informed is what I live for."

"You're wise beyond your years, Officer LaMond," said Charles.

I would have used another word after wise, but no one asked me.

She laughed. "I'll leave on that lie," she said and slipped out of the booth.

"I'll get your drink," said my generous friend.

She sighed and then walked toward the exit.

Charles looked down at the photo. "She's pretty," he said and then pushed the paper over to me.

I glanced at it. "A beauty queen," I said.

"Think Samuel would recognize her?"

I smiled. "Not without a red bikini. His attention wasn't on her face."

Charles took the photo back and asked me what time it was. The room was one table shy of full, and we had overextended our welcome. He asked if I wanted to walk with him to see if Melinda was done at the beauty shop. My appointment calendar had a couple of holes in it, and I told him I would if we would be done by Friday morning. He looked at his imaginary watch and said he thought we'd make it. It was Monday.

We had walked a block before Charles spoke. "Think Cindy would have a photo of the first dead woman?"

"Nicole Sallee," I said. "I don't know if Cindy would, but since she's been identified, I would think her hometown paper would have run one. We can check the Internet. Why?"

"Just curious," he said and then spoke to a heavily tattooed, middle-aged gentleman walking a pug.

*Just curious is often the start of something much worse*, I thought.

Folly Curls was in a small, red, one-story building a half block off Center Street. The building had housed many failed businesses over its thirty-five-year history. Its most recent incarnation opened a couple of years ago and was owned by a young couple, Anne and Cameron Potterfield. Anne was a hairdresser who worked in the shop six days a week and rented chairs to two other stylists. Cameron was a carpenter with Edelen Construction on James Island. I wouldn't have known any of this if I hadn't gotten my hair cut at Millie's and learned about the competing salons through osmosis.

I asked Charles if he had ever been in the salon as we headed up its sand and crushed-shell walk. He said "sure" but then added that it had only been once and that had been this morning when he delivered Melinda.

We were greeted by an attractive stylist in her late twenties. She had her left hand tangled in a middle-aged woman's mane and her right hand gripping a hair dryer. She said her name was Anne and asked if she could do anything for us. Before she could answer, I heard the familiar voice of Melinda from behind a portable bamboo partition. "Is that you Charles?"

"As sure as the ocean's wet," he said.

I would have been more impressed with his poetic answer if my eyes hadn't been directed to the right side of the room, where there were five Styrofoam heads covered with a variety of wigs in colors ranging from glow-in-the-dark blond to pitch black. None of them was more attention-grabbing than the Carolina-blue wig in the center of the room, snugly placed on Melinda's head. I had no idea what to say. To my amazement, neither did Charles.

"Didn't he work wonders?" said Melinda. She turned her head so we could get a view of all sides. The hairdresser who stood behind her raised both hands over his head and clapped. He reminded me of a trained seal begging for a fish.

"Aunt Melinda," said Charles, "*wonders* doesn't do it justice."

Charles had said it all.

"Oh, I'm being rude," said Melinda. "Meet Damian, umm—"

"Sharp," said the midthirties hairdresser. He walked around the chair and shook my hand and then Charles's.

"Ain't he a doll?" said Melinda. "He said he'd never colored a wig quite like this before, but when I told him it had been my dream for years, he said he'd do it."

Damian grinned and bowed at his trim waist. But when Melinda turned toward Charles, he rolled his eyes. I was in agreement.

"Your aunt's quite a lady," said the dirty-blond-haired wonder worker. "It'll be fun having her around—I hope it's for a long time."

Charles cringed. I hoped Damian was right.

"Think we could get a taxi back to my place?" said Melinda as she looked at Charles. We stood outside the salon, and she leaned against the side of the building.

Charles looked at me. The nearest taxi was in Charleston, so I volunteered to get my SUV and pick them up. Melinda looked exhausted and slowly lowered herself to the step.

By the time it took me to walk home and get Melinda's ride, she had perked up and was in animated conversation with Charles about a couple of the other customers and how even she thought they were a bit nutty. She whispered that one of the customers, Sylvia, was "nuttier than a squirrel turd" and then asked Charles if he had solved the murders. Charles told her with great confidence that he and I had been working on the case and had a "hot lead."

"It's only a matter of time before we catch him," he said.

I stared straight ahead at the road and thought that perhaps Sylvia wasn't the only nutty person Melinda had encountered today.

# CHAPTER 25

"Only a matter of time … only a matter of time before *we* catch him," I mumbled to Charles.

We had dropped Melinda off at her apartment, and Charles had suggested that we go to my house and get on the Internet. He said that Melinda may not have much more time around and *we* had to solve the murders before she went on to meet other *angelic alcoholics in distilled-spirits heaven.* He reminded me that I had mentioned that my calendar was clear for the next four days, and he planned to fill them with "killer-catchin' stuff."

It didn't take long to find a photo of the late Nicole Sallee in the *Valdosta Daily Times.* The image was wrapped in the tragic story about the death of the beautiful master's degree holder from Valdosta State University. The photo was a glamour shot pulled from her modeling portfolio. Nicole was as pretty as Kendra Corman-Eades. The article shed little additional light on her death. It did say that she had married right after college but that it had only lasted a year. He ex-husband said her death was "beyond belief" and that he hadn't seen her in months. The Charleston police were not commenting on the death other than that foul play hadn't been ruled out.

I printed a half-dozen copies of the photo. Charles also asked me to "copy it to a thumb thing." He said that while I was at it, I could scan the photo of Ms. Corman-Eades he had received from Cindy and add it to the "thumb thing." I asked why and he said, "You never know when you might need more copies." I gave him a sideways glance and started to scan the image.

"Umm," he said and pointed to the computer. "While you're at it, could we use your computer magic and add some words?"

"We could," I said and stared at him. The ball was in his court.

"Then why don't *we* say something like, 'Do you know anything about,' and then you could add their names."

I said, "*We* could."

And then he mumbled, "Then under the photo we could add, 'If so, please contact Charles Fowler at,' and then you could put my phone number."

"*We* could."

"Great idea," he said and then pointed at the keyboard. "Then you could stick all that on the thumb-thing doohickey, and we could go over to Pack & Mail and get a couple hundred flyers printed."

I knew it was a terrible idea. Pursuing the issue was the wrong thing to do, and it could only lead to trouble. I also knew Charles.

"You bet," I said and started Photoshop.

It took an hour before amateur graphic designer and faux detective Charles was satisfied with the layout. The photo of Kendra Corman-Eades was sharp but in black and white. The low-resolution image of Nicole Sallee taken from the newspaper website wasn't as clear, but she was recognizable. Charles had urged me to add my name and phone number as a second contact, but I declined. I controlled the keyboard, so I won a minor victory.

An hour later, we were back on Folly Beach with two hundred and fifty flyers. Charles wanted to get started distributing them to every business on the island and attaching them to every light pole, announcement board, and store window. I wished him well and chose a nap over covering the island with images of the two deceased women.

Naps and I don't get along. The phone rang before my eyes were closed, and I heard the calm, cheerful voice of Chief Brian Newman. "What in blue blazes is that damned friend of yours trying to do? Don't answer!" he yelled. "I don't want to know. Damn, go ahead and tell me. This had better be good."

This would be a perfect time for me to play ignorant. "I'm sorry, Brian, what do you mean?"

"You … you know damned well what I mean. Frickin' flyers stuck on poles down Center Street. Charles doesn't have a computer or a way to make anything as nice as what's stuck all over. You do."

Brian wasn't the chief by accident. "He wanted some flyers to see if anyone knew about the two women. He wanted to get information to turn over to the police. How'd you hear about it?"

He made a noise that sounded like a snarl and then said, "Oh, could be because in the last half hour I've received calls from two restaurants, one city council member, two of my officers, and, best of all, our mayor."

"Oh," I said.

"Yeah," said Brian. "And our mayor said that if he sees one of those blankety-blank flyers on any surface on *his* island after eight a.m. tomorrow, the world will come to a screeching halt for two people."

"I'll share that message with Charles," I said.

"I would have told him myself, but the idiot who's asking people to call doesn't have an answering machine. He's not sitting by the phone waiting for calls—probably still out plastering what'll be my termination notice on telephone poles. I'd go looking for him, but I'm afraid if I found him, I'd shoot first and ask questions later. Oh yeah, when you find him, you might *suggest* that first he removes the two copies from the window at city hall. Damn, my head hurts." The phone went dead.

I realized that my head didn't feel so well either and headed to Bert's to get something for it. I was tempted to seek relief in the wine department but instead headed down the medicine aisle.

"Yo, Christer," came a squeaky voice from the next aisle. "Got datum for you."

Dude and his glow-in-the-dark, peace-symbol-adorned, tie-dyed shirt were instantly recognizable, but hearing the surfer say "datum" threw me. I supposed he had gleaned it from the pages of *Astronomy* magazine. "Hey, Dude," I said. "What would that be?"

Instead of answering, he scampered down the aisle and around to where I was standing in front of the headache medicines and then looked around. "Me be careful about who's nosin' in," he whispered. He had a jar of mayonnaise in his left hand and a pack of fishhooks in

"Funny," he said and then shook his head. "It was Oscar—"

"Oscar from the gas station?"

Charles stared at me. "How many Oscars do you know?"

"Just checking," I said. Oscar was in his midtwenties with hair that matched his personality. It went all directions without any plan or semblance of order.

"Now, if you'll let me finish, I'll lay a big clue on you."

I nodded.

"Oscar said Kendra Corman-Eades bought gas from him a few days before she turned up missing."

"How'd he know it was her?"

"Good question," said Charles. "I asked him the same thing." He nodded.

"Well?"

A large construction truck rumbled down Center Street and interrupted his concentration. He stared at the truck until the sound level fell below that of a jetliner taking off.

"Oscar might be a bit scattered—okay, seriously scattered—but one thing he can focus on is young, pretty women."

"How—"

"Hang on," said Charles, "I'm getting there. Apparently she came in around midnight. That gave Oscar time to give her his full attention. She started to pay by credit card, but then she pulled it back, giggled, and said she'd better use cash. Astute, sharp-eyed Oscar saw the name on the card. Said he couldn't remember what it was, but it had a hyphen. Seemed funny to poor Oscar, and he committed it to whatever memory he has left."

"Did he tell the police?" I asked.

"Oscar has an extensive *history* that's intertwined with law enforcement. Said he has a serious allergy to fuzz in any shape, form, or uniform."

"That mean no?"

"Yep," he said.

"Say anything else?"

"Yep," said Charles, who then took off his Tilley, wiped his brow, and turned back to me. "Here's the big clue."

He looked at the road and leaned back on the bench. The phrase "pulling teeth" came to mind. I decided to wait him out.

"Don't you want to know what it is?"

I grinned. "Yep."

He smiled. "Guess what she bought? Never mind, you'll never guess. She bought a package of popsicles."

"Would've been my first guess," I said.

He shook his head and mumbled something and I said, "So?"

Charles nodded. "Nobody knows where she was staying. Right?"

"True."

"Her sister said she was going to a beach near Charleston. Right?"

"Yes."

"So what's the only beach she could have driven to before the popsicles melted?"

"Good point," I said. Maybe he actually did have a clue. "What about the other call?"

"What call?"

"You said you got three good calls."

"Oh yeah," he said and hit the side of his head with the palm of his right hand.

"Eric, at Bert's, told me that a cute, African American lady came in the store a couple of times when he was at work the week before she turned up dead. Now Eric, being a good, law-abiding citizen, actually did tell the police. They showed him the photo of Nicole, and he said it 'definitely could have been her.' She didn't say much, and Eric didn't know anything about where she was staying."

"But," I said, "if she was in Bert's more than once, most likely she was staying nearby. If it was her, that is."

"Clue two," he said and grinned like he had solved the crime of the century.

"Then we need to tell the police," I said.

"Detective Burton?" said Charles.

"No way," I said. "And it wouldn't do any good to tell Karen. She would have to tell her superiors, and that would end up with Burton."

"And go nowhere from there?"

"Yep."

"So what are you waiting for?" said Charles.

The chief answered on the third ring.

# CHAPTER 27

Brian joined us on the shaded park bench. He said it wouldn't have been good for us to come to city hall. We didn't have to ask why.

"So there you have it," I said after Charles, with countless side trips and a lecture by Brian on defacing public property with missing-person flyers, walked him through what he had learned from Ada, Oscar, and Eric. "The two women had been on Folly. They probably stayed here."

Brian stared at a bright red Corvette as its driver stomped on the gas and headed across the river. Since it was headed off-island, Brian simply cursed under his breath instead of grabbing his radio to have one of his officers light up the sports car.

"Okay, where was I?" he said. "Yeah, your super-duper clues." He glanced over at me and then stared at Charles. "About Ada. First, she has cataracts. The dear lady couldn't tell the difference between Bigfoot and the Loch Ness Monster if one of them ambled through her door."

"Don't think the Loch Ness Monster can amble," interrupted Charles.

Brian shook his head and then continued, "She's also a little, how shall I say it, prejudiced. Combine that with her eyesight and all African Americans who graced her door would look alike. I wouldn't go to court with her as a witness."

"Doesn't mean she's wrong, does it?" said Charles.

"No," said Brian. "So let's look at your big clue from Oscar. That would be the Oscar who left a life of sanity a half-dozen years ago, who has worked the night shift at Kangaroo for the last two years, and who thinks that Folly Beach is between Guam and Rota Island?"

"Where's Rota Island?" asked Charles, the trivia collector.

"Never mind," said Brian. "It's far away."

"That would be the same Oscar," I said.

"And all he remembered was a hyphen and a pack of popsicles?"

"Clues galore," said Charles.

"Uh huh," said Brian. "What was the third phenomenal clue again?"

"Eric at Bert's," I said.

"Yeah," said Charles. "Eric talked to her, and he's as sane as they come. I bet he never heard of Rota."

"I don't disagree with that," said Brian, "but what did he say that made you think that *both* women stayed on Folly? For that matter, what proved that even one stayed here?"

"He saw the Sallee lady twice," said Charles. He had crossed his arms and glared at the chief, almost as if daring him to challenge his "proof."

"I believe you said he 'thought it was her,' and even if it was, she could have been visiting, not staying here."

Charles exhaled loudly and kicked the ground. Brian then asked him to repeat what he had said once more. This time, Brian took notes.

"Bottom line," said Charles, "is that you don't believe the two ladies were staying here?"

"Didn't say that. All I'm saying is that there's nothing to prove they were. I'll share this with my guys and tell them to snoop around some. They have some contacts and something might shake out. I'll also take this to Detective Burton and—"

"Crapola," interrupted Charles. "Why don't you just throw those notes in the river?" He pointed over his shoulder to the Folly River.

"I know you have to share this with Burton," I said. "But it may be a good idea not to tell him where you heard it."

Brian laughed. "So you and Burton are still not BFFs?"

"Depends on what the Fs stand for," interrupted Charles, again.

Brian ignored Charles. "I'll keep your names out of it."

"Thanks, I guess," said Charles. "So, what about the missing girl from Buckhead?"

Brian didn't ask how Charles knew about her. "All we know is that she was supposed to be over here somewhere. We're asking around."

"You'll let us know if you find out anything," said Charles.

Brian smiled. "No."

"Hmm," said Charles.

For the second time since Brian had joined us, one of his patrol cars circled the block. I saw the chief glance at it out of the corner of his eye during the first pass. This time, he stared at it with his police glare. "Officer O'Hara," he mumbled after the car turned down Indian Avenue. "El numero uno, asshole spy for *your* mayor."

"Guess you're stuck with him," brilliantly observed Charles.

"No comment," said Brian. "Oh yeah, Charles, speaking of the mayor, another thing about your flyers. He reminded me yesterday that if I found any of them plastered on any public surface on *his* island, I was to arrest you." He pointed his forefinger at Charles. "You have removed all of them, haven't you?"

"Ask me in a couple of hours," said Charles.

Brian then said he had to get back to his office and plot how to stop all drinking on the island and, if the mayor was to have his way, vanquish all citizens with tattoos. We wished him luck. He said he would need more than that.

"Up to flyer removal?" Charles asked as soon as Brian pulled back on Center Street.

"If they're in the shade," I said.

"If only," he said. He swatted a fly off his face with his hat, picked up his cane from beside the bench, and waved for me to follow. The good thing about retirement was that I didn't have anything else to do. The bad thing was that I didn't have a good excuse to say no.

The saving grace for two gentlemen in their early sixties was that the weather gods had provided a much cooler day than what had encapsulated the island recently. It didn't take us many steps to find the first of Charles's flyers. Two were stapled on a telephone pole in front of the post office across the street from our bench. Between there and the Catholic church a block away were five telephone poles adorned with six flyers. He rationalized that since there wasn't home mail delivery on the island, everyone passed the poles to get the mail. What better place to put them? I'm sure the mayor would have had a suggestion, but I nodded and kept walking.

The decorative light poles that lined both sides of Center Street from the bridge off Folly to the Tides were Charles's second-favorite flyer holders. He moaned about how he'd had to tape each one to the steel poles the entire time we were carefully removing the paper and tape without damaging the surface.

"You do know that those two women were staying on Folly, don't you?" said Charles. He nearly hit a passerby as he waved his cane around to cover all four corners of the island.

"I don't know it," I said, "but I don't think Brian took your information as seriously as he should have. It would be beyond a coincidence for both of them to be visiting here within a couple of weeks of each other and then winding up dead."

"So," he said, "how are we going to prove it? You owe it to Samuel."

Charles was great at finding weak spots and zooming in on them. I ignored his attempt at instilling guilt. "Let's say you're right," I said. "They had to stay at the Tides, or a bed and breakfast, or with a friend, or in a rented house or condo. If they visited Bert's and Ada's, they had to buy food or go into some of the other shops, frequent the bars, get their hair done, get manicures or pedicures or beanstalk wraps, or whatever young women get done to themselves."

We had reached the end of the main drag, and I said I'd check with the Tides and a friend, Bob Howard, with Island Realty. His company handled a good portion of the vacation rentals, and he had contacts in the other two island realty firms.

Once Charles realized that I was taking his theories seriously, he said, "What's going to happen to Aunt Melinda? I didn't hear from her for decades, but she's all I have left." He tilted his head. "Think the docs could be wrong?"

"She seemed certain about the diagnosis," I said. "Anything's possible, but I wouldn't get your hopes up."

"I know," he said as his voice cracked. "I know."

# CHAPTER 28

"Look what the damned polecat dragged in," came a booming voice from behind an old army surplus desk.

The voice, and affiliated attitude, came from Bob Howard, a friend who was part owner of Island Realty, which was, as Bob described it, "The second largest of three very small island realty firms." Charles had gone off to interrogate each employee of each retail establishment on Folly Beach, and I had walked four blocks back up Center Street to the frame house that had gone commercial years ago. The lobby reminded me more of a mom-and-pop motel in a remote section of Idaho than a successful real estate agency.

Bob walked around the metal desk and squeezed between an ancient filing cabinet and the battleship gray secretary's desk that held a beer stein of pencils and an IBM Selectric typewriter, surely the only operating model in Charleston County, perhaps in the universe. Behind the desk was Louise Carson, Bob's aunt, who, at eighty-five, had to be Folly's most senior real estate employee and was, without competition, the island's prime busybody. In addition to the beer stein pencil holder and ancient typewriter, the desk held a modern police scanner; that electronic gadget got far more use than the typewriter. Louise wore the a loud, green and yellow floral-patterned dress that I would have sworn she was in the first time I'd met her some six years ago.

Bob sucked in his ample stomach to slip around the wood-paneled counter to greet me. He was over six foot vertically and about two-thirds of that horizontally. He referred to himself as burly—one of the few things he understated. He wore his summer casual outfit of tattered shorts to compliment his food-stained, orange, short-sleeved polo shirt.

Bob waddled around the office to get to me as I winked at Louise and asked how my favorite senior citizen was doing. She looked at her nephew and said she was as well as could be expected given that she had to put up with a "potty-mouthed walrus." Bob grinned and said that it beat being dead. Louise said she wasn't sure.

"You here to buy a *casa* on the beach?"

"Don't think so," I said.

"Is this visit going to put a satchel-full of money in my bank account?"

"Probably not," I said and grinned.

"Holy hell, you're sticking your nose into something it has no business sniffin' around in—again!"

I pointed my forefinger at him and said, "You got it."

"Then I got myself a hankrin' for a couple of those monster chef salads at Planet Follywood," he said and rubbed his stomach.

Bob usually wasn't that friendly, so I took it as a good sign. "Two," I said, knowing that would be the minimum bribe I could get away with for the favor I was going to ask.

"Where's your car?" he said and looked out the window.

"I'm walking," I said.

"You damned well expect me to walk miles to the Planet?"

*Miles* equaled shy of three blocks. I smiled and said, "Take it or leave it."

Truth be told, Bob was one of my favorite people. He had been my Realtor when I'd bought my house and rented the gallery. Over the years, he had provided invaluable assistance in helping me catch some unsavory individuals, and some things he'd discovered had saved my life on one occasion. He's also an extremely kind, compassionate person if you can wade through his bluster.

He bitched another minute but followed me out the door on my way to the restaurant. Bob was in his early seventies and not quite the poster child for *Healthy Living* magazine, so the walk was slow, to put it kindly.

It was midafternoon, but the Planet was nearly full. The waitress directed us to a bar-height round table in the corner. Bob looked around the room for one of the larger tables where he could spread out; they were full. He grumbled about how they expected a "real man" to fit at this piddlin'-tiny excuse for a table. He took a couple of deep breaths and reminded me that regardless of the size of the table, he'd manage to get two—or more—meals to fit. The interior was an eclectic mix of tropical doodads, mismatched tables, and the casual feel of a friendly beach bar. We were seated under a mural of familiar Low Country scenes painted on the concrete block wall.

A waitress with zombie-white skin and bleached-blonde, spiked hair smiled as she headed to our table. Bob gave her a big Realtor smile. "Hey, cutie pie," he said, a comment politically correct for Bob. "My puny friend here's going to buy me a couple of your Alamo burgers, extra fries—what the hell, throw in an order of onion rings too, and two Buds for me, and a glass of that fruity white wine for him." He turned to me, "Want anything to eat?"

I wondered what had happened to the chef's salads he'd mentioned earlier. I also realized that I was hungry and knew this wouldn't be a short meeting. "Chicken fingers."

She wrote it all down, as if she would forget such a complicated order, and headed to the kitchen. Bob watched her go and then turned to me. "Okay, what shit pile have you stuck your fallen arches in this time?"

I started with Samuel's visit to the house and walked Bob through everything I could remember about what my young friend had said, the two deaths, Charles's theory about both of them having stayed on Folly Beach, and how I thought Bob could help.

Bob's first Alamo burger had come and gone, as had his first and second Bud, before I finished the monologue. He only interrupted to make sure that "cutie pie" was working on his second burger and third beer.

"Let's see if I have this right," he said and took a sip. "You are taking the word of a teenager who already admitted to lying and are conspiring with your airhead friend Charles to find where two chicks stayed on Folly when no one knows that they ever stayed here, to find a man who is thin with long, dark hair who killed both of them, even though no one has said that one of them was murdered." He looked at the ceiling as if there would be wisdom to be found there and then back at me. "How am I doing?"

"Couldn't have said it better myself," I said and grinned.

"Holy crapoly," he said. "Think that deserves a third burger. And now you expect your kind, wonderful, generous buddy Bob to pull a rabbit out of your ass and save the day. Again!"

I nodded. "If you aren't too busy selling all those multimillion-dollar houses in this bustling economy."

"If you put it that way, I could spare a few minutes to save your ass. I could have the staff check if anyone named Nicole or that hyphen person rented anything from us. Hell, if you're real nice, I could check with the two *inferior* realty firms and see if they show anything. They owe me a few favors."

I couldn't imagine what Bob could possibly have done to garner favor from his competitors. He asked me to write down the names of the deceased women and then surprised me by saying that he'd heard that Charles actually had a relative who would claim him. I asked where he had heard it, although I figured it probably was from Louise, the busybody. He said it was none of my damn business, and that he wasn't about to "burn" his source.

I told him about Melinda's visit and what the doctors had said. The softer side of Bob finally made an appearance, and he said to let him know if there was anything he could do. He offered that he could find a small house for her if she was uncomfortable at the boarding house. I thanked him, and he said, "Hell, stuff it."

Bob had returned to normal.

# Chapter 29

Wednesday started as one of those days that never stuck in your memory. Errands had to be run, and although the gallery was open only four days a week, expenses didn't take a break. I spent the morning writing checks for taxes, utilities, insurance, and repairs to the air conditioner. I experienced a tinge of guilt knowing that Charles was canvassing businesses to learn if anyone had seen or talked with the two women. With luck, Bob was checking records to see if they had stayed on the island. And here I was, writing checks and trying not to think about the fate of the two young women and whether Samuel had actually witnessed an abduction.

Charles called around two to say that Melinda wanted to go Walmart shopping. I thanked him for the update, which forced him to ask if I could take them. I considered it a small victory. A large victory would be if I'd convinced him to buy his own car or get his Saab repaired. I doubted that win would come soon.

I didn't mind taking Melinda shopping. It was fun to see her in her Carolina-blue hair being pushed around the superstore by her nephew. A blender and a set of four tall, plastic champagne flutes were the items she *needed*. She didn't say why.

We dropped her at Mariner's Breeze and drove the additional half block to Charles's apartment. The mild temperatures had continued, and he asked if I wanted to walk and take photos. We had spent many hours over the years traipsing around the island. We'd taken photos, talked, and laughed, and I'd watched him talk to every person he saw, friend, foe, or stranger. He also never passed a dog, cat, squirrel, or mouse without sharing a kind word.

Charles was more hyper than usual. He didn't say it, but he was worried about Melinda. He insisted on telling me about his visit to each business. I listened to what, if anything, the clerks and owners knew about the dead women, whether the stores were busy, and whether they were having any specials. He spewed a lot of words, but the bottom line was that no one seemed to know more than what they had heard on the news or from others. It was nearly dark, and we were several blocks from his apartment, so I suggested that we head back. We had passed Melinda's building, and I stopped to shake some pesky gravel from my shoes. Charles had walked ahead. I rounded the corner of his building and saw him twenty feet from his door, where he had stooped to take a photo of a candy wrapper—one of his specialties. I rushed to catch up.

I smiled as he focused on the discarded piece of paper and used his flash to take the photo. A sudden movement near his door caught my attention. The closest light was four apartments away, and I barely made out the shape of someone crouched down behind a row of straggly shrubs beside his entryway.

My friend finished taking the photo and was a couple of paces from the shadowed figure. Charles was oblivious to the newcomer, but the stranger was turned toward him and didn't see me.

I thought it was Heather waiting to surprise him until I saw the silhouetted figure slip around behind Charles. The stranger held a three-foot-long, thin piece of something in his right hand. It was rigid, and the thought *rebar* flashed through my mind. Charles was still oblivious to what was happening as the intruder got in a baseball stance and was about to drill Charles's head into right field.

"Charles, duck!" I yelled.

He looked over his shoulder at me and then obediently fell to the gravel lot. I was still five paces away.

The deadly steel missed Charles by inches. The wind whistled as the weapon zipped through the air. The assailant stayed focused on Charles and raised the weapon to bring it down on him.

I grabbed the end of the steel rod as he started to swing. He seemed surprised that I had reacted so quickly. That made two of us. He let go of the rod, and it threw me off balance. I fell back and tripped over Charles, who was pushing himself up from the parking lot.

I landed on my back, hitting my head hard. I gasped for a breath. Charles stood and looked around. I inhaled as he helped me up.

The steel-swinging intruder ran toward the far corner of the building. He was still in deep shadows and had a ball cap pulled down around his ears. Long, dark hair stuck out from under the edges of the cap. His face was hidden.

Charles wiped gravel from his knees, looked at me, and shrugged. I waved for him to follow and started to jog after the intruder. Charles was a step behind, but I quickly realized that we weren't going to close the gap. The assailant was young and swift, and he had a head start.

I stopped, and Charles pulled up beside me. My back and head hurt from the awkward landing, and Charles was bent over with his hands resting on his thighs. We stood in silence. Cars crossing the Folly River and our gasping breaths were the only sounds that I heard. We waited long enough to catch our breaths and then slowly walked back to the car and drove up Sandbar Lane toward town. The odds were a million to one that we'd find him. There were countless places to hide, and it was dark. All he had to do was to stand near any building and we wouldn't have seen him.

"Did you recognize him?" I asked as I tightly gripped the steering wheel. I tried to watch both sides of the road.

"No," said Charles as he brushed the last few pebbles off his sweaty knees. "Never got a clear look. Danged hat covered most of his face. Couldn't even tell if it was a man or woman."

We crisscrossed the downtown stretch twice and hoped that the attacker was dumb enough to walk down one of the well-lit streets. No luck. I drove back to Charles's door and found the three-foot-long section of rusty steel rebar. The closely spaced ridges around the weapon would make it impossible to pull any useful fingerprints. We debated briefly but decided against calling the police. What could we have told them that would be useful?

"I have a bottle of cheap wine in here. Interested?" said Charles. We stood in front of his apartment and stared at the weapon.

"How could I resist such a generous offer?" My lower back ached from bouncing off the lot. The pain in my head had moved from an ouch to a headache. It could have been much worse.

I moved the stack of books off a battered restaurant chair in front of one of his bookcases and gingerly lowered myself into it. Charles returned from his tiny kitchen with a Styrofoam cup of box wine and a Bud Light. He cleared a spot on the floor and sat with his back leaned against a shelf of history textbooks. He claimed to have read all the books in his apartment with the exception of a row of cookbooks. I had no reason to doubt him.

Charles took a gulp, stared at his knee like he had never seen it before, and said, "You know President Calvin Coolidge once said, 'Never go out to meet trouble. If you will just sit still, nine cases out of ten someone will intercept it before it reaches you.'" He looked up at me. "Thanks for the interception."

I didn't know if Coolidge had said that, but the tenth case could have been terribly tragic for Charles. "You know what that was about," I said.

Charles nodded and hopped to his feet. He walked to the small front window and looked out and then over the bookcases on the far wall. "It means that Samuel saw someone abducted. It means that the two dead women stayed right here on Folly Beach. It means that they were murdered by a short, thin, dark-haired man or woman." He took a quick breath and continued. "It means that someone I talked to in the last two days told him about me." He paused. "Or maybe I actually talked to the killer. And, it means that we're getting close to figuring out who it is. Finally, it means that the killer was going to make me his next victim." He picked his cane up off the floor and pointed it at the door. "He was going to add me to the list tonight, right outside that door."

For once, I couldn't argue with anything he'd said. I had to act, and act quickly. Too much was at stake.

# CHAPTER 30

To say that I had a restless night would be like saying there are a lot of grains of sand on the beach. I couldn't get comfortable. My back hurt whenever I turned, and I turned a lot. My mind flashed back to the person lifting the rebar to attack Charles and how close he came to being gravely injured or killed—and for what? What did my friend know? What had he stirred up? If his attacker was the person who had killed the two women, he wouldn't hesitate to kill anyone who could stand in his way. Charles and I were within inches of him, but we didn't see his face. The frightening thing was, he didn't know that we didn't see him.

I told myself that the police, particularly Detective Burton would be unlikely to take us seriously and would do as little as possible to investigate. I found it ironic that it might take Charles getting killed to raise the issue to a level where someone paid attention. I then wondered if I was in danger. Would Charles or I be as lucky if the assailant tried again?

Since the death of my ex-wife earlier in the year, I'd been haunted by the thought that I could have done something to save her life. Everyone told me that I couldn't have prevented what had happened. It didn't help. I couldn't help my ex, but friends were now in danger. Could I help them?

The clock slowly rolled around to six a.m., and sleep didn't return. I walked to Bert's for coffee and hopefully a friendly conversation with a clerk. My back still hurt, but it felt good to stretch it by walking.

Eric, who camouflaged a keen wit and intellect behind the appearance of a hippy who had forgotten to leave the 1970s, greeted me with a cheerful welcome and the latest gossip. He shared a couple of funny stories about a dyslexic tattoo artist he knew and his latest adventures on the river in his small sailboat. What he didn't share was anything new about the two dead women.

I was carrying my coffee in my right hand with a copy of the Charleston *Post and Courier* and a small bag of donuts in my left when I nearly collided with Marc Salmon. Coffee sloshed from my cup and splashed onto his shoes but missed his slacks.

"Not where I prefer my morning coffee," said Marc. He smiled when he said it.

I gave a halfhearted apology, and he patted my shoulder. "No prob," he said. "I'd been meaning to run into you anyway—get it, run into you?"

I grinned, and he seemed satisfied that I appreciated his rapier wit. "Got a minute?"

"Sure," I said.

He waved for me to step outside. Apparently Eric's presence in the otherwise empty store wasn't private enough for what he had to say. I followed him to the side parking area. A supersized likeness of Bert stared down at us from a mural on the building. The only other living things present were hundreds of bugs attracted to the lights.

"Are your business licenses up to date?" he asked, barely above a whisper.

Definitely a question I wouldn't have anticipated. "I guess. Why?"

He looked around again and appeared satisfied that Bert's likeness wasn't eavesdropping. "I was over at city hall yesterday. City's business never ends, you know. Well, I was in the second-floor corridor outside the mayor's office. His door was open, and I heard him talking— actually, he was yelling—and so I stopped beside the door. Wanted to be there to help him if he was in trouble, you know. Some angry citizen could've threatened him harm."

I nodded like I actually believed that story rather than jumping to the conclusion that Marc was doing what he does best, being nosy.

"And then I heard your name." He paused and nodded back at me. I didn't respond immediately, so he continued. "He was saying 'f-word

Landrum' was a thorn in his side and that he was stirring up trouble again, except he didn't say 'f-word.' Some of the mayor's supporters thought Folly would be better off if that 'f-word Landrum' would go back to wherever he came from."

I wasn't surprised after my recent almost-lunch with the mayor. "Who was he talking to?"

Marc shook his head and swatted a bug away from his cheek. "Don't know. If I had moved past the door to see who was in there, the mayor would've seen me. Didn't think that would be wise since he knows I'm not a supporter."

"Hear anything else?"

"That's when he said *we* need to find something wrong with you. Catch you with expired licenses, or some piddlin' building code violation, or health code infraction, or anything." Marc smiled. "He even said they needed to check your criminal record to see if there are some outstanding warrants for 'porn, perversion, or mass murder.' Aren't any of those, are there?"

I kicked the sand in the lot. "What did the other person say?"

"Don't think I heard anyone answer. The mayor was on a roll and didn't leave any breaks for responses." Marc slapped his face again. "Bugs!"

I waited. If he had heard anything else, he wouldn't hesitate to share it.

"Oh yeah, I heard one other thing," he said. "I didn't hear all of it. The elevator started to rumble and I knew someone was heading up, so I walked toward the council chamber instead of past the mayor's door."

"But you heard?" I prompted.

"The mayor said something about starting rumors about Chief Newman; something to get him 'run out of town on a rail.'"

"You didn't hear what the rumor was?"

"Nope, too busy keeping from getting caught snoop—waiting to help if the mayor needed saving."

"You said the mayor kept saying 'we,' so it must have been someone who worked for the city, especially if they were going to access my records."

Marc looked up at Bert's likeness and then back at me. "Likely."

"But you don't know who?"

"Somebody who doesn't talk loudly. I'd suggest you watch your butt, my friend."

Oh great, just what I needed. And Marc didn't even know about the rebar-wielding assailant.

I was nearing the house and a healthy breakfast of donuts and more donuts when Charles called, "Aunt Melinda and I've decided we'd let you have breakfast with us at the Dog." He giggled. "She said she'd even let you buy."

*Donuts or Dog, Donuts or Dog?* I thought. "When?"

"Now," he said. "We've saved you a seat." He then said something I couldn't understand and said, "Gotta go. They want their phone back."

It was near the overnight low temperature, and Charles had decided that we would sit on the deck in front of the restaurant. He waved as I approached. At least, I think he waved. My attention was more drawn to Melinda. Her hair had miraculously changed from Carolina blue to a red that was more illuminating than a stoplight. I held my stare to see if it would switch to green and then to yellow. She saw me, smiled widely, tapped the top of her head, and turned it so I could get the side view. I smiled back and mouthed, "Wow!"

I walked to the far end of the patio and entered. There was one empty chair at the table, and Charles pointed to it like I wouldn't have figured out where to sit. I continued to smile at Melinda. "Good morning, Melinda," I said. "Is that a new blouse you're wearing? Something looks different."

She giggled. "Silly boy. How about the new color?"

"Stunning," I said. "What happened with the fetching blue?"

"I was afraid to ask," said Charles, who then sat back in the chair.

Melinda frowned at Charles and then smiled at me. "People kept pointing at me and saying, 'Carolina blue.' I didn't know what they meant, and then the nice man pushing the rusty grocery cart around town with empty gas cans in it told me that it was the University of North Carolina's school color. Then he said they were called Tar Heels and the more intelligent people around here didn't like them." She shook her head. "How was I to know? And who wants tar associated with their hair?"

*Who indeed*, I thought. But Melinda didn't wait for me to say anything.

"So while you and Charles were out causing a ruckus yesterday after you dumped me at the apartment, I walked to Folly Curls and shared my dilemma with dear Damian. He was so nice—he's gay, you know. He said that a lot of his clients, especially the young ones like me"—she giggled—"change their hair color all the time and asked me what color I wanted. I said I didn't know, and he showed me a book with a thousand colors. I chose rambunctious red."

"You chose that out of a thousand colors?" said Charles.

Her smile disappeared. "So?"

He glanced over at me. I wasn't going to bail him out.

"Beats Carolina blue," he said and waited for her to respond. Her smile didn't reappear. "I like it," he finally said.

"I think it makes me look younger. What do you think, Chris?"

The beginning of a grin appeared in the corner of Charles's mouth; he turned toward me.

*Think it will make it a lot easier to cross the road in traffic*, I thought. "I agree with Charles. But you didn't need it to look younger; you already do."

Charles head dropped, and he mumbled something undistinguishable.

She smiled and then turned to Charles; her smile disappeared. "Chris," she said, continuing to look at Charles, "Charles tells me that things got a bit interesting last night. He said that he had to save you from almost getting decapitated and then chased a bad guy away before he could come after you again."

I looked at Charles, who stared into his water glass. "That's not exactly how I remember it," I said.

Melinda continued to look at Charles. "I suspected it wasn't exactly like that," she said. "Whatever happened, let me put my foot down. I packed all my belongings and took that god-awful bus ride down here to be with my only living relative and enjoy a wonderful rest of my life with him."

"Now, Aunt M.," said Charles.

"Now nothing, Charles. Hush. The key word in what I said was *living*. That means you not being dead."

"Nothing's going to happen to me," said Charles. "Now don't you worry your sweet, rambunctious red head about it."

"Why not?" she asked. I wondered that as well. "I'm not the brightest lightning bug in the woods—heck, I didn't even know what color Carolina blue was—but it seems like you are sniffing too close to a killer and he's wanting to do something about it. Now why doesn't that put you in danger? Just asking."

Amber refilled our coffee mugs and grinned at Melinda's hair.

Charles waited for her to leave the table. "That's why Chris and I have a plan to end this madness."

That got my attention.

"We're going to catch the killer real soon-like," he said.

And I doubted he had a plan.

"How?" she asked.

"Now don't you clutter your sweet mind with all that," said Charles. "We've got it under control."

I should have chosen donuts.

# CHAPTER 31

Karen called in midafternoon to say that she was sick of the grime of the city and the lowlifes she had spent all morning running down while gathering leads on a double homicide off Meeting Street. She hinted that a picnic on the beach overlooking the Morris Island Lighthouse would be a pleasant way to wash the *crime grime* away. I readily took the hint and offered that if she picked up sandwiches, I'd provide the libation, transportation, and scrub brush. I asked if her hair would be the same color as it was the last time I saw her. She asked why. I said that if she was good, I'd tell her later. She asked me to define "good." I saw a pleasant night ahead.

"So, what's with the question about my hair color?"

The temperature was still mild, and it was an hour until sunset. We were walking along the paved road that had gone through the middle of the coast guard station before it had been decommissioned. Stanchions blocked motorized traffic about a quarter of a mile before the road switched to sand and led down a hill to the beach. Labor Day was still a week away, and several groups of vacationers walked toward us on their way to their cars or houses.

I gave her an abbreviated description of Melinda's wig metamorphosis and told her to leave her hair the color it was; it contrasted nicely with her sea-green blouse and tan shorts. She said that she was more of a tempestuous teal girl. I suggested that she hold the teal, but if she wanted to be tempestuous, I wouldn't object. Even before we reached the shore line, she said that she felt the crime grime waning. I asked her to leave some for me to scrub off.

"I will, but you'll have to find it," she said with a sultry growl.

We spread an old blanket that I kept in the SUV for … well, for any time I needed an old blanket. It took up little space and was handy. Karen had picked up two box suppers at a neighborhood deli close to her house, and I contributed a bottle of midpriced Chardonnay from Bert's.

There was only a handful of people on the beach. Two women in their early twenties leaned against a row of Mini Cooper–sized boulders off to our right. They giggled and smoked something. They found humor in everything, and I suspected that their smoke of choice wasn't tobacco. Karen glanced their way once and said, "Whatever." A young mother with twin boys walked off to our left. The lighthouse looked lonely as water lapped its base. The roar of waves crashing on the beach provided soothing background music.

Karen started quickly on the wine but slowed after the first refill of her plastic cup. I debated telling her about the attack and decided I'd wait until a more appropriate time. She didn't need to hear more about crime.

She scooted close, her shoulder touching mine. "I've been thinking about this ever since early this morning," she said. "Thanks for the shoulder to lean on." She giggled. "Regardless of how clichéd it is."

"I suppose you could have easily leaned on that driftwood over there." I pointed to a large tree that had washed ashore years ago.

"I could, but it didn't bring wine."

"True," I said. "Or a scrub brush."

"Guess you'll do," she said and elbowed my shoulder.

The sun setting behind us lit the undersides of a flock of seagulls gracefully flying low between us and the lighthouse.

We spent the next hour talking about absolutely nothing before noticing that the sun had disappeared and the only light was reflected off low, puffy clouds. We walked hand in hand back to civilization.

An hour later, I had scrubbed the remaining crime grime off Karen and we sat in matching shirts, both mine, in my living room listening to a Four Seasons CD and finishing off the second bottle of Chardonnay.

"I forgot to tell you earlier," she said and yawned, "remember the missing girl, Chelsea Hall?"

I winced. "Dead?"

Karen smiled. "Far from it. She called home from Spokane, Washington. Seems that she'd decided she wanted to see the Pacific Northwest and didn't think that anyone would care if she was gone. In a millisecond her parents went from worry, to relief, to anger, to 'I'll kill you if you ever do anything like that again.'"

"It's still good news," I said.

Karen nodded and then yawned again. I was about to tell her about the incident with Charles but figured sleep was more important.

It was the first good night's sleep I'd had since Samuel appeared on my doorstep. My back didn't even ache. The sun had already peeked over the Atlantic when Bob jarred me out of a peaceful sleep. I grabbed the phone so it wouldn't wake Karen but discovered that her side of the bed was empty. Bob said that he had some information and wanted me to meet him at his office. In the six-plus years that I had known him, I had been in his office once, so I was surprised and curious about his request.

A note by the coffee pot let me know that Karen had to be in the office early. A strong cup of coffee would be critical to putting up with Bob this early in the morning. Some of our mutual friends would say that a shot of bourbon would work better.

# Chapter 32

Bob's PT Cruiser convertible was in the gravel lot when I arrived. I smiled when I saw its top down. I recalled the first time I had met the curmudgeonly Realtor when he appeared in his convertible, top down, and he drove me around the island in the rain as we looked for a house. He had said that "come holy hell or hurricane" he was going to drive his car "as God intended," top down—and "don't call it purple; it's dark plum," he had added.

The small lot held two other cars, Louise Carson's quarter-of-a-century-old, rusting Oldsmobile and a relatively new, black Chrysler 300, owner unknown. Louise was the only person I saw as I opened the front door. Her left ear leaned close to the police scanner. She looked up, broke into a wide smile, and stood to greet me. I walked around the counter and gave her a hug.

"Is you-know-who here?" I asked as I stood back and admired her dress. which looked almost identical to the one she had worn the last time I'd seen her.

She pointed her finger toward the back. "In his luxurious office suite. Go on back. He said some worthless geezer would be in. Guess that was you."

"He sure makes visitors feel welcome," I said.

"Part of his charm," she said and then winked.

Bob's *luxurious office suite* was an eight-by-ten room in a newer four-office addition behind the main building. To maintain the character of the original structure, the walls were covered with the same whitewashed wooden panels, a small window was high up on the wall, and Bob's desk and bookshelf continued the outer office theme—beat-up, battleship gray surplus store rejects. Two side chairs that looked like they'd had an earlier life in a greasy-spoon diner took up most of the remaining floor space.

"Welcome to my humble abode," growled Bob, who matched the decor. He was wedged between the desk and the wall and made no effort to stand.

"I wouldn't have wanted to start my day any other way," I said and smiled.

A corkboard behind him held a handful of fact sheets on oceanfront properties and an oval sticker that said, "Wag more, bark less."

"You training dogs now?" I said and pointed to the sticker.

He turned and looked. "Damned staff gave it to me. They thought it would remind my snotty-nosed, whiney clients to be nicer to me."

*Yeah, right*, I thought. "No doubt," I said.

He turned back to me and then looked at his watch. "Didn't ask you here to waste time. I could be selling houses, condos, horse farms, and skyscrapers."

I smiled again and patiently waited.

"Got someone for you to meet," he said and then bellowed, "Alexander, get your ass in here!"

Thirty seconds later, a young man stood in the doorway. He was in his late twenties, trim with sharp features; his dark brown hair was pulled back in a ponytail, and he looked as nervous as a goldfish at a cat show.

"Yes, Mr. Howard."

I'd never heard anyone call Bob Mr. Howard.

"Park your butt," said Bob in his least *wag more* voice.

Alexander obeyed, and his knees nearly touched mine.

Bob pointed to the new arrival. "That's Alexander. He's a wet-behind-the-ears Realtor I hired last summer. Damned if I know why." He then pointed at me. "Chris Landrum, a very good friend of mine. Damned if I know why."

With both of our egos boosted, I nodded to Alexander, and he returned the gesture.

"Alexander," said Bob, "tell my bud what you told me yesterday. Don't leave anything out or you'll be flipping burgers again."

Bob, despite his bluster, was an outstanding Realtor. If he had hired Alexander, the young man was talented and could be an asset to Island Realty. I also knew Bob enough to know that Alexander probably had reason to be nervous around the gruff Realtor.

Alexander glanced at Bob and then turned to me. "Mr. Howard showed me the photos of the girls that have been … well, are dead." He looked at his hands that were folded in his lap. "I recognized one of them. She—"

"Alexander's assigned to new renters," interrupted Bob. "Don't want him talking to the regulars; can't hurt the newbies too much." He flicked his wrist at his protégé. "Go on."

"Kendra Corman-Eades came in mid-July and wanted a condo for three weeks. She didn't have a lot of money, so I knew it would have to be away from the beach. Real cute; had a great smile, but there was something behind the smile. Sad, maybe. I'm not sure."

"Get on with it," said Bob. "Chris here doesn't have all day. He's got to open his gallery and not sell any pictures."

Alexander turned away from Bob and rolled his eyes. I knew he was smart.

"I rented her a condo on East Huron, a small, but neat, second-floor unit. She said it would do just fine and paid cash."

"She say why she was here?" I asked.

Alexander looked at Bob like he had to get permission to speak. Bob shrugged.

"Not really," said Alexander as he turned back to me. "Kind of vague. I didn't get the impression that she was just here on vacation."

"Isn't it unusual for someone to pay cash, especially for three weeks?"

"You bet your sweet checkbook," said Bob.

I ignored him and asked Alexander, "Did you get any identification? Credit card, anything?"

"Umm, no, didn't think it was necessary. I didn't figure the cash would bounce." He gave a tentative smile.

He started to say something, but the roar of a leaf blower outside the one window in the office drowned him out. We sat in silence until the landscaper moved away from the building.

"Were you going to say something else?" I asked.

He looked at Bob again and then back to me. "Nothing other than a feeling. Most ladies her age say that I'm, umm, handsome, or at least, good to talk to, but—"

"Holy damned Helios," interrupted Bob. "I see McDonald's in your future; you'll be behind the counter, saying 'That'll be four ninety-five, ma'am.'"

I ignored Bob again. I did wonder what Helios was, but I didn't ask. "But what?"

"I tried to be all social-like with her. You know, to make her feel welcome, asking if there's anything I could do to make her stay more pleasant."

"And she kicked your charming, stuck-on-yourself ass out the door?" said Bob.

"Nothing like that," he said, head turned my way. "She seemed distant. She was extremely attractive, but cold, if you know what I mean."

*Probably*, I thought. "Did you see her again?"

"Once at Bert's and once going into Mr. John's Beach Store. Umm, I think that's all."

While Alexander was stammering and stuttering though his story, Bob pulled the rental agreement. From the dates on the reservation, her third week ended two days after Samuel had seen the woman abducted.

"Was either of you here when she checked out?" I asked.

"No, not even nosy Nelly out there," said Bob. He pointed his chubby forefinger toward the reception area. "Ms. What's-her-name dropped her key in the box outside the front door here like most of the tenants who try to beat the traffic off-island."

"You mean somebody dropped her key in the box," I said.

"Huh?" said Alexander. He leaned closer until our knees touched.

"The key was left two days after my friend saw someone, probably her, abducted from a walkway from the beach. According to the police, there's a chance she was already dead."

"Damned dead people don't drop keys in the box," added Bob, insensitively but accurately.

"Oh," said Alexander. "I never thought of that."

I wondered why he hadn't. Bob had told him why I was curious. Interesting.

I waited to see if he said anything else. He didn't, so I asked, "Did the cleaning crew notice anything unusual when they cleaned the condo?"

"Now let's see," said Bob. "There was a dead body on the couch, but they cleaned around it." He stretched his arms over his head. "Damn, Chris, of course they didn't find anything bad, anything suspicious."

"Umm," said Alexander. I turned to him. "I inspected the condo after the cleaning crew was finished. Mr. Howard taught me to do that to make sure the unit's ready for the next renter." He turned toward Bob and nodded. "We had no reason to think anything was wrong ... we really didn't."

# CHAPTER 33

"Yummy," said Cindy. "Sure you don't want anything?"

I was in the Black Magic Café off Center Street watching Cindy gobble down a bagel. I had called her after leaving Island Realty. She said that she was on duty but taking a break and that I could join her if I didn't try to steal her food.

"I'm fascinating, and people usually line up to watch me eat bagels," she said with a grin. "But I don't think that's why you're here."

I agreed with her on both points. "Cindy, I've got a problem, and maybe you can help."

"Then this is on you," she said and then raised the remaining part of the bagel and pointed it at me.

She'd already paid, so I told her I'd get the next one if she didn't order more than a bagel. She agreed and told me how big a spender I was, and then I gave her a brief summary of what I had learned from Bob and Alexander.

"Now to the problem," I said. "I'm afraid if I talk to the chief, my name would get connected with the investigation, and with the chief's relationship with the mayor—"

Cindy shook her head. "Hate relationship!"

"Yeah," I said. "The mayor had already told me in clear, concise terms to butt out, or else."

"He's good with that clear, concise crap," she said. "Why not go to your girl-toy?"

I smiled. "Because Karen would have to share it with Detective Burton, and—"

"And he'd file it under *so what, I'm retiring.*"

"You got it," I said.

"What am I supposed to do?"

I looked at the painting of a coffee cup and saucer on the green wall behind Cindy and then glanced at a couple at the next table. "I thought that possibly you, or your buddy Officer Spencer, could accidently run into Bob and he would mention that Corman-Eades had stayed in one of their rentals and then you could tell the chief."

"Leaving you out of it?"

I nodded.

"And you think there's nothing I'd like to do more than hear blustery Bob cuss, rant and rave, and grumble about how Chris Landrum can't mind his own blankety-blank business?"

"Yep," I said and smiled.

"And what reason would I have for going to see big, bad Bob in the first place? You know the chief will ask."

"Tell him that Bob was in your hubby's hardware store and mentioned it. Larry told you, and then like a good cop, you went to follow up with Bob."

Cindy took a bite of bagel and then looked at the ceiling. "You ever thought about writing fiction?" she asked.

I smiled. "I don't even read fiction."

She shook her head. "Okay, I'll give it a try. You owe me more than a hunk of dough." She stuffed the last bite in her month, stood, and mumbled that she had to go serve and protect. She saluted me and left.

I should have opened the gallery an hour ago, but I figured that Charles would be there with the door open, lights on, and no customers within a hundred yards. I ordered a Greek omelet at the counter and settled in for a hearty breakfast surrounded by the soothing aroma of freshly brewed coffee. Now that I knew that one of the dead girls had rented on Folly and that someone felt the need to try to eliminate Charles, it seemed logical that the other woman, Nicole Sallee, had also rented here. How could I find where she lived? And even if I knew, what good would it do?

Thoughts turned to Melinda. How far along was her cancer? Did she have days, weeks, months? How would Charles take her death? They hadn't been close for all these years, but she was the only family he had. A chill ran down my spine when I wondered what would happen if something happened to Charles—or to me. All were thoughts that ruined the taste of a Greek omelet.

My mental meandering was interrupted. "Yo, Christer."

I looked up from breakfast and saw Dude headed my way. He looked like he always did. His long, gray-white hair was asunder, his tie-dyed shirt covered his scrawny chest, and his blue cargo shorts nearly slipped off his hips.

He looked at the table and then under the table and said, "You be solo?"

I grinned at the retro-looking surf shop owner. "Unless ghosts are hanging around."

He looked under the table again. "Nope," he said with the confidence of someone who would recognize any nearby apparition.

"Join me," I said. He had the uncanny knack of sucking words out of the air around him. A couple of minutes with Dude and most people's sentences shortened.

He sat and wiped away a couple of crumbs from Cindy's bagel.

"Haven't seen you here before," I said, mainly to make conversation.

"Me be equal opportunity tea buyer," he said as if that explained it. "Enough 'bout Dude's shopping. How be Melinda?"

I wasn't aware that he knew that Melinda existed, much less her condition.

"Seems okay," I said. "I haven't seen her in a couple of days."

"Me be praying to sun gods for her," he said reverently.

"Thank you," I said.

If Dude had enough contacts to know about Melinda, I wondered if he had heard anything else about the two women. I asked.

"Been askin'," he said. "No news not always good news."

*Good point*, I thought. I told him what I had learned about Corman-Eades staying on Folly and that I suspected that Nicole Sallee had been also.

"All me be knowin', she not been in surf shop."

"Why so sure?" I asked. "Could've been in while you were out—like now."

"Two tatted peeps on payroll would've told me. Surfing black dudette on Folly be as rare as bumblebee on Boogie Board."

Dude's two *tatted peeps* are, from what I can tell, his only employees. They have enough words tattooed on their bodies to write the US Constitution and the first three books of the Bible. Their attitude toward customers, especially the more mature—okay, old—customers, would indicate that they weren't familiar with the Bible. A snarl was the friendliest greeting in their repertoire.

"Would they have told you if she had been in?"

"You bet," he said. "They tell me all. More than me wants. Sure would." He nodded and took a sip of tea. "Jabbered all yesterday about Folly being *police state*. Narco dicks pestering God-fearing, law-abiding surfers at Washout, yada-yada-yada."

I shook my head in sympathy. "Of course none of the surfers had anything to do with drugs, right?"

"'Course they did," he said. "Not the point. Should be laws about cops-a-pesterin'."

I thought back to my conversation with the mayor and decided the law should extend to all city officials. "I agree."

"While readin', writin', and removin' laws, add one for fuzz not to try to pick up chicks by flashin' badge."

I held my arms out, asking for an explanation.

"Tatt Earl be bitchin' about Fuzz O'Hara trying to pick up his chick." He took another sip of tea, looked around the room, and then continued. "He stopped her—blue lights a-flashin'—for walking down middle of Ashley Avenue carrying surfboard."

"Middle of the street?" I said. I was on O'Hara's side on this one.

"She be quick. See car, jumps out of way," he said. "Problem be, Fuzz O'Hara gave longing look at her. Asked for phone number."

"Oh," I said. There are advantages for being the mayor's pet. "Sorry."

"O'Hara be chick collector. Police state … ugh."

I nodded, and Dude said he had to get to the store to save the surfing world from his two employees. I nodded again, and he was gone.

Officer O'Hara, the chick collector and Mayor Lally's pet. Can anything else go wrong?

# CHAPTER 34

I finally made it to the gallery. Instead of giving me the usual chiding for being late, Charles was seated in the back wearing a University of Alabama long-sleeved T-shirt and a frown. I asked if I'd missed any customers, and instead of making up a story about the hundreds of visitors to the gallery, he shook his head. I asked what was wrong. He said it was Melinda.

"What's the matter?"

"Don't know," he said without looking up from the table. "One minute she's all bubbly, throwing out some of her corny sayings. The next minute, she flops down in the chair and barely has enough energy to lift her hand."

"She say anything?"

"Yeah," he said and looked up at me. "She gets real still and then talks so low that I have to move close to hear. Says that she doesn't have many days left. She has this sweet grin and says that she'll be sure to tell Jesus to keep a keen eye out for me in thirty years or so."

"Is she serious?"

He tilted his head. "People don't joke about this kind of thing, do they?" he said.

"Don't suppose so," I said and sat across from him. "Think she should go to a doctor?"

"Should, yes. Will, no. I made the mistake of saying that to her," he said. He blinked and then grinned. "She said that if I said it again, she'd abandon her vow of no profanity and then take up nephew-whuppin'."

"Suppose that meant no," I said.

He nodded. "See the problem?"

I asked what he thought he should do. He said that at her age and stubbornness about not seeking medical help, he didn't see where there was anything he could do. Before he left this morning, she'd told him she wanted to go to the Surf Bar tonight. She said it looked just like the kind of place she would have liked to hang out when she was younger—much younger, she added. Charles then looked at me and asked if I would join them. That was a no-brainer. I nodded.

Charles walked to the near-antique Mr. Coffee and refilled his mug. He looked through the door to the customer-free gallery and then stared at me. "Now, with the cheery stuff out of the way, where were you this morning, and why were you hours late for work?"

I had been way too optimistic. Elephants, bookies, and Charles never forgot. I shared my conversations with Bob and Alexander, Cindy, and Dude. He interrupted me no fewer than fifty times with insightful, critical questions like, "Did any of them ask about me?" Or, "Has Cindy dumped her hardware store husband and gotten ready to run off to Venice with me?"

There's a fine line between ridiculous and remarkable in Charles's questions and comments. Somewhere after one of his stupid questions and before one of his more-stupid questions, he said, "One of the girls actually stayed here, most likely the other one did, and someone tried to shut me up with a piece of rebar. Your friend Samuel didn't see what he told you he saw, but he saw something. The killer thinks I know who he is. If I do, I don't know it. Unless he's caught soon, I'll be visiting earlier than Jesus will be looking for me." He paused and stared at me. "And Samuel is in trouble."

Fortunately we didn't have much time to hash and rehash what little we knew. The afternoon was filled with customers actually buying photos and visits from a couple of locals who stopped by to get out of the heat.

\* \* \*

Charles, Melinda, and I were on the rustic patio at the Surf Bar. A large-screen television and a room full of boisterous, college-aged patrons inside convinced us that if we were going to have a conversation that our aging ears could understand, the patio was our best choice—correction, our only choice.

"Charles," said Melinda after she took a gulp of Budweiser from the bottle, "you probably don't know this since you were reared by your old, stuffy, librarian granny, but I spent many a night in fine establishments like this in my younger day."

Charles sipped his beer and nodded. "Didn't know that," he said. "Granny did say that you had a rather active social life." He winked at her and then grinned.

"I bet she did," said Melinda. "The closest that dear old lady ever came to a bar was lunch at the Motor City Salad Bar on State Street." She giggled. "The old biddy—sorry, dear sweet lady—never approved of anything I did. 'Course, she wasn't always wrong."

Melinda's movements were slow, her words rapid. She had talked almost nonstop since I picked them up at her apartment and made the short drive to the bar. I sat back and drank house white wine from a six-ounce Ball jar as I listened to Charles and Melinda reminisce about the bad old days in Detroit.

She took a deep breath and looked at the television showing a video of a surfer wiping out under a humongous wave somewhere in Australia. "Never tried that," she said. "Dam ... danged Detroit River never did much waving." She turned to Charles. "Think your hippy buddy, Dude, will teach me?"

"Whenever you're ready, Aunt M.," said Charles. He gave her a forced grin. "Whenever you're ready."

"How are you feeling?" I asked her.

"You know darned well," she said. Not quite the answer I expected. "I know my big blabbermouth nephew's told you how he thinks I am." She turned to Charles and frowned.

Charles shrugged. "I'm worried about you, Aunt M."

She looked at Charles, turned to me, and then stared at the large television screen. "Let me tell you boys something." She then finally looked back at Charles. "I've had a good life ... maybe even better than good. I've had the pleasure of knowing—if you get my drift—all sorts of men. Heck, I married four of them." She giggled.

Charles leaned back in his chair and nodded.

"In my earlier days, I birthed a bunch of babies into this world—loved each of them dearly."

"I didn't know you had any children," said a clearly surprised Charles.

Melinda laughed. "Not mine. I was a midwife and gained quite a reputation around Detroit—a good one, that is."

Charles shook his head. "I didn't even know you ever worked."

Melinda reached over and put her hand on his. "That's another reason your granny didn't approve of me. She thought all babies should be born in the sterile hospital environment with a real medical doctor there." She hesitated and shook her head. "Don't think she ever understood the beauty and naturalness of nature and the birth of babies."

"Granny was mighty stuffy," agreed Charles. "Think the only nature she appreciated was in the books she read. Don't think she ever went outside."

Melinda nodded and then said, "I've enjoyed nature. Not only helping bring precious bundles into the world but also sipping every kind of squashed grape imaginable and savoring natural hops." She raised her beer bottle in the air and tilted it toward us to toast.

Charles lifted his bottle and I raised my Ball jar to toast her love of nature, and, I supposed, four marriages.

A tear rolled down her cheek. "I've found the Lord," she whispered. "He wasn't hiding. I was. The older I got, the funnier people looked at me when I blurted a batch of four-letter words, so I've given up that danged cussing."

Charles started to say something, and I nudged him. He took the hint, proving that an old dog can learn new tricks, and closed his mouth.

Melinda wiped the tear from her cheek and then grinned at Charles. "Best of all," she said, "I'm now reunited with my favorite relative."

Charles smiled.

Melinda set the beer bottle down and raised her right hand toward the roof. "I'm ready to leave anytime the good Lord wants me."

"Now Melinda," said Charles, "you know he won't be ready for you for a long time."

"Don't bet your left kidney on that," she said. "But let me tell you boys one thing. I'm not about to check out with Charles in danger." She glared at Charles and then at me. "We've got to find the lady killer and Charles almost-killer—and soon."

*If only it were that easy,* I thought. "We've shared everything we know with the police. They'll figure it out." I had little confidence in what I had just said, but I thought it was what Melinda needed to hear.

"Chris," said Melinda, "Charles says you're a fairly bright fellow, and I've seen glimmers of it. That was a bunch of malarkey about the police catching the bad guy. Charles says the Folly chief's hands are tied by an idiot mayor, your girlfriend's stuck in the middle and can't do anything, and the detective on the case is a lot closer to retiring than he is to the killer. Did I get that all right?"

"Yes," I said, "but—"

"Don't go butin' me," she interrupted. "It's up to us to catch him. Now let's figure it out."

# CHAPTER 35

Our second round of drinks had arrived; our second hour at the Surf Bar had begun, and Melinda had found her second wind.

"I've been thinking about the two murders," she said.

"Now, Aunt Melinda, we only know that one of them was murder," said Charles.

She stared at him. "Two murders. Now, as I said before being interrupted, I've been thinking. Doesn't it seem strange that no one—family, friends, pets—knew where the two girls were or how long they'd be gone?"

I shared that Charles and I had discussed that.

"The poor girl in the water could *mistakenly* be ruled as an accident. And the other one probably would never have been found if it weren't for that beachcomber with a metal-detecting gizmo."

"True," said Charles.

I suspected he wanted to say more but didn't want to incur the wrath of Melinda.

"So, my young friends, how did the killer know that no one would be looking for the poor, dead young women?"

Charles looked at me and then at Melinda. "Umm ... he—"

"Whoa," interrupted Melinda. "Don't confuse me with guesses. Let me continue."

Charles wisely said, "Yes, Aunt M."

"I figure there are two ways he could have known—the girls told him or he read about it somewhere. They're from different places, so he would have read it here or they told him here."

"How would he have read about them?" I asked.

"Nary a clue," she said. "So I didn't go down that trail. Spent the rest of the time figuring out who they might have told." She looked at Charles. "You've given out those flyers to everyone and their dogs and talked to all of the shop folks. Did anyone say that they'd seen both girls?"

"No."

"Then wouldn't you guess the killer talked to each of them at a different time?"

"Maybe, but—"

"Let's assume he did. So who would two, young, lovely, unattached females tell enough of their story to so he'd know they were alone and no one would miss them for a while if they woke up dead?"

"It could be several people if they were here long enough," I added.

"It doesn't sound like they were here long," said Melinda. "Let's try categories of folks."

Before we started playing *Jeopardy*, I asked what she meant.

"For example," said Melinda, "I haven't been here long, and I've already visited my cute, gay wig dresser twice. Just sitting in his chair brings out my life story. Those folks are good listeners."

"Gays or hairdressers?" asked Charles.

"Don't know much about gays, but hairdressers hear more confessions in a day than most priests."

"How about cops?" I said, thinking about some of the stories Cindy and Karen had shared with me.

"Add cops to the list," said Charles. "Hey, how about what you said about Officer O'Hara trying to pick up chicks?"

"There you go. You've already got a suspect," said Melinda.

Not a bad thought. I also started thinking about real estate agents. They need to know how long the renter will be around and how many people will be staying. Most people like to talk and often jabber on about their lives, saying why they are here and giving other information to a friendly rental agent. Alexander had seemed unusually nervous when he was telling me about renting to Kendra Corman-Eades. I thought his jitters were because of Bob. Could it have been something else, something more sinister?

"How about rent—"

"Bartenders," interrupted Charles. He pointed his cane toward the inside bar.

"Good," said Melinda. "That narrows it down to, let's see, you have about a dozen bars, five or so bartenders at each. Add about sixty more suspects. Doesn't help much, does it?"

"No, but it's a start," said Charles.

"Since we're going the wrong way with narrowing the list down," said Melinda, "let's add preachers and priests."

"Might as well stick lifeguards on the list," said Charles, "Chicks're always hanging around the boys in red."

Melinda started to say something, but suddenly she looked down at the table and then slowly lifted her head. Her face had gone from its regular pale, chalky white to bright white. "I think I've had about all the partying I can stand tonight. Think I could hitch a ride home?"

"I was getting tired myself," said Charles the diplomat. "Besides, Chris here has to be at work *on time* tomorrow."

Yes, he never forgets.

# CHAPTER 36

I was determined to beat Charles to the gallery and arrived at nine thirty, a half hour before opening. My determination was admirable but wasted. Charles had already opened the door, brewed coffee, and wrinkled his face into a scowl.

"Late again," he said and looked at his watchless wrist.

I gave him my best faux-sincere smile. "And a pleasant good morning to you as well," I said.

We alternated throwing a few good-natured darts and then Charles said, "Aunt M. made some good points last night. We need to look closer—"

The bell over the front door jingled. "Mr. Landrum, Mr. Landrum," yelled Samuel's familiar voice.

"It's for you," said Charles as he lowered his body into the chair by the wooden table.

Samuel rushed in the back room before I had time to greet him in the showroom. "Thank God you're here," he said.

"Calm down," I said. "Come in. You know Charles Fowler, don't you?"

Samuel noticed Charles for the first time. "Oh, hi, Mr. Fowler."

Charles wiggled his cane at Samuel.

"Have you heard?" asked Samuel. He looked around the room to be sure there were no other surprise visitors.

"Heard what?" said Charles, beating me to the question.

Samuel paced from the gallery door to the refrigerator and to the back door. My neck was getting sore just watching him. "Have a seat. Get you something to drink?" I asked.

He inhaled and said no, but he did sit.

"Heard what?" Charles repeated.

"They found another body ... a lady ... young." He looked at his hand tapping on the table. "He killed another one, Mr. Landrum."

"Who found a body?" I asked. "When? Where?"

"Some workers found her. They were sort of replacing an old pier behind a house over by the marsh, out near the county park." He looked at the florescent light in the ceiling. "Hmm, not far from the first body."

"How'd you hear about it?" asked Charles.

"I was in Mr. John's Beach Store buying a new T-shirt. I was back in an aisle and heard one of the EMTs telling the man behind the counter. He was saying the body was buried real deep. Said they knew who she was, but I didn't catch the name. Didn't want to butt in."

"Anything else?" I asked.

"No, Mr. Landrum, but I'm really scared. What if he knows I saw him? What would he do?" His hands continued to tap on the table. "What should I do?"

I smiled and tried to remain calm. "Don't worry, Samuel. I don't think he'd find out what you told the police. The police will get him."

"I wish I was that sure," he said and abruptly stood. "I didn't mean to bother you. Just thought you'd want to know."

I thanked him and told him again not to worry. I hoped it helped. He was calmer when he left—but not much. I wished I believed what I told him.

Charles had my cell phone in his hand before Samuel closed the front door. He hit Karen's number from my contacts list and handed the device to me. He was getting good at deciding whom I should call.

"Hear they found another body," I said.

"I wish I had sources as good as you have," she said. "Yeah, another woman. Hang on a second while I find some privacy."

I heard people speaking in the background and waited. A door slammed, and she returned.

"How'd you hear?" asked Karen.

"Samuel heard an EMT talking. He got some of the details, but not much."

"Guess it's not a secret," she sighed.

"What happened?"

"Around seven this morning, a groggy, coffee-deprived backhoe operator hit something that would ruin anyone's day. The body was buried three feet deep. It was buried not to be found." She hesitated. "Wait a second, let me get some notes."

Charles, with the patience of a fruit fly, tapped my arm and kept saying, "What?" I shooed him away as I would a fly.

"Okay," said Karen. "The victim was Felicia Gildehous, thirty-one, five foot two, 135, from Greenville, North Carolina."

The information surprised me. "How do you know all that so quick?"

"Would you believe outstanding work on the part of Detective Burton?"

"Umm, no," I said.

"Me either," said Karen. "Her purse was buried with her. Her driver's license and credit cards were still in it."

"Then the killer didn't care if her identity was known?"

"The spot where she was found was pretty isolated; everything's overgrown. Somebody recently bought the property that'd been vacant for a couple of years and wanted to replace an old screened-in gazebo near the end of the walk out to the marsh. Then they decided to replace the whole wooden walkway. Otherwise the body would never have been found."

"How long had she been there?" I asked.

"Don't know, but it's been months and not weeks."

"Has her family been contacted?" I asked.

"A couple of hours ago."

"Hadn't they missed her?"

"Here's the interesting part," said Karen. "Her parents hadn't heard from here in the last six months; they hadn't expected to. They said that she had resigned from a teaching job in Greenville and said she was going to travel across the country. Her mother said that even though she was beautiful, she had almost resigned herself to a life as an old-maid schoolteacher. She said Felicia thought the travels might help her find a new lease on life."

"And," I said, "now we have three deaths with one thing in common—no one knew where they were and no one expected to hear from them. What are the chances of that being a coincidence?"

"Zero," said Karen. "I said the same thing to *Detective* Burton, and he said, 'Interesting, but it doesn't mean anything.'"

I huffed, "What an idiot."

"I won't share that with him," she said. "But I wouldn't argue with it."

"Will you let me know if you learn anything?"

She laughed. "I should ask you that. You seem to find out more than the cops—especially the detective on this case."

We agreed to share information, regardless of the source, and she said she was about ready for another good meal and an evening of working off the calories. I let my imagination run for a second and said, "Me too."

"No," I said. "And what I find most interesting is that none of them told folks back home where they were going or when they'd be back. That's more than a coincidence. The killer found out somehow."

Bob couldn't stay out of the conversation. "And that's where you came up with the harebrained theory that each of them told a cop, hairdresser, bartender, priest, monk, or Cherokee holy man?"

"Yes," I said. "Don't forget rental agent."

"I was avoiding that one," said Bob.

Al said this was getting interesting and wanted to know if we wanted another drink.

"One, hell," said Bob as he held up two chubby fingers.

Al had finally trusted me behind the bar, so I jumped up before he could push his pained body out of the chair. I got two more Buds for Bob, one for Al, and another glass of wine for myself.

George Jones's version of "Almost Persuaded" flowed from the jukebox.

Al frowned at Bob and then turned to me and smiled. "Thank you, kind gentleman."

"Suck-up," said Bob in my direction.

"Now, I don't wish to defend bartenders. Lord knows they're many bad ones, but I've been in this business a long time, and—"

"Amen to that," interrupted Bob.

"A long time," continued Al without skipping a beat. "I've stood behind that old, rickety bar thousands of nights—yes, thousands. I've heard many lonely men or woman bare their soul and entire life history to someone they met minutes earlier, yes I have." He caught his breath. "There's something about a dark room, alcohol, and a stranger willing to listen that brings out stuff that a person wouldn't tell her husband, his wife, or anyone close."

"That's good, Al," said Bob. "Now you've expanded Chris's list of suspects to everyone who's been in a bar on Folly Beach over the last few months." He turned to me, "There you go. Hop in that SUV of yours and zip over to the beach and point out the killer to the cops."

"What else do you know, Chris?" asked Al.

I started to answer, but Bob grabbed my cell phone from the table and punched in some numbers. "Oh hi, Louise ... of course it's Bob ... yeah, whatever. Alexander there? ... Disturb him anyway ... of course it's important." Bob took another sip and then started humming along with George Jones, who was now singing, "Even the Bad Times Are Good."

"Well, tell them this is more important than them finding a condo," said Bob. I assumed he was talking to Alexander. "Put your brain in gear. Did you rent a condo to Felicia, umm—" Bob pointed to me.

"Gildehous," I said.

He pointed at me. "Spell it."

I did, and he repeated it to Alexander.

"Okay, hurry." Bob started humming again. Country was the only kind of music Bob acknowledged, and he knew most every song recorded from the 1930s through the seventies.

"You did?" His eyes widened. "When, where, for how long? Yeah … okay … you sure? Get any other information on her?" He paused. "Okay." He punched the *end call* button and slid the phone across the table at me.

"Well?" said Al.

Bob yawned. "Wrong number."

"And you think my comedy act needs work?" I said.

"It does," he said and took another sip of beer. "You're now three for three."

I knew what he meant.

# CHAPTER 38

Gene Watson's "Nothing Sure Looked Good on You" played in the background, Al grimaced as he massaged his arthritic knee, and Bob stuffed another handful of fries in his mouth. I tried to assimilate what Bob had said about Alexander renting the condo to Gildehous. Could it simply have been a coincidence that the young rental agent rented condos to two of the three victims? Should I tell Cindy? It may mean nothing; after all, there were only three rental agencies, and few agents worked in each.

"Chris," said Al, "Chris."

"Sorry," I said. "I was daydreaming."

"Al does that to you," interrupted Bob.

Al glared at Bob and turned to me. "I was curious," he said, "if you or the budding detective, Charles, had any suspects?"

*Isn't that what the police are supposed to be doing?* I thought. "I wish I did. I'm really scared for Samuel—and Charles, of course. The guy with the rebar wasn't kidding. Samuel doesn't know anything, but the killer doesn't know that." I turned to Bob, "What does Alexander drive?"

Bob swallowed another handful of fries. "Chrysler 300, big ol' black thing. Why?"

"Just thinking," I said. "He has hair like Samuel described. He rented condos to two of the girls, so he would have learned things about them."

"Like that they were there alone and no one would miss them," said Al.

"Yeah," I said. "And I could see how Samuel would have thought the Chrysler was a Ford Crown Vic in the dark. Both are large cars, and he did say it was a dark color."

Al turned to Bob. "What do you know about him other than that he has to be a borderline nutcase to be working for you?"

Bob frowned. "You used to be a lot nicer, old man."

Al smiled. "Nope. You never shut up long enough to listen to anything I said." He laughed. "I've always been a crank."

"Takes one to know one," I added.

Bob pointed a finger at each of us. "You two finished?"

I looked at Al. He smiled and nodded. "We are," I said. "For now."

"I'm on his case a lot," said Bob, "but Alexander's a good agent. He's new to the area. He followed some chick here and then she left him for a lifeguard—brawn over brain. He brought some good experience with him. He worked two years at a resort in Palm Desert—that's in California, for the geography-challenged folks in the room. You tell him I said this and I'll key your SUV. He's good at his job, cares for the clients, has potential. He could be with us a long time."

*Unless he's the killer*, I thought. "Any red flags?"

"None that I know of." He hesitated and then smiled. "Busybody Louise says he has too many girlfriends. Think he made the mistake of telling her that he had dated two people since arriving."

"Anybody else?" asked Al.

I told them about Officer O'Hara and what Dude had said about him being a "chick collector." Al asked what color his hair was. I told him it was brown, and Bob said that so was the hair on the majority of the male population on Folly. When I told them that he had been on Folly for less than a year, I remembered how relieved he had appeared to be when Samuel told him that he probably couldn't identify the abductor. Bob asked what kind of car O'Hara drove. I didn't know, but it was a good question.

Bob said he'd love to waste the rest of the day talking to two old, boring has-beens, but he had to go sell an overpriced house south of Broad to some sucker from New York, New York. He told Al that I'd take care of the check and to add a thirty-percent tip, even though he hadn't done anything to earn it, and waddled out the door.

Rickey Van Shelton's version of "Don't We All Have the Right" played from Al's colorblind jukebox as only Al and I remained in the dark bar. We spent some time catching up without the constant interruptions and insults from Bob. Al shared the latest news from his nine kids. His wife had passed away a few years ago, so he lived through his children. I had met one, Tanesa, an emergency room doctor at Charleston Memorial Hospital. The others ranged from teachers to college students to an inmate somewhere in California.

When Al wasn't around, Bob bragged on him for taking on "stray kids" and because he saved seven soldiers during the Korean conflict. Al had reciprocated by salting his jukebox with many of Bob's favorite country classics even though most of his clientele complained about the musical selections. Al also worried about Bob and shared that his doctors had told him that he needed to lose fifty pounds. He had diabetes and high blood pressure. Al said he felt guilty fixing cheeseburgers for Bob, but that if he didn't, someone else would. He did say that Bob had actually cut back some. "Some ain't much, but better than none," said Al.

Al also said that he was worried about Charles and me. He knew how much we butted into police business. I said I was worried about Charles and especially Samuel.

On the way out, Al told me to be careful.

I wish I'd paid attention.

# CHAPTER 39

By Monday, more information emerged about Felicia Gildehous, the "backhoe body," as the local wags referred to her. She had earned a degree in elementary education from East Carolina University in her hometown, Greenville, North Carolina. Her parents reported that she had been upbeat after she resigned her teaching position to take a year off to travel. A color photo of her was on her local newspaper's website. She had an optimistic smile, blonde hair with a one-inch-wide red stripe down one side, and a colorful, patterned blouse. Her parents had to be devastated. The principal of the elementary school where she had worked said she was always outgoing and would do anything for her fourth-grade students. He said, "I thought it was a terribly sad day for the school when she resigned, but nothing could compare to the tragic news of her death. We're in shock. Grief counselors have been brought in to meet with her former students and colleagues."

I had stopped by the gallery to pick up some tax forms I'd forgotten to take home over the weekend. The bell over the front door rang, and I stopped going through the folders in back to see who'd stopped by on my day off.

"Are you Christopher Landrum?" asked a tall, hefty gentleman with a neatly groomed beard. He wore a highly starched, long-sleeved dress shirt and navy slacks. He glanced at me and then around the gallery.

"Yes," I said. "May I help you?"

"I'm L. E. Edwards, code enforcement." He looked toward the back room and made no effort to shake my hand. "I've received complaints about egregious code violations, and I'm here to inspect your premises."

"What kind of violations?"

He looked at me. His eyes narrowed. "I'll inspect first, and then I'll discuss the results with you."

I didn't know there was even a code enforcement person, so I clearly didn't know the proper protocol.

He then took a clipboard out from under his left arm and walked to the back room. He stopped in the doorway and wrote something on a form clipped to the board. I couldn't see what he wrote, but I didn't figure it was a commendation. He looked around and then moved to the back door and tried the knob. The door was locked with a deadbolt, the way it always was when I'm closed.

"Where's the key?" he said in a flat voice.

I took the key ring out of my pocket, segregated the lock's key, and handed him the ring. He unlocked the door and stepped outside. I waited inside. A couple of minutes later, he returned and scribbled something else on the form. I offered him a seat so he could write more comfortably. He shook his head and said that he was finished. Then he removed the multipart form from under the clip, pulled off the pink second copy, and handed it to me.

He returned the original copy to the clipboard and looked down at it. "Mr. Landrum," he said, again in an emotionless voice, "I have found two violations and one probable infraction." He looked back down at the form as if he had already forgotten what they were. "The law clearly prohibits a means of egress being locked when a business is open." He turned and pointed at the back door. "That's a serious violation."

"The business is not open," I protested. "When I—"

He held up his right hand to stop me. "Mr. Landrum, your front door was open, and I walked in. There was nothing to indicate that you were closed. Now let me continue."

I clamped my jaw closed and nodded.

"Secondly, the gas meter out back is rusting. It is required to be rust-free." He looked back down at the sheet and then up at the four-tube florescent light fixture. Two tubes were burned out, and I had been telling myself for weeks that I needed to get to Larry's for new ones. "That inoperative light could be an electrical issue and fire hazard. You have five work days to repair the meter and also provide my office with a notarized statement from a certified electrician indicating that the electrical system is in proper operating order. You will also be subject to increased inspections to make sure that you do not endanger your customers by illegally blocking the rear mode of egress."

He started toward the front door and then abruptly stopped. "Any questions, Mr. Landrum?"

I took a deep breath, looked down at the pink sheet, and then looked back at him. "Only one, Mr. Edwards. Who complained?"

"Mr. Landrum, that's confidential." He then pivoted and left as quickly as he had arrived.

I followed him to the door and locked it behind him. I folded the pink paper and then ripped it in half. *Confidential!* During my six years in the gallery, this was the first visit from any inspector. I looked down at the torn paper, carried it to the back room, unfolded it on the table, and grabbed the tape dispenser to tape it back together. The entire time, I cussed both Mr. Edwards and the person who—I would wager my entire estate on—had sicced the inspector on me: Mayor Lally.

*       *       *

It took me fifteen minutes to get over my mini-temper tantrum. Then I locked the gallery, regretted that I had gone there in the first place, and headed home. I hadn't been in the house for an hour when Charles pounded on the door. He had on a silver, long-sleeved T-shirt with a strange wolf-looking thing on the front and "University of New Mexico" written in block letters below it, tattered shorts, and a frown. His ever-present cane was in his left hand and his Nikon strap draped over his right shoulder.

I waved him in. "What's wrong?"

"Don't know," he said and grabbed a mug from the counter and poured some coffee. "Maybe it's my imagination—don't know." He took a sip.

I sat silently and waited for him to elaborate.

"Something woke me up at four this morning," he said. "Thought I heard a noise and then thought I imagined it. To be honest, the rebar guy's got me spooked."

"Something outside or in your apartment?"

"Think outside, just not sure. Could've been something as simple as a car turning around in the lot."

"You don't believe that, do you?" I asked. "You've lived there for years, and you know what that sounds like."

"I guess. It did seem closer, like someone trying to get in. I looked out the window and didn't see anything. Was afraid to go out."

Charles doesn't get worried easily, and I can't remember him ever being scared. He had heard something.

He pointed his cane at the front door. "Thought you might want to walk around and take some photos."

We both valued the time we had spent walking around Folly and photographing whatever seemed interesting at the time. But he didn't show up at the door unless something bothered him.

"Let's go to your apartment and see if we find anything."

"Okay," he mumbled.

It was still a few hours before the heat of the day, and I thought it would do both of us good to walk. He stopped to take some photos along the way, but his heart wasn't in it. He talked about Melinda and her deteriorating condition. He didn't handle being helpless well, and he used that word a dozen times along the way. I told him that simply being there for her helped. He said that he wanted to do more, but we both knew that wasn't possible.

I changed the subject and told him what I'd learned about Gildehous. He asked if I'd print her photo so he could add it to the images of the other two women that he was still showing shopkeepers and anyone else he saw. I then shared news of the visit by Mr. Edwards and the petty alleged violations.

"Mickey Mouse manure," said Charles. "You know it was Lally."

"Sure," I said. "I can't prove it, and even if I could, what good would it do?"

"Mickey Mouse manure," he repeated.

It was hotter than I had anticipated, and by the time we reached his apartment, sweat was rolling down my back. The front of Charles's T-shirt was soaked. His window air conditioner churned as hard as it could, but it couldn't keep the room comfortable. I didn't see evidence of tampering on his front door, but the door was nearly as old as the apartment's occupant, and the lock wasn't much younger. It had undergone much abuse over the years. Someone probably could have taken a crowbar to it and it wouldn't have looked much worse. The front window had been painted closed before Charles moved in, and it would have taken more than a crowbar to open it.

Charles leaned over and slowly inspected each rock, shell, and piece of trash within twenty feet of his door. He looked at everything like he expected to find a calling card reading "Murderer" with a phone number. He was finally satisfied that the trash was either his or his neighbor's and asked if I wanted to continue our walk.

*I'm sweating, and it's only going to get hotter and more miserable,* I thought. "Why not," I said. He needed to talk and was too upset to sit in the claustrophobic apartment.

"I thought I saw you boys walk by," said Melinda. She had been waiting for us on the front step of her building. "Where're *we* going?"

After what Charles had told me about her condition, I didn't think she needed to be going anywhere but to the hospital. Charles said, "Come on, walk a spell with us. Chris here'll buy us something to drink in town."

She beamed. "Think I can work it in."

Charles put his arm around her and helped her down the last step, and we slowly headed toward town. I was a step behind the two of them. "So," said Melinda, "what're we going—"

Gunfire blasted a hole in her sentence. Charles's Nikon exploded into hundreds of pieces. And Melinda screamed, "Shit!"

# CHAPTER 40

Charles grabbed for the camera. His hands flailed around, catching nothing but air. Camera fragments flew everywhere, and Melinda's knees buckled. She collapsed as if the air had been let out of her. She hit the pavement hard.

I looked in the direction of the shot. All I saw was a six-foot-high privacy fence at the far side of the property—no shooter, no movement.

Charles then ignored the camera and bent over Melinda's still body. A resident of Melinda's building cautiously opened the front door and asked what was going on. I yelled for him to call the police and an ambulance. Charles wasn't going to leave Melinda, so I continued to look toward the fence that divided the parking lot from a row of townhouses. Several of the fence slats had rotted, and there were gaps where a weapon could have poked through. I didn't hear a vehicle leave. In fact, I didn't hear anything from the other side of the fence. The residents were either used to gunfire in their backyard or weren't home. I suspected the latter.

"Was she hit?" I asked.

"Don't think so. No blood," said Charles. He then rolled her onto her side. "Think she fainted."

"You okay?" I asked.

"Better than my camera. Now I'm pissed!"

The expensive camera had been the only significant item Charles bought after his substantial inheritance a couple of years ago.

The resident who had called for help hurried over and leaned close to Melinda. "She okay?" he said to Charles.

Charles looked down at Melinda. She started to move her left arm and opened her right eye. "Did I hurt my new britches?" she said.

Charles looked toward the sky and then leaned over and kissed her forehead. "Anything hurt?"

She ignored his question and tried to sit. "What in the Sam Hill happened?" She looked around but then lowered her head. "Whoa," she said and closed her eyes. "I'm dizzier than a termite in a yo-yo."

Screaming sirens filled the air. A silver City of Folly Beach patrol car skidded around the corner of Indian Avenue onto Sandbar Lane. A second police car was close behind and nearly rear-ended the first vehicle.

Officer Spencer jumped out of the car and rushed to Melinda. Fortunately, he knew Charles and me and listened as we tried to explain what had happened. He looked toward the fence as we talked and yelled for the second officer to go around behind the barrier and see if anyone was there. The odds were slim, but at least they were looking.

Spencer said that an ambulance was on the way and grabbed a blanket out of the patrol car to put behind Melinda's head. She was conscious but stared at the sky and didn't appear to understand what had happened.

A Folly Beach fire engine arrived next. The city's firefighters multitasked as EMTs and were usually on the scene before an ambulance arrived from Charleston. Chief Newman pulled around the corner. The officer who had gone to the other side of the fence returned and talked briefly to the chief as they walked over to us.

Two EMTs loomed over Melinda. They checked her vitals and asked questions to see if she knew where she was. The chief waved for us to follow him out of their way. He looked back at the pieces of the camera on the ground. "I gather someone didn't like your pictures," he said with a slight grin.

Charles pointed his cane at the camera—or what was left of it. "You know how much I paid for that?" he asked. "I'm not only pissed, I'm royally pissed. They almost shot Aunt M.," he said and then pointed to Melinda, who was now sitting and giggling at something one of the firefighters had said.

Charles finally got it out of his system about the camera, and we shared what we could about the shooting. The chief then walked to the other side of the fence. The ambulance lumbered past the police cars, and the driver conferred with the Folly Beach EMT and then unlatched the stretcher from the emergency vehicle.

Charles had returned to Melinda, and I stood in the middle of the parking lot wondering what to do. Charles was on his knees beside his aunt. "Yes," he said loudly.

"No," replied Melinda, equally as loud.

Charles reached down, put his hand on her shoulder, and whispered something.

She shook her head. He nodded. She shook her head again.

The EMT leaned down between Charles and Melinda and said something I couldn't hear. She grinned, patted him on the knee, and shook her head.

I got the gist of the conversation and would put money on Melinda. I stepped closer, and she turned to the second EMT and said, "You bet your sweet posterior I'll sign it."

Two police officers, one chief of police, two firefighters doubling as EMTs, two EMTs from Charleston, and one nephew were no match for one sweet little old lady with terminal cancer sitting gracefully in the middle of the street as if she sat there on a regular basis. Melinda was not going anywhere in an ambulance. That was final.

I stood back and watched the battle of wills. I then realized how close it had come to Charles being loaded into the back of the ambulance. Or a coroner's wagon.

# Chapter 41

Monday morning shootings weren't regular happenings on Folly Beach. By now a dozen neighbors and a car full of vacationers, apparently from Tennessee since each of them wore an orange T-shirt with "Go Vols!" on the front, had gathered about thirty feet from the action. One of the helpful neighbors set a green and white lawn chair on the side of the road, and the two EMTs carefully helped Melinda out of the street. With the signed Refusal to Transport form in hand, they wished her well and were off. The helpful neighbor also handed Melinda an umbrella to block the blazing sun. Nothing was humorous, but I couldn't help smiling at Melinda casually sitting in a colorful lawn chair at the side of the road while holding a light blue umbrella with the Aflac duck logo on top.

The fire engine slowly backed out of Sandbar Lane, and three officers were sent to canvass the neighborhood to see if anyone had heard or seen anything. I didn't expect much from the effort. Charles hovered over Melinda, and I picked up the pieces of the ruined camera. Chief Newman helped with the impossible task of gathering the remains.

"Suppose you think it was the person who killed the women?" said the chief.

"Who else?" I said, stating the obvious.

He threw pieces of the shattered lens to the side of the road. "You're certain you didn't see anyone?" he asked.

"Didn't see anyone and didn't hear a car after the shot. He was on foot."

"You and Charles walked from your house, so he must have followed. I doubt he'd been waiting here long. Too many people in the townhouses could have seen him." He pointed toward the fence and then looked back toward Indian Avenue. "He must have used a handgun; it would be way too conspicuous for him to carry a rifle around town. From that distance, he would have had to be an expert marksman to hit any of you."

"What now?" I asked. Charles had walked Melinda to her apartment, and the responders had gone their separate ways.

"I'll call Detective Burton," he said. "He'll probably deny it, but we all know this is related to Charles's butting in the investigation. Your friend's stirred up a powerful nest of hornets."

I smiled. "We do what we're good at," I said.

The chief shook his head.

By the time I got to Melinda's apartment, she was asleep. Charles was seated in her living room with his feet up on a gray fabric-covered ottoman with a dark stain on the top. His Tilley was on the floor beside the chair, and the Nikon camera strap, sans camera, sat lonely on top of the hat.

I nodded toward the bedroom. "She okay?"

"Poor thing puts on a good front, but she's shaken, weak, and confused about what happened." He looked toward the front door. "So am I."

"Stop talking about me out there," came a weak voice from the bedroom. "I ain't in a coffin."

Charles rubbed his eyes and shook his head. He looked at me and then got up and walked toward the bedroom. Melinda almost ran into him. She was out of the bed and on her way to see what we were talking about.

She slowly lowered herself into the chair Charles had vacated. "So, who tried to bump off my favorite living relative?"

"It was most likely an accident," said Charles. "A stray bullet from someone shooting—could've even been from off-island."

Melinda looked at me, gave an exasperated sigh, and then gazed at Charles. "My dear nephew," she said, "I may be old, I may be dying, and I may have the stupidest nephew in these here United States, Mexico, and Canada if he thinks I believe it was an accident."

"Aunt M.," said Charles, "I don't want you to worry. Everything'll be fine."

"Charles," she said and put her hand on the top of the ottoman, "when you were no taller than this, you'd scamper around the house on all fours saying that you were a collie. Heck, you even barked like one."

This sounded interesting. I had been standing in the corner of the room but moved closer.

"Your granny kept telling you to stop acting like a nut," continued Melinda. "I'd call you over and say I wanted to pet the prettiest collie I'd ever seen. All your granny ever wanted to do was stifle your creativity. I wanted to encourage it."

Charles patted her foot. "Other than to embarrass me in front of Chris, what's your point?"

She reached down and squeezed his hand. "Two points, my dear nephew. First, I can tell the difference between fact and fantasy even though I pretended that you were a dog." She let go of his hand and then slapped it. "Someone just tried to kill you, sure as I'm sitting here. That's a fact. And second, you've still got more creativity in you all these years later than all the cops in South Carolina. So get your rear end out of this building and figure out who's killing those women."

"Aunt M.," said Charles, "the police are on it."

"Brian's going to call Detective Burton," I added. "He'll probably be contacting us later today."

"Great, that's a conversation I'm looking forward to," said Charles.

"Am I supposed to be comforted by that?" asked Melinda. "You've already said he's an idiot dressed in imbecile's clothing."

"Now, Aunt M., we have to let him do his job. There's nothing to worry about; he can take care of it."

I looked at Charles—two lies in one sentence.

"Perhaps I was a bit vague," said Melinda. She glared at Charles. "And Lord forgive me for making an exception to my no-profanity rule. Charles, you take Chris here and get your wrinkly, old ass out of here and find the freakin' shit-eater who's killing those sweet ladies. And do it before he kills you."

I thought her message was quite clear as Charles and I left Melinda's apartment.

What wasn't clear was how we were going to catch a killer.

# CHAPTER 42

"Hear picture takin' contraption wiped out," said Dude before he reached our table at the Lost Dog Café.

Charles had still been too shaken to return to his claustrophobic apartment, so we had walked to the restaurant. A light mist filled the air, and the temperature had cooled slightly, so we sat on the covered patio.

Charles was surprised that Dude knew, but I would have been more surprised if he hadn't. After all, it had been a couple hours since the "picture takin' contraption" had been vaporized. Dude nodded at the empty seat. Charles took the hint and asked him to join us.

"Hear fuzz found zero shooters," Dude added.

That was one hundred percent accurate. I asked if he'd heard anything else.

He took a sip of water from the jar that Amber had placed in front of him. "Not about the Chuckster's rough surfin' this a.m."

Charles tilted his head and looked at Dude. "About something else?"

"Hear bulldozed chick be hanging out at Crab Shack," said Dude. "She been all gussied up, hair shiny blonde with red streak, attracting dudes."

I assumed he meant before she was killed. "Hear about her paying attention to anyone in particular?"

"Me not *Entertainment Tonight*," said Dude.

My phone rang before I could find out what else Dude didn't know. The caller ID read, "CCS." If I were quicker, I would have realized it was the Charleston County Sheriff's office and not answered. Too late, so I got to hear the crotchety voice of Detective Brad Burton. "I wanted to talk to the alleged victim first, but your friend's apparently too cheap to have an answering machine. You were next in line."

I was tempted, sorely tempted, to hand the phone to Charles, but instead I asked what I could do for Detective Grumpy.

"Just got off the phone with Chief Newman, and he filled me in on what happened. Is Mrs. Beale okay?"

That's Burton. Charles was almost killed, and he asked about Melinda. "Yes, and so is Charles."

"Yeah, whatever," he said. "And you didn't see anything? No idea who it was?"

"It's obvious that it's the person who's killed those women and who tried to kill Charles a few days ago," I said. "Detective, Charles has been asking questions, and a killer thinks he's getting too close."

There was a pause. "You may be right," he said.

That surprised me, so I tried to take advantage of the slight concession. "Any leads on the murders?"

"None that I'll tell you about," he said, back to his gruff self. "Have Charles call me." He gave me his number and hung up.

Dude took another sip of water and said, "Fuzz?"

I nodded.

"Burton?" asked Charles.

"Yes. He wants you to call him," I said.

Charles looked out at the mist and then at me. "It's cool out here, but not cold enough for hell to freeze over. He'll have to wait."

Before I could encourage Charles to give Burton the benefit of the doubt, the door from the patio to the dining room opened, and Marc Salmon peeked around the corner. The soothing smell of frying hamburgers followed him out.

"Thought I saw you walk through," he said in our direction. "I was in a deep political discussion with Houston and didn't get to tell you the news."

Instead of commenting on the deep political discussion, which probably was something like how they could get more comfortable chairs in the council chamber, I said, "What news?"

Marc looked around to see who else was on the patio and then walked to the table. Only two tables were occupied, and a large Great Dane at one of the tables got more attention than the three of us. Dude stood and said something about being too close to government. He bent over for the huge dog to lick his cheek and then slipped out the side exit.

Marc watched Dude and the dog, said "Yuck," looked around again, and then sat in the chair that Dude had vacated. "I hear your friend, Chief Newman, handed his resignation to Mayor Lally."

I was shocked. "Are you sure? When?"

"Not certain," said Marc. "But a *source close to the police department* told me. She's usually accurate. Said it happened yesterday." He sat back in the chair and basked in knowing something about my friend that I didn't know.

"We saw him a little while ago," said Charles. "He didn't say anything."

"He was busy trying to figure out who was trying to kill you," I said. I thought it sounded like a reasonable explanation, but I was still disappointed.

Marc put his elbows on the metal table and leaned closer to Charles and me. "I also hear *the mayor* is still determined to run you out of town. You'd better watch your p's, q's, and permits."

I flashed back to the visit from code enforcement but didn't tell Marc. There was already enough fuel on the fire without my adding more gas.

"Don't suppose you'd divulge your source?" asked Charles.

Marc smiled. "Nope. But here's a hint: mayor's pet cop."

"O'Hara," I said.

He smiled again. "Didn't hear that from me."

That reminded me. When I was talking to Bob at Al's, I wondered what kind of car O'Hara drove. What better source?

I turned to Marc. "What's the mayor's pet cop drive?" I asked, as nonchalant as possible.

Marc tilted his head in my direction. "Cop car."

I sighed. "When he's not working?"

"That's what I'm talking about. He drives an old cop car," said Marc. "Ten-year-old Crown Vic. He brags about it all the time. Says he got it at auction for fifteen hundred bucks."

Charles perked up. "Color?"

"Dark gray," said Marc. "Big white primer spots on the driver's side door where they sprayed out the markings. Looks terrible to me, but O'Hara treats it like it's his baby." He hesitated and then said, "Why?"

"Just curious," I said and changed the subject. "What important city business were you and Houston talking about?"

"Oh, nothing controversial," he said.

Charles had been quiet for too long. "As President Kennedy said, 'My experience in government is that when things are noncontroversial, beautifully coordinated and all the rest, it must be because there is not much going on.'"

Marc looked at Charles like he couldn't figure out if he'd been insulted and then said. "Kennedy was never on the Folly Beach City Council."

Charles and I nodded. Marc took the moment of silence to announce his departure. "City's business is waiting."

Charles and I nodded again, and Marc headed inside to discuss more of the city's important business with Houston. As soon as the council member was out of sight, Charles scooped up my phone from the table, scrolled through the contacts, hit *dial*, and then handed the phone to me. I was ready to tell him how much his new maneuver irritated me but instead looked at the screen and saw that it was calling Brian Newman.

"Did someone try to kill you or Charles again, or has some blabbermouth been talking about my job?"

I renewed my hatred for caller ID. "Charles and I are just fine, thanks for asking."

"Cut the BS," interrupted the chief. "Where are you?"

I told him.

"Be there in five." The phone went dead.

# CHAPTER 43

"So what busybody told you?" Chief Newman had made the five-minute trip in two and took the seat formerly occupied by Dude and Marc Salmon. He would have been quicker, but he stopped and fawned over the Great Dane.

I didn't want to get Marc in trouble and said we had heard it through the grapevine.

"Is it true?" asked Charles.

Brian sat military straight and sipped the iced tea that Amber handed him before he arrived at the table. "Yes. I've been in this job eighteen years. I spent thirty in the military, most in law enforcement." He hesitated and smiled. "My hair was black when I arrived on Folly." His short military cut was mostly gray. "This is a young man's game, and I'm sixty-eight."

"Brian," I said, "you're the youngest sixty-eight-year-old I've known, and you know more about Folly than anyone. Do you really want to retire?"

He looked over at the dog and then toward the street. "The mayor wants me out. The majority of the council probably agrees. Why fight it?"

"That's not what Chris asked," said Charles.

"I know," said Brian. He took a sip of tea and turned to Charles. "How's your aunt?"

Charles nodded. "Good try. That's the topic after the next commercial break. Now, back to Chris's question."

Brian blinked twice and turned back to me. "I'd rather not. What would I do? You're right. I feel great, still have lots of energy, and still think I can contribute." He hesitated and then smiled. "I have some good friends here." He looked at Charles and then at me. "Other than a couple of troublemakers who keep butting into my business, most of my friends are good folks."

Charles didn't ask who the troublemakers were but asked, "Are you sure most of the council members want you out?"

"No, but I can't go around asking them. The mayor says he has what he needs to get rid of me. That's why I resigned instead of being fired."

Charles aimed the brim of his hat at Brian. "If most of the council members wanted you to stay, would you rescind your resignation?"

"I've—"

"Yes or no?" said Charles.

Brian shook his head and turned to me for support. I pointed at Charles.

"Yes," said Brian.

"Then don't pack your bags for an around-the-world cruise," said Charles, who then tapped the metal table. "Now about Melinda. I think she's okay—as okay as she can be in her condition. There is one thing that she said would make her better."

"What?" asked Brian.

"She said that you needed to find the killer—and find him fast." Charles pointed his right index finger at the chief. "Tell you what, Brian, you don't want to disappoint my dear, sweet aunt."

Amber brought drink refills and told the chief she'd missed him the last couple of times he'd been in. She also glanced at me and opened her mouth as if she wanted to say something but instead waved to the three of us and headed inside.

Brian sipped his refreshed drink and then shared that the mayor had hinted that he wanted the local police to stay out of the investigation. The mayor had confidence in the detectives in the sheriff's office to find the killer. He also said that the mayor didn't specifically say "cover-up," but he made it clear that he didn't want any undue attention to anything bad that happened on Folly. It was bad for vacationers and upstanding citizens—those wealthy newcomers that strongly supported the mayor.

"What do you know about Officer O'Hara?" I asked the chief after he had run out of steam complaining about the mayor.

He looked at me and around the patio to see who was near. "You mean other than that he's a cocky, connected prick?"

"Already knew that," I said. "What about his background? Problems in the past? Complaints against him?"

Brian gave me his patented police stare. "Why?"

I shrugged. "Is he working today?" I continued. "I noticed that he wasn't at the shooting."

"No," said Brian. "He's off. Why?"

I looked down at the table and then said, "Just curio—"

"Whoa," interrupted Brian. "You're not thinking he could be the killer?"

"Are you?" blurted Charles.

"Bear with me, guys," I said. "I'm not accusing him of anything, but he's about the same size as the guy Samuel saw and the guy who tried to bludgeon Charles the other day. When Samuel and I went to the police station, O'Hara seemed nervous at first, but after Samuel said that he didn't think he would recognize the abductor, he was more at ease."

"Hardly anything to scream guilt," said Brian.

"Hold on," I said. "And then Dude told me about O'Hara trying to pick up girls at the Washout. He called him a chick collector."

Brian frowned.

I held up my hand. "All three of the dead females were attractive, and neither their friends nor their relatives knew where they were or when they would be returning home. In other words, no one would miss them. That's the kind of information O'Hara could easily have gotten." I took a sip of water. "Add to that, doesn't O'Hara drive a dark Crown Vic, the same kind of car Samuel saw the night of the abduction?"

Brian shook his head. "Yes, but—"

"Let the man finish," interrupted Charles. "This is getting good."

"All I have left is this morning," I said. "It's his day off, so he could have been the shooter. He knew Charles was putting up the signs and talking to everyone who would listen to him about the girls. Charles was doing more investigating than the entire sheriff's office. He's getting close."

Brian sighed again. "One question. Motive?"

"Good question," said Charles.

"I agree," I said. "Here's my guess."

Charles leaned back in his chair, and Brian leaned closer.

"O'Hara either pulled each of them over for some minor infraction or talked to them on the street. He used his badge to ask questions that the women wouldn't normally answer for a stranger."

"Such as?" asked Brian.

"Where were they staying," I said, "or who was with them, how long they would be on Folly, and who knew they were here."

"And then?" said Brian.

"And then he hit on them," I said. "Could be one or more of them went out with him."

"Quite a leap from a date to murder," said Brian, but he still leaned toward me.

"I know," I said. "The only reason to kill them I can think of is if they rejected him or made him angry." I looked at the large dog lapping water from a bowl near the exit and back at Brian. "Or he's simply a very sick puppy. Whoever is killing the girls is either a psychopath or has serious anger issues. He doesn't need a logical reason for his actions, does he?"

Brian thought about it. "No."

"Does O'Hara have a temper?" asked Charles.

"I haven't seen it," said Brian.

"I'm not saying it's him," I said. "Seems he would be in a good position to learn about the girls, and his reputation doesn't help."

"Tell you what," said Brian. He hesitated and then looked down at his glass. "I can check to see if he was working when Samuel saw the alleged abduction."

"And when the rebar-wielding guy met me at my apartment?" said Charles.

"Then too," said Brian. "But I've got to tell you: I don't like the guy. He's an egomaniacal jerk. But I don't see him as a killer."

"But—" said Charles.

Brian held up his hand. "I said I'll check."

"Fair enough," I said and shook his hand.

Brian walked off the patio, and Amber headed to the table. She had been watching for the chief to leave. "Chris, could I talk to you a minute?"

Charles took the hint and said he had to check on Melinda. He told Amber that I would take care of the check—no surprise—and said he'd call me later. I was relieved that Charles hadn't invited the entire Baptist church choir to breakfast.

"Let's not talk here," she said. I paid for Dude's, Brian's, Charles's, and my morning refreshments and followed Amber.

*Curious,* I thought.

# CHAPTER 44

I followed Amber off the patio and around the restaurant to the small city park behind the combined library and community center. I smiled as I read "It's Okay To Drool" on the back of her yellow Lost Dog Café T-shirt. I smiled, but I was still curious about her mysterious request and need for privacy.

"Thought you ought to know," she said as she leaned on the wooden rail of the small bridge that overlooked a pond in the park. "Jason said that Samuel is telling everyone in school that he saw the 'lady killer' abduct Corman-Eades." Jason was Amber's son and was also Samuel's best friend.

"You sure?"

"No reason for Jason to lie about it, is there?" she said through clenched teeth.

The reason Amber and I had stopped dating was that she felt that I had put her son in danger after I got mixed up in a murder case a couple of years ago. Jason had been with me when I discovered one of the victims. She was afraid for her son. I didn't think he was in danger, but I understood—he was all she had. The last thing I wanted to do was to dredge up feelings of those terrible days.

"Of course not," I said. "I'm not questioning Jason. Just thought maybe whoever told him was confused. You know how rumors get started."

"Samuel told him. Would've been hard to get confused, don't you think?" She gripped the handrail and glared at me.

In fewer than two minutes, I had irritated Amber by questioning her son. I didn't mean to accuse him of anything. "Oh," I said. "Sorry, I didn't mean he misunderstood. I'm confused. Samuel told me that he didn't see the person. He heard a girl scream. He caught a glimpse of a man earlier who he later thought may have taken her, and he had seen a car drive away." I shrugged. "He said he couldn't identify the abductor."

She loosened her grip and hesitated before speaking. "You know how boys are," she said, her voice calmer. "Everyone at school's talking about the murders. Samuel's a big man in school with his story. I hate it when you get involved in this horrible stuff, but I'm resigned to the fact that you will. Charles has shown pictures of the victims to everyone who lives, works, and visits Folly, so the two of you are already neck deep in it."

I started to protest, but she touched my arm and shook her head. "Don't say anything. You'll do what you have to do." She smiled. "That's why I love and hate you at the same time."

"I only—"

She squeezed my arm and continued, "Jason made a good point. He said if everyone in school believes that Samuel saw the killer, he was afraid that the killer would find out." She looked out on the small pond and then back at me. "He's afraid for Samuel. So am I."

I would love to have reassured her and said that Samuel wasn't in danger, but I knew better. This was a small community. Kids tell their parents and parents tell their friends. Pretty soon, everyone knows. Samuel didn't get a clear look at the killer and couldn't identify him, but the killer didn't know that.

"I'm worried too," I said and put my hand on her shoulder.

She looked back toward the Dog. "Wanted you to know. Got to get back to work. Good luck." She kissed me on the cheek and hurried back to the restaurant.

I watched her go and knew that she was right. Samuel was in danger. The killer had already made two attempts on Charles's life. What would stop him from going after a teenager who could possibly identify him?

The phone rang before I could think about Samuel's exaggeration, a teenager's tale that could get him killed.

"So what'd she want to tell you that she couldn't say in front of me?" said Charles.

If he had owned a cell phone, I would have sworn that he was hiding behind a nearby tree watching for Amber to leave. He couldn't let her story linger.

"She said you were the sweetest, most kind and generous man on earth. She didn't want to say it in front of you; she was afraid she'd blush," I said.

"Wow, really?" said Charles.

"In your dreams," I said. "I'll tell you later."

"Good," he said. "So here's our plan. Melinda told me she's feeling chipper and wants a night on the town. Heather says it's about time I spent some money on her. And I bet Karen could use a good meal."

Unless I had drifted during it, I had missed the plan, but I had a hunch I was involved. "The plan?"

"The plan is that you call Karen and invite her out to dinner and then you head over this way later and take us to Blu."

The upscale restaurant was in the Tides. The food was great, but it was probably the most expensive restaurant on Folly. Even though it was Charles's party, the odds were high that the check would be mine. "Why Blu?"

"Melinda said that she had a hankerin' for a good meal at the resort hotel where we put her up her first night here." He laughed. "She said she knew her *wonderful* and *generous* nephew would want to splurge on her."

I wondered if she had another nephew but said, "What time?"

I had just started to punch in Karen's number when the phone rang again. The caller ID read, "Mayor Lally." My first reaction was to think, *what an ego.* Then I wanted to throw the phone in the pond, but curiosity won out.

"Mr. Landrum," said the mayor, "meet me for lunch tomorrow. Our regular meeting spot." He cackled at his feeble joke.

I sighed, regretted not throwing the phone in the water, and said that I'd be there.

I didn't know what he wanted but was certain that *our* mayor didn't want to give me a good citizenship award.

Heather had nothing on me when it came to being psychic.

# CHAPTER 45

The humidity was stifling, but we managed to get an inside table beside the large windows overlooking the ocean. It was seven o'clock, but the summer sun was still high in the sky, and the beach had no shortage of couples and walkers. A few preschoolers jumped and squealed as each wave slapped their legs. Two surfers optimistically waited for the perfect wave.

"Don't see many surfers back home," said Melinda. She had been staring at two young men sitting on their boards waiting for something to happen. It seldom did. Her eyes sparkled, and she seemed more alert than I had seen her in the last few days. She stared at the surfers. I stared at her shamrock-green hair and thought she'd give M&M's a run for their color choices. I wasn't going to mention her ever-changing locks, but I hoped that Charles or Heather would ask about it.

"Guess that's why Chuckie's not a surfer," said Heather. I thought she was kidding, but with her, I could never tell. She and Charles were made for each other.

A waitress interrupted our intellectually stimulating conversation. Melinda hadn't looked at the menu, and Heather said she didn't know how to order from such an exotic selection. Everyone knew how to order drinks.

"I thought Karen was coming," said Melinda. She looked around as if Karen might be at another table.

"She may stop by later," I said. "Something came up at work." I didn't want to ruin a perfectly pleasant evening by telling Melinda that someone had the nerve to get murdered in Charleston just to keep Karen from joining us.

"Ho, ho! There you are," came a familiar voice from across the room.

I turned and saw Chester Carr hobble our way. He wore a white short-sleeved dress shirt and something no human in his late eighties should wear in public: shorts. The purple veins in his legs reminded me of a road map of Florida. Thankfully, his white tube socks covered Miami. A broad smile peeked through his Magoo glasses.

Melinda stood and pointed at the chair that had been saved for Karen. I glanced at Charles, who seemed as surprised as I was to see Chester. Charles looked at Melinda, and she gave him a wide grin.

"Thanks for the invite," said Chester, who then gave Melinda a peck on the cheek. He patted her on the head. "I do like that color—quite fetching. Puts me in the holiday spirit."

*Halloween?* I wondered.

Melinda turned her head so he could see the back. "St. Patty's Day," she said.

"Little early for that," said Heather. "Isn't it a half year away?"

"It's never too early, my dear," said Melinda.

"Fetching," repeated Chester.

My stomach knotted as I wondered if it was green because she figured she wouldn't be around in March for St. Patrick's Day. I took a deep breath and decided to enjoy the moment. Melinda had a way of brightening the dreariest day.

"Folly Curls is the greatest," she said. "Damian said he'd change the color any old time I wanted."

Heather leaned toward the table and whispered something. Chester put his hand behind his ear and said, "Huh?"

Melinda said, "What?"

My hearing was on the slow path toward deafness, so I appreciated their questions.

"I said,"—Heather spoke more loudly but clearly didn't want anyone at nearby tables to hear—"rumor is that Anne's been running around on poor Cameron."

"Who?" said Chester.

"Anne Potterfield, the lady who owns Folly Curls," said Charles in a tone that implied everyone should know.

"Oh," said Chester. "I get my hair cut there and never knew her name. Cute little thing. Who's Cameron?"

"Her husband, duh," said Heather.

"Oh yeah, the woodcutter," said Chester.

"Carpenter," said the always-accurate Charles. "Where'd you hear it?"

He wanted to be able to footnote the rumor.

"Millie's," she said. "Tongues are a-waggin'. All the ladies have been talking about it."

"She seems so nice," said Melinda. "Sort of reminds me of two of those poor dead girls from the picture you're showing around, Charles." She paused. "Yes, she's so nice and—"

"That's the problem," interrupted Heather. "She's too nice. Hear she ran off to St. Thomas with one of her clients. He's that real estate hunk who's always primping. His picture is always in the ads in the paper, standing in front of the Cooper River Bridge like he'd just sold it. Anne told poor Cameron that she was at a stylists' convention in Las Vegas. Hear it wasn't her first trip with the creep—few days here, few there." She shook her head. "Poor hubby. He'd kill her if he found out."

Charles had heard enough about the salacious life of half the Potterfield family. "So, Melinda, it was nice of you to invite Chester to supper. Did you forget to mention it to me?"

"Nope," she said and then sipped her gin and tonic.

Chester leaned toward me. "Have the police caught the maniac who's killing those cute *muchachas*?"

Heather piped in, "Chuckie says there's not a snowball's chance in Laredo, Mexico, that that detective in Charleston will figure it out."

Melinda reached over and pinched her nephew's cheek. "Charles is right. But, don't worry your adorable hairless head about it, Chester. My nephew, the detective, and his friend here almost have it solved." She pointed at me.

Heather gave two oversized nods. "They sure do."

Chester turned to Charles. "Who is it?"

"Don't want to say just yet," said Charles.

"Sort of like that priest thing," added Heather. "He can't tell."

"Oh," said Chester.

"It's that creepy cop," said Melinda. "The Irish one, O something."

Chester cupped his left hand behind his ear. "Who?"

"O'Hara," said Heather. "Whoops, sorry, Chuckie. It just flew out."

He looked at her like she'd stepped on his toe but said, "That's okay. We're all friends. Besides, we're not exactly sure."

"Hope you're right," said Chester. "I was talking to some of the guys at Bert's yesterday, and we all figured it must be a bartender. You know, someone the girls would open up to. They were here alone, weren't they? Someone said that not even their families knew where they were."

"He's not gay," said Melinda.

I glanced at Charles. He looked at Chester, who said, "I most definitely am not."

"Not you, silly," said Melinda, who then winked at him. "Never thought you were."

"Who, Aunt M.?" asked Charles for all of us.

"Damian, of course."

"What brought that up?" I asked.

"Chester mentioned bartenders which reminded me of Damian. Hairdressers learn all sorts of stuff about their clients; they're like bartenders with scissors."

"Anne sure did," said Heather.

*Couldn't argue with that*, I thought. "How do you know he's not gay?" I asked.

Chester turned to Melinda. "Put a move on you, didn't he?"

She giggled. "No. Charles isn't the only detective in the family. I know a thing or two about detecting."

"See him kiss a girl?" asked Chester. "Watch women's beach volleyball?"

"Nope," she said. "When I was in there yesterday getting my hair ready for St. Patty's Day, I looked him in the eye and said, 'Are you gay?'"

I nearly choked on my wine, Charles put his head down on the table, and Heather said, "Great detecting?"

Chester added, "Beauty and brains. You've got it all."

Two hours later, bolstered by alcohol, Melinda's high spirits, and Heather's impromptu reading of Chester's palm, we had become the loudest, most festive group in Blu. Chester also regaled us with stories of ghosts on Folly Beach, his years growing up on the small island, and stories he had heard about various politicians who came to convince Folly voters that they were the greatest thing since sliced fudge. He said the residents would listen, smile, and ignore whatever was said. I didn't think it was much different now.

It was nice getting my mind off murder, a hostile mayor, code enforcement, Melinda's cancer, and worrying about Charles and Samuel. Melinda said it was the best meal she had had since husband number two, or maybe it was number three, took her to a ritzy steakhouse in Chicago. I was sorry that Karen didn't make it. I was also sorry to get stuck with the check, which was more than I had paid for my first car.

# CHAPTER 46

Only two restaurants on the barrier island were beachfront. Blu had provided me with a fantastic evening, and now I was entering the other beachfront restaurant, Locklear's, to meet the mayor. I had no illusions that the experience would come close to the last night's gathering. Storm clouds blanketed the sky, and it wouldn't stretch the imagination to foresee a torrential rain ruining a morning at the beach for hundreds of vacationers.

Mayor Lally's first words reinforced my fears; the storm had moved indoors. "Mr. Landrum," he snarled, "I thought I had been clear about your butting in *my* city's business."

Lally was at the same table where we'd had our earlier "pleasant" conversation. He still looked as out of place as an elephant at a funeral. His dark-gray suit and heavily starched white dress shirt looked identical to what he had worn the first time we had met. The bright red tie was different, and he had a glass of water in front of him instead of iced tea. It had two slices of lemon. I hoped that the waiter had gotten it right the first time.

"I most certainly—"

He lifted his glass and clicked it back on the table. "I'm not done," he said. "You were warned, and now I hear that you and your beachcombing, straggly bum of a friend, Fowler, are continuing to harass my fine citizens—passing out those handouts with pictures of the dead girls, pestering shop owners about whether they've seen the poor dead souls." He pounded his fist on the table. The waiter heard the noise and started to the table but saw the look on the mayor's face and retreated. "I thought asking you nicely the last time to refrain from such behavior would be enough. Clearly, I was mistaken."

Clearly, I'd missed the *asking me nicely* part. "Mr. Mayor, my friend is trying to help the police by asking the people if they had contact with the deceased women. He is concerned and wants to help."

I chose not to mention that neither Charles nor I believed that the police had taken the murders seriously at first and that we thought the lead detective had little chance of solving the horrific crimes. I also chose not to mention that I thought the mayor was a pompous, bullying ass who didn't know how to dress at the beach.

"Mr. Landrum, I'm being patient, but make no mistake: this is your final warning. If you or your friend chooses to foolishly continue meddling, I promise I will find a way to run you out of town. Your friend, Fowler, is a bum. I have little clout over him. God knows, if I could run all the bums off *my* island, it would have happened long ago."

A bolt of lightning over the pier illuminated the room. A loud clap of thunder vibrated the large window overlooking the beach. Lally looked toward the pier and then back at me. "You, on the other hand, are a businessman and come under several city regulations—regulations I control." He lifted his glass, and I thought he was going to use it again like a hammer. Instead he calmly took a sip and slowly lowered it back to the table. "Is that clear? Is that perfectly clear?"

"Quite," I said.

"One more thing," he continued. "Don't waste your time running to your buddy, Newman." He paused, took another sip, and then grinned. "He's wiser than I thought." Lally nodded. "He slinked out, tail between his legs, rather than having his ass canned." He sat back in the chair and smiled like he had just taken the pot with a pair of deuces.

"That's too bad," I said.

He tilted his head. "Too bad for you."

What would he have said if he had known that Charles was canvassing members of the council to see if they would support keeping the chief? I wondered it but didn't dare ask.

A heavy downpour began to pelt the pier, and several fishermen scrambled to get their gear to cover. A lone surfer continued to sit on his board, oblivious to the rain. Water was water, and he knew the perfect wave would be along any second. And Mayor Lally stood, picked up the umbrella that he had leaned against the window, and walked toward the entrance without saying another word. I remained seated and stared at the two lemon slices in his glass.

For the first time I wondered if Mayor Lally was simply a total jerk or if he could possibly have other reasons for wanting Charles to butt out. I knew he was close to Officer O'Hara, our top suspect.

So, butt out? Not Charles. Not me. Not a chance. But unless we stopped the killer soon, the chance of something terrible happening to Charles or Samuel was too high to contemplate. Sorry, Mr. Mayor, your threats were a waste of time.

# CHAPTER 47

I waited to walk home until the seasonal thunderstorm took its rain and lightning and rumbled out to sea. I called Charles to see if he'd heard from Melinda. He said that he had just left her apartment and that she was exhausted from last night. Charles said he'd teased her about sneaking off with Chester after supper and suggested that was why she was tired. He said Melinda told him that he had a dirty mind—and besides, Chester couldn't keep up with her. She was afraid she'd give him a heart attack.

I gave Charles an abridged version of my conversation with the mayor and asked if he'd talked to any of the council members about Chief Newman. I waited while he ranted and raved about Lally being the worst mayor "in the history of mayorhood." He then calmed down enough to say that he'd talked to three council members and learned that two were strongly in the chief's corner. I asked what the chances were of one of the remaining three standing behind the chief. "Hell if I know," was his in-depth, highly honed political analysis.

Charles wasn't a fan of telephone conversations. He often said that people communicated more with their gestures and expressions than with words. He started to say something else and then stopped. "I hate phones. I'm on my way over. Don't run away." The line went dead before I could say whether I'd run away or not.

The temperature had dropped drastically with the passing storm, and I was sitting on the front step when Charles rode his classic Schwinn bicycle up to the door and then leaned it against the porch. He loosened the bungee cord that held his cane to the rear fender and set it by the step. He wore a green, long-sleeved T-shirt with "Delta State" on the front under something that looked like—well, looked like something wearing boxing gloves. I usually bit my tongue before asking but threw my rule to the wind this time.

I pointed to the shirt. "What's that?"

He looked down and pulled the shirt away from his body. "A fighting okra, of course."

"You're kidding," I said.

"I don't kid about college mascots," he said. "Think it's a Mississippi thing."

I'd already gone too far with the conversation and asked if he wanted a drink. He said that he not only wanted a drink but also thought we ought to call for a pizza. "We've had way too few pizza parties this summer."

Neither of us needed pizza, but he pointed out that we weren't spring chicks and most likely something other than pizza would do us in. Considering recent events, I agreed. We went in, and he grabbed a beer and a poured a glass of wine for me in one of my finest plastic wine glasses. I called for a pizza.

"Something Aunt M. said last night got me thinking," he said and then sipped his beer. "Remember she said—"

A loud knock on the door interrupted Charles. It was too soon for the pizza, and we looked at each other.

"Hello, hello! Anyone in there? Mr. Landrum, you there?"

I opened the door, and Samuel nearly fell inside. "Come in," I said, needlessly.

"I'm glad you're here. I saw the car and Mr. Fowler's bike, so I figured you had to be around."

"How come you're not in school?" I asked.

He looked sheepishly at the floor. "I cut school today to tell you what I saw."

"Must be important," said Charles. Want a soft drink?"

Samuel nodded, and Charles went to the refrigerator for a Pepsi.

"Mr. Landrum," said Samuel as Charles gave him the drink, "can you come with me?"

"Where?" I asked.

"I saw him again," said Samuel. He looked back at the door.

"The abductor?" said Charles.

"Yeah … um, the killer," said Samuel. It was still cool outside and about the same in the house, but Samuel had sweat on his forehead.

"Where?" I asked again.

"Behind Rita's," he said. "Will you go with me?"

"Did you just see him?" I asked.

"No, last night," he said. "Will you go?"

"Under one condition," said Charles. "We have a pizza coming. You stay and help us eat it and then we'll go wherever you want."

The pizza arrived fifteen minutes later. Charles and I ate half while Samuel wolfed down the other half. We asked about last night, but he said he would rather wait until we could see exactly where he was and what he saw. He wanted to make sure that he wasn't accused of being somewhere where he couldn't see the person—once burned, and all that. Samuel was an excellent student who wouldn't cut school unless it was for a good reason.

*   *   *

"I'd been out on the pier watching two friends of mine fishing. I caught as much without a pole as they did with big ol' expensive rods." He grinned and looked toward the step that led up to the pier. We had walked the three blocks from the house and were on the sidewalk across the street from Rita's. The large gravel lot behind it was crammed with cars in season, but only a dozen or so were there now.

"And?" said impatient Charles.

Samuel looked at my friend. "Sorry. It was after eight, sun heading down." He nodded toward the west. "I had to get home and do homework before bed, so I was in a hurry." He hesitated. "Then this big car came around Dude's surf shop and right across the lot there." He pointed to the rear corner of the lot.

"It was the man from the abduction?" I asked.

"Think so," he said. "From the angle I was to the car, it looked sort of like him."

"Sort of?" said Charles.

"Said I couldn't be sure. I thought it was, but something looked different."

"Same car?" I asked.

"Think so," said Samuel.

"Ford Crown Vic? Like a cop car?" said Charles.

"Pretty sure," said Samuel, who then lowered his head. "Pretty sure."

"Could it have been a Chrysler?" asked Charles.

*Where'd that come from?* I wondered.

"Umm, maybe," said Samuel. "I'm not a big expert on cars. I really wasn't paying that much attention. I was trying to see the driver."

Then it struck me. Bob had told me that Alexander Bishop, his young associate, drove a black Chrysler 300. I must have told Charles, but I didn't remember.

"Did the driver see you?" I asked.

"Let me think," said Samuel. He looked to the empty spot where he had seen the car and then back toward the pier, toward Rita's, and back at me. "Don't know for sure. If he did, he didn't let on."

Samuel asked if we thought he should tell the police. Experience from our previous trip to the police station and my current relationship with the mayor told me it would be one of the worst things he could do. I said that I would share the information with them. He finally said that he wanted me to see where he had been so I'd believe him and indicated that he felt terrible about lying to me the first time. I told him not to worry.

He thanked us for going to the lot with him and said he'd taken enough of our time and should be going. He then asked if we thought he was in danger. I said that I didn't think so but that he needed to be careful. My fingers were crossed.

We were already on the street where Samuel had allegedly seen the abduction, so I convinced Charles to walk with me to the site. I didn't expect any significant findings, but I had nothing else to do.

"Why did you ask him about a Chrysler?" I asked as we passed Loggerheads.

Charles looked at a Doberman and its owner on the other side of the street and growled at the dog. Yes, Charles growled. I grinned, thinking of Melinda's story about Charles acting like a collie. The dog stopped and looked at my friend and tilted its head like it couldn't decide whether to bark at Charles or run away as fast as its four strong legs would carry it.

Charles smiled and then turned back to me. "I was awake at four o'clock thinking about the killings." He hesitated. "Hard to sleep when someone's out to kill you."

I nodded.

"Well, anyway," he said, "I was thinking that the only person we know for certain who'd talked to more than one of the ladies was Alexander, Bob Howard's understudy, or whatever you call the person who has to put up with Bob."

"True," I said.

Charles stopped in the middle of the lightly travelled road and made a fist with his right hand. He extended his thumb. "First, he would know that they were staying here alone, and with a little innocent questioning, would know that no one else knew where they were." He extended his forefinger. "Second, the guy we saw and the one Samuel thinks he saw had dark hair. So does Alexander." The middle finger popped out. "Third, he drives a big, dark-colored car. Unless you know cars, there's not that much difference between the big Ford and the Chrysler." He looked at his hand and then extended his ring finger. "Fourth, umm … I think I fell asleep when I got to four. Anyway, three's enough. While you were goofing off at four this morning, I was figuring that the killer is Mr. Alexander Bishop."

I couldn't find any obvious faults with his reasoning. "Those three things could also be true about Officer O'Hara," I said. We had reached the spot where Samuel said he had stood.

"Yeah," said Charles. "But we know they're true about Alexander. You want it to be O'Hara because you don't like him." He looked at the sandy berm as if there would be a telltale clue waiting to be discovered.

Partially true, I'd concede. "What were you going to tell me that Melinda said last night before Samuel knocked?"

"Umm, I forgot," he said and shook his head. "Brian's checking if O'Hara was on duty when the rebar swinger visited the apartment and when Samuel saw whatever he saw here?"

"He should know soon," I said.

"Yep," said Charles. "So how are we going to find out where Alexander was those two times and when the Nikon killer attacked?" He shook his head and then turned back toward town.

"Good question," I said and followed my friend. The walk to Samuel's crime scene produced a minimal amount of exercise and little else.

"Have a good answer?" asked Charles.

"Seldom."

# CHAPTER 48

Charles needed to make a delivery for Dude and rolled off. Delivering small packages for the surf shop was another source of his limited income. Deliveries, of course, had to be within bicycle range. I walked to Bert's to bum a cup of coffee and pick up the Charleston newspaper. On the way out, Brian Newman's unmarked car pulled into a space on the side of the building. He waved me over.

"Hop in," he said.

I walked around the passenger side and slid onto the front seat. He didn't say anything but pulled on Ashley Avenue and headed toward the old coast guard station.

"Aren't you afraid the mayor will see you colluding with the enemy?" I asked as he stepped on the accelerator.

He glanced over at me. "I've resigned," he said. "What's he going to do?"

"Where're we going?" I asked.

He smiled. "Just riding around; that's what cops do."

"And I'm riding around with you why?"

"You're playing cop all the time, so I thought you'd like the ride." He smirked in my direction.

"You know I don't want to meddle in your business," I said.

He laughed. "Just teasing. I wanted to tell you something and didn't want everyone around Bert's to hear."

We were passing the quarter-mile-long Washout section where surfers were parked along the right side of the road. Two of them saluted as the car passed. So much for an unmarked car.

"You can wipe lover boy off your list," he said.

"O'Hara?"

"Yeah, sorry," said Brian. "He was working when someone almost knocked some sense into Charles."

"You sure?"

"Afraid so." He shook his head. "I wanted it to be him too. The roster showed he was on duty." He waved to the left. "For what it's worth, although not much, he was off when Samuel said he saw the abduction. You already knew he wasn't working when someone assassinated Charles's camera."

"It was worth a try," I said. It would have been almost perfect if it'd been him. Not only would a dangerous person be taken off the street but it would also have been a welcomed slap in the face of the mayor.

We turned around at the east end of the street and headed back toward town. Brian pulled off the pavement at the beginning of the Washout. He put the car in park and looked in the rearview mirror and then turned toward me. The smile had disappeared.

"What in the hell is meddling Charles doing?" he said.

I knew what he was talking about but shrugged.

He sighed. "I get this call from a member of the council who will remain nameless," he said. "Seems that he was visited by you-know-who and asked if he would support me if it came to a vote about me keeping my job." He stared at me. "Know anything about it?"

I looked at him and didn't see a hint of friendliness. "I recall that Charles said something about talking to some of the council members."

"Recall?" he said.

"You know we don't want you to quit. And remember, you said that if the council supported you, you'd reconsider," I said and shrugged again.

"Stop him," he said in a tone that sounded more like an order than a request.

"May be too late," I said and held out my hands. "Think he's already talked to most of them. You know Charles when he's on a mission."

Brian shook his head and then looked in the rearview mirror and started the ignition. He sighed. "If you can't stop him, then thank him."

He accelerated, and I grabbed the armrest. "Okay," I said.

Two minutes later, I was back in my front yard wondering what to do now. The top suspect—my favorite suspect—had an alibi. If you can't believe the chief of police, who can you believe? I didn't have much time to think about it. The phone rang.

"Hey, Sherlock Holmes, listen up," came the gravelly voice of Bob. Words like "hello," or "hi," or most anything civil, were buried deep in his vocabulary. "Is your sorry mug somewhere where you can pay full attention to me? Don't want to be interrupted by a checkout clerk."

I assured him that he had my full attention. He said he doubted it, but continued. "You got me thinking about Alexander, and my razor-sharp mind has been pondering the possible involvement of my young rental agent."

I unlocked the front door with my right hand and pushed it open. A welcome blast of cold air slapped my face. "And what wisdom did that razor-sharp mind spew?"

"Are you being a damned smart-ass again?" he said.

I grinned and walked to the refrigerator for a Pepsi. "Yep," I said.

He snorted. "Thought so."

"So," I said, "you called me to discuss your mind?"

"You're no fun," he said. "Okay, now here's the thing. My sweet Aunt Louise cornered me when I came in this morning. I knew it had to be something important because she turned down the volume on her scanner." He growled. "Sure hope there weren't any damn juicy crimes when she had it down. It'd be my fault."

Bob was beginning to sound like Charles telling a story. "And she wanted?"

"She wanted to tell me that my young protégé confided in her that he was 'a-hankerin' to lasso himself a girlfriend.'"

I took my drink to the living room and plopped down in my favorite chair. I couldn't see this story ending soon, so I might as well be comfortable.

"I'm sure you will get around to telling me what's so interesting about that," I said and took a sip.

"I'm almost there. Chill," he said.

"Uh-huh," I said.

"Okay, here's the kinky part," he said. "Alexander told Louise that it 'would be peachy' if she steered his way any single women who wanted to rent on the island. He told her that he'd already checked out all the singles who lived on Folly 'and some others' and they were lacking 'that certain something' that he was looking for."

I hated to admit it, but Bob—with the help of Louise—did actually seem to have a point about Alexander.

"He rented condos to two of the women," I said.

"There you go, Sherlock," he said.

"Did he tell her anything else?" I asked.

"Not that she could recall," said Bob. "And when it comes to crime and nosiness, Louise has the damned market cornered. If she said nothing, nothing was said. Know what she wanted me to do?"

I didn't, but Bob would tell me whether I asked or not. I remained silent.

"She told me to go to the police and tell them what he'd said."

"What'd you say?"

"Said, damn, old lady, you want me to sidle up to a cop and give him the earth-shattering news that a red-blooded young male stud likes girls?"

I guess that he told her no, but I knew there was more—otherwise, he wouldn't still be on the line. "So what did you say you'd do?"

"Tell you."

"And what am I supposed to do with it?"

"Damned if I know," he said. "I'm handing you a big-ass clue. You figure it out."

The line went dead. Bob's phone etiquette doesn't improve with the length of the call.

# Chapter 49

When I was a taxpaying contributor to the economy, I would spend hours at work scribbling notes. When confronted with a problem, I'd wade through it and eventually arrive at a solution. It wasn't always the correct solution, but it was a solution nevertheless. I put away my notepad and pen the day I retired and have waded through most issues without major problems since.

I realized when listening to Bob that more than anything, I was confused. I dug through the *stick everything I don't know where else to put it* drawer, found a gray notepad and ballpoint pen, and then stared at the blank page. I decided that wasn't quite enough of a plan, so I went to the refrigerator, grabbed a Diet Pepsi, returned to the blank page, and began writing what I did know. There were three deaths, and two were definitely murder; most likely, so was the third. All of the victims had rented on Folly Beach. None of their relatives or friends knew where they were. And they were all beauty-queen attractive. My best friend and a young acquaintance were in danger—serious danger. One suspect appeared to top the list. The police, in my opinion, were far from a resolution. The mayor had forced the police chief out of office. And, for some unknown reason, he hated me.

Listing what I knew was easy. What I didn't know, other than the most obvious—the identity of the killer—was more difficult. What was the motive? How did the killer learn about the victims? What did Charles know that had earned him two attempts on his life? And was Samuel really in danger?

I turned the pad over and stared at the soft drink can. It didn't take long to figure out that no great inspirations were knocking on the door. Perhaps a ride around town would help. Schools were in session, but the streets were still busy. I followed stop-and-go traffic to where Samuel saw the abduction and where Charles and I were earlier today. True, Samuel's facts were not totally accurate, but he was certain that Kendra Corman-Eades had been taken against her will. I believed him. I didn't know what I expected to see or find, but nothing had changed—it would have been nice for there to be a sign on the dune listing the abductor's name. That fantasy faded, and I turned left on Arctic Avenue and drove to the spot where the traumatized backhoe operator had uncovered Felicia Gildehous. The crime scene tape was gone, and construction of the pier continued as if nothing untoward had happened.

A Folly Beach patrol car slowly drove by as I stared at the pier under construction. I couldn't see who was driving, but it reminded me how much I had hoped Officer O'Hara was the killer. On the way back to town, I passed Island Realty. Only two cars were in the lot—Alexander's black Chrysler and Louise's Oldsmobile.

I'd taken one of the residential streets when I heard a siren blast behind me and glanced in the rearview mirror. A Folly Beach patrol car was tailgating me. I pulled over for him to pass, but the car stayed on my bumper.

Officer O'Hara stepped out of the cruiser and swaggered to my door. I sighed, hit the down window button, and put my hands on the steering wheel.

O'Hara looked in the open window. "License and proof of insurance, sir," he said without a hint of recognition.

I took the documents from my wallet. "What did I do, officer?" I asked as I handed them to him. Two can play the *I don't recognize you* game.

He took the papers, ignored my question, and said that he would be back.

Ten minutes passed, and so did at least forty drivers who stared at me before he returned and handed me the paperwork and a citation. "You, sir," he said, "committed a rolling stop at the stop sign back there."

He maintained eye contact and pointed toward the stop sign behind me.

I caught myself before I let out a loud sigh. "You mean you stopped—"

He abruptly stepped back from the door and said, "Thank you, sir. Drive safely." He then walked back to the cruiser and pulled around me back into the flow of traffic.

I pounded the steering wheel. *A rolling stop.* How many people had been ticketed for that horrific offense on Folly in the last year? My guess would be fewer than had been written up for illegal bungee jumping off city hall. Mayor Lally was a man of his word.

I also wondered if a computer time sheet showing that O'Hara had been working when Charles was attacked really proved that he was.

I drove down a couple more residential streets to calm my jittery nerves and then parked in the post office lot. I dialed Brian Newman's cell to tell him about what Bob had said. He was in a meeting with two of his officers and said he'd call me "in a few." I watched a handful of residents enter the small post office and two men empty trash cans along the street before Brian called. I shared what Bob had told me that he had learned from Louise. I was tempted to tell him about the traffic stop, but I didn't.

Brian laughed. It was not exactly the response I had hoped for, but it was one I understood. I asked if he was laughing at me. He said no and then, "partially." He said that if Louise was fifty years younger, he would name her deputy chief. And then he added he would if he was still chief. Her information was weak, but he said that he would pass it along to Detective Burton. I said "whoop-de-do," and then he said that I should remember that Detective Burton couldn't be as bad as I thought or he never would have made detective. I asked Brian if he was trying to convince me or himself. He didn't answer.

I had little confidence in Detective Burton's getting to the bottom of anything other than his pension, but I was slightly encouraged when Brian said he would talk to a few of his officers and try to see if they could establish an alibi for the rental agent for any of the times of death. I hoped he wouldn't waste time confiding in Officer O'Hara.

# CHAPTER 50

I was still fuming about my ticket when the phone rang.

"Meet us," said Charles.

During my fuming, I must have missed a few minor details—like when, where, and who. "Details?" I said.

He sighed. "Now, of course. City park by the bridge."

I could learn the rest when I got there. "On my way," I said.

I pulled in the small parking lot in front of the city park and saw Charles sitting on one of the metal picnic tables under the pavilion. Melinda stood in front of the structure and stared at a six-foot-tall metal sculpture of a frog standing on its hind legs and strumming a guitar. I waved at Charles and hugged Melinda. She appeared more stooped than before, and her Walmart wardrobe had begun to sag on her shoulders.

She pointed to the strumming amphibian. "Think all frogs are left-legged?"

I looked at the sculpture and smiled. It was strumming the strings with its left hand—left leg. "Just Folly frogs," I said.

"Makes sense," she said with a straight face.

I could picture myself having the same nonsensical conversation with her nephew.

"You two, get over here and out of the sun," said Charles. "It's beginning to fry your green hair. And your bald spot, Chris," he added.

Charles and Melinda sat on one side of the table, and I sat on the other. We turned to face the Folly River and the marsh. We were the only people in the small park, and there was one person on the far end of the pier that extended over the edge of the river.

Melinda pointed at the person on the pier and asked what he was doing. Charles told her he was crabbing. She said that didn't sound like an ounce of fun. I agreed with her. She continued to look at the pier but said, "Figured out who the killer is?"

"Afraid not," I said.

"Neither has my nephew, the detective." She punched Charles on the arm.

"I'm surprised," I said. "Here's what I did learn."

I proceeded to tell them about Louise, Bob, and Alexander. I reluctantly shared that the murderer couldn't be O'Hara but told them about the ticket. Melinda said, "Hmm." Charles, chimed in with, "Mickey Mouse manure." I could also tell that Charles was peeved that he had to hear about Alexander and O'Hara the same time that Melinda did, but he didn't say anything.

"Hmm," said Melinda. "Sounds like you've got something there. Could be right."

Charles tilted his head toward her. "What's that mean, Aunt M.?"

She nodded. "Means I've got a better suspect," she said.

Charles and I turned to Melinda and waited. She turned to me and then to Charles and then grinned.

"Who?" said Charles.

"Straight Damian," she said and then folded her arms.

"Your hairdresser?" said Charles.

"You know any other nongay Damians?" she asked.

"Why him?" I asked.

"Well," she said. She put her elbows on the table and took a deep breath. "I went in there around noon. Wanted to ask if he thought it was too soon to change the color of my wig. He was snipping on the long, brown hair of some woman who looked like she just rolled in on a boxcar. Well anyway, I was trying to make conversation, and since I knew he wasn't gay anymore, I asked if he'd dated any lovely lasses lately. Just trying to be polite, you know."

"And?" said Charles.

"And he said, 'A couple of fine young ladies.'"

She hesitated too long for Charles's taste. "And?"

She glared at her nephew. "Patience, Charles. Anne, the affair lady, was standing behind him when he said it. She shook her head and made a circle with her thumb and forefinger. Your detective skills are rubbing off on me." Melinda looked at Charles. "I detected that meant zero."

Charles held his hands out toward Melinda. "Is that it?"

She squished her nose at him. "Now, now, Charles, I've only been a detective for a few days. I thought I was doing good to find out that he wasn't gay."

"You have a hunch," I said. "What makes you think it's him?"

She looked at Charles and then back at me. "You keep saying that the killer had a way of finding out about the girls—where they were staying, if anyone knew where they were, that kind of stuff."

"And you've said hairdressers are like bartenders with scissors," I added.

She nodded. "I was thinking that he asked the girls for dates." She nodded again. "Heck, they could have pooh-poohed him and made him mad." She nodded again. "Or, they may have said yes and then when they were out, said no when he wanted to explore their terrain, if you get my drift."

Charles and I nodded.

"Anything else?" I asked.

She looked toward the river and closed her eyes. "Not yet, but if I hang around you two more, I might learn how to detect better."

Charles started to stand and then sat back down. "Wouldn't Anne have known if the three women came in and if Damian had worked on their hair?"

*Good question*, I thought and turned to Melinda.

Melinda opened her eyes and looked at Charles. "Would that be the same Anne who's having an affair with the real estate guy? The one who was gallivanting around St. Thomas and taking off days at a time to do you-know-what with Realtor-stud?"

"True," conceded Charles.

"Bigfoot could've come in for a trim and she would've missed him. She was out doing you-know-what." She grinned. "That activity will cloud your mind—it sure will."

She wiped the smile off her face and said, "Her husband ought to kill her."

"Then how about this," said Charles. "The guy who Samuel saw and the guy who tried to knock my block off had long, dark hair. Your not-gay hair snipper is blond."

"Dirty blond," corrected Melinda.

"Okay, dirty blond," agreed Charles. "Short, dirty-blond hair."

Melinda looked at her nephew, at the river, and then back at Charles. "What color's my hair?" she asked.

Charles looked at her head. "Green."

Melinda tilted her head. "And you call yourself a detective." She reached up and yanked on her bright-green locks. The wig came off in her hand. She shook it in Charles's face like a feather duster. A coating of fuzzy, gray hair covered her scalp. "Did you forget that Damian was a master at dying wigs? He has more wigs in the salon than you have T-shirts." She looked at Charles's long-sleeved Texas Tech shirt. "Well, maybe not more, but he has a bunch."

She had a point, but I stayed out of the conversation—or, more accurately, family feud. Damian was also about the same size as the guy we chased at Charles's apartment.

"Aunt M.," said Charles, "that's a fine bit of detecting." He hugged her shoulder. "Now I know where I get my hidden talents."

She was backlit, and I couldn't tell for sure, but I thought she blushed. She then turned toward the far end of the small pier. "Think I'd like crabbing?"

"Don't know," said Charles. "Want to go sometime?"

"Nah," she said. "Looks boring. This detecting stuff's more fun."

I nearly fell off the bench. She was so wrong.

"Tell you what, Aunt M., I think Chris here should call his bud the chief and tell him what you found." Charles turned to me.

She smiled. "Now?"

The last thing I wanted to do was to call Brian with her suspicions, so I did what most red-blooded Americans would do in a similar situation. I lied, again. "He's in a meeting. I'll call tonight."

"Promise?" she said.

"Promise."

Melinda seemed satisfied and had turned her attention once again to the lone crabber. Charles looked at me and shrugged. I snapped my fingers.

"Melinda," I said, "since you're getting so good at this detecting stuff, do you happen to know what Damian drives?"

"Huh?" she asked as she turned back to Charles and me.

I repeated the question, and she rubbed her chin. "Yeah, sort of," she said.

"Sort of?" said Charles.

"I know it's one of those little Jap cars—excuse me, now we're supposed to call them Asian vehicles. By sort of, I mean I don't know what kind it us. All those little cars look alike to me."

Charles turned to me. "There goes that theory."

Melinda looked at Charles and then turned to me. "Just because it's little and not a big black car like Samuel saw doesn't mean he drives it all the time. I don't know what kind it is, but it's old. Seems that it would break a lot. Maybe he has another car or borrows one when his is in the shop or when he gets a hankering to abduct a young lady. Just a thought."

And not a bad one at that. I reinforced that I would call the chief later and tell him her suspicions. Charles nodded and told Melinda that we had gone to the chief with more far-fetched theories.

Could we be getting closer? Or were we adding suspects beyond the far-fetched?

# Chapter 51

I caught the chief on his way home. He said he'd had a "delightful" two-hour meeting with the mayor and was debating between treating himself to bourbon or Scotch. He didn't ask me to help him decide or invite me to join him, so I jumped right into the reason for the call. He patiently listened as I shared Melinda's theory about Damian. I heard announcements in the background about a two-for-one special and assumed he was in the Pig. He mumbled something about "watch where you're going with that cart" and then asked what I thought of Melinda's idea. I said it made as much sense as anything else we had.

"Thanks for adding another suspect," he said.

"You're welcome. We just want to help you serve and protect."

"At this rate," he said, "you'll have the entire male population of Folly Beach in the suspect pool."

I'd begun to wonder if we should limit it to males considering the small stature of the assailant and the long hair. I also gathered that he wasn't excited about Melinda's suspicions. "So what do you think?"

"You've brought me more far-fetched theories before," he said and laughed.

Did he have the park bench bugged?

"Some of them helped you catch a killer," I reminded him.

"And that's why I'm going to pass this information on to Burton," he said. There was some talk in the background and then he said, "Debit."

I took that as a hint to get off the phone so he could pay for his groceries.

"Bourbon," I said and then hit the *end call* button.

*   *   *

The humidity and excessive temperatures had moved off the coast, and the early morning sun's rays reflected off high, puffy clouds. I started the coffee and told myself that it was going to be a glorious day—glorious if I could avoid Mayor Lally, the code enforcement cops, or any *Mickey Mouse manure* traffic stops. I was determined to enjoy it to the fullest. I willed myself not to think of a killer on the loose, Melinda's deteriorating health, or the arthritis causing increased pain in four of my fingers.

I had just poured a cup of coffee when someone pounded on the front door. The saying "where there's a will, there's a way" was rudely interrupted by Charleston County Sheriff's Office Detective Brad Burton.

"Good morning, Mr. Landrum," said Burton. His disheveled hair matched his suit, and the look on his face fell somewhere between a snarl and a smirk. "May I come in?"

I motioned him in and asked if he wanted coffee. His nod surprised me. He followed me to the kitchen and sat at the table. I poured his coffee into a chipped mug I had "borrowed" from the Dog. I pointed to the refrigerator and he said, "Black."

I set the mug in front of him, and he surprised me again when he said, "Thanks." Maybe we were becoming BFFs after all.

He looked around the room. I figured he was looking for my Superman suit or, at least, my secret decoder ring.

"Nice," he said. "It needs a lady's touch, though."

I couldn't tell if he was a location scout for HGTV or making small talk. Neither option fit my impression of Detective Burton. I smiled. "You're right about that," I said.

He continued to look around. "Umm," he said and then turned to me. "I thought it would be better to talk directly to you rather than keep hearing your theories from others."

I was heartened that he felt that way but needed to get something out in the open. "Detective," I said, "it's no secret that you hold me in disdain. I can see your point, but you need to know that I don't intentionally stick my nose where it doesn't belong. When—"

"Mr. Landrum—"

I held my hand up. "Wait," I interrupted. "Let me finish. When a friend of mine is in danger and the *police*"—I paused and looked him in the eye—"When the police don't appear to take it seriously, I'm going to get involved."

He leaned forward in the chair and glared at me. "The police—"

I returned his stare and interrupted again. "Please let me finish." He blinked and then leaned back in his chair and waved his hand toward me.

"My young friend, Samuel, is convinced he saw a crime. My friend Charles was almost killed—twice. And three women, and who knows how many others, have been murdered on this island." I waved toward the front door. "We've tried to take information to the local police. You've received the same information they have, and from what I can tell, nothing has been done." I looked down at the table and then back at Burton. "My friends are in danger, and I'm not going to sit here and do nothing. Sorry, but I'm not." I took a deep breath and exhaled.

Burton nodded. "Done?" he asked.

I returned his nod.

"Mr. Landrum," he said, "I've never been a dues-paying member of your fan club."

"I know—" I said.

"Wait," he interrupted. "My turn. I've not been a member of your fan club. If you remember, the first time we met, you were standing over a body out by the lighthouse. I had no reason to think of you as anything but a suspect. You were cleared, but you were a smart-ass even then. It rubbed me wrong."

I smiled. "Sorry."

He shook his head. "Anyway, since then you've been nosing around every murder on this island. You, and some of your idiot friends, have interfered with our investigations. You've almost gotten killed. And you've been a constant burr under my saddle."

"And helped you catch some really bad folks," I said. He appeared to want to forget that.

He nodded. "Mr. Landrum, that's why I'm here. I don't have to like you to respect what you bring to the table. I also have a great deal of admiration for Chief Newman. He does a great job, and—umm, never mind. When you and your friend went to the local police, you talked to an officer who, for whatever reason, never told the chief. He didn't find out until later."

I sat back in the chair and looked him in the eyes. "Would you have done anything if you had known earlier?"

Burton blinked twice and then sighed. "To be honest, probably not." He shook his head. "Look what I would have had to work with—a teenager thinking he saw a female being taken against her will. The kid didn't recognize anyone, he couldn't recognize the car, and there wasn't anyone else who saw anything. And, oh yeah, no one was missing."

He was right, but it still irritated me. "So what are you doing now?"

"Sitting here watching you stare at me like you'd like to crush me like a Palmetto bug," he said and then smiled.

That wasn't what I'd expected, but he was right. "Sorry," I said. "I just don't think you've taken this as seriously as you should have."

"You may be right," he said. "The point is that I am here now. Tell me what—" he hesitated and took a small notebook out of his suit coat pocket. "Tell me what, umm, Melinda Beale—that's Charles's aunt, right?" I nodded. "What did she see, say, and think about the gay, now straight, hairdresser?"

I walked Burton through Melinda's experiences at the salon and what she thought about Damian. Burton took a few notes and listened attentively. It was a strange feeling watching the man paying attention when he had ignored me or snarled at me every time we were together and for the last six years. I also knew that much of what I was relaying was speculation. Burton could dismiss it as the ramblings of an elderly woman letting her imagination run wild while she was getting her wig dyed.

I'd better take advantage of his listening. I then told him about Alexander Bishop and how he had been the rental agent when two of the dead women came to Folly and about what he had told Louise about pushing single women to him when they wanted a rental. I shared about Samuel coming to me after seeing someone he believed was the abductor in the parking lot behind Rita's and Charles's theory that it was Alexander because Samuel said the car might have been a Chrysler, the kind of vehicle the rental agent drove.

Burton asked me if I agreed with Charles. I said that it could have been him but that I wasn't convinced based on the car he drove. My thought was that if Samuel said it was a Ford Crown Vic then it was. The Ford model was common with police forces. Most boys, even if they weren't experts on cars, wouldn't mistake another make for it.

And for some reason, I remembered what Melinda had said twice about Anne's husband killing her if he found out about her affair. I told him how much the owner of Folly Curls looked like two of the victims and wondered if her husband could have been taking his rage out on other women rather than his wife. I didn't tell him that despite what the duty roster showed, I was still suspicious of Officer O'Hara.

Burton jotted down a couple of notes and only said, "Interesting theories." He then nodded, seeming satisfied that he had gotten all he could out of me, and closed the notebook. He thanked me for the drink and walked toward the front door.

He hesitated and turned back to me. "Mr. Landrum," he said. "I'm a year away from retiring. I've done this job for more years than I want to remember. I've put up with killers, crooks, liars, and politicians."

"That's redundant, isn't it?" I said.

He chuckled. "Anyway," he continued, "I've seen and taken about all the shit I can." He took a deep breath and then looked around the room as if he thought someone else was there. "I shouldn't tell you this ... hell, why not. Your mayor's doing everything he can to get rid of Chief Newman."

That, of course, was no surprise since I had heard it from the mayor himself. I didn't tell him that Brian had already resigned. I nodded.

"It's not right," he said.

I nodded again.

He hesitated, bit his lower lip, and then looked me in the eye. "If you say you heard this from me, I'll deny it on a stack of Bibles and may shoot you." I nodded, and he continued, "Five years ago, your upstanding, better-than-God mayor was accused of stealing millions of dollars that should have belonged to one of his employees."

I sat up straighter. "Wouldn't he have been taking his own money? Didn't he make millions when he sold his company?"

"I'm just a police detective," said Burton. "I deal with the dregs of society. I'm clueless about the big-time finances of companies. Apparently, this was before he sold to some conglomerate. It had something to do with Lally taking credit for a patent for software that one of the company's vice presidents had created. The other guy created the off-track betting software that put the company on the map. Lally wasn't about to let him have it, so he planted some cocaine in the guy's company-furnished apartment and then had his security people find it. He held that over the vice president's head. Basically, your mayor stole the software and tore up the intellectual property rights of the true creator."

"Why didn't the guy sue?" I asked.

He opened his notebook again and removed a folded piece of paper. He unfolded the paper, looked at it, and then handed it to me. "It's all in here."

I looked down at the paper. But Burton stopped me from reading it. He took it back and then said, "He had a drug conviction and didn't think anyone would believe him."

"Where did this come from?" I took the paper back and held it up.

"That's the sad part," he said and then shook his head. "The inventor was so torn up that he killed himself. Hanged himself a year to the day after Lally sold the company for millions."

I held the paper back in front of Burton.

He pointed at it. "He wrote that four days before his death and mailed it to his sister in Charleston. He attached a note saying that nothing could be proven but wanted her to know his reason for the suicide. He didn't want her to feel like it was her fault."

"Why would she have thought that?"

"Not certain. But apparently they had a history of fighting over their parents' estate. Poor guy—it seems that his sister won that battle too."

"How'd you get it?"

"The sister's brother-in-law works as a civilian clerk in our office. He gave it to me three months ago, saying he knew there was nothing

I could do but wanted to get my take on it. He wanted to see if I knew any way it could be used to indict Lally."

"And you couldn't?" I said.

"Nothing in there except the word of a dead former employee—no evidence, no proof of authorship of the software code, no nothing."

I scanned the single-spaced, typed document. I didn't read it all, but Burton was right. There wasn't anything that could be proven. I looked up at him. "So you think there's a way I could use it to keep the mayor from firing the chief."

"I'd like it if you could get him thrown in jail," said Burton. "But that's not going to happen. Next best thing is to save the chief."

"Why me?" I asked.

"Because you're Newman's friend." He hesitated and then grinned. "And because you are such a pain in the ass that you probably would be able to do something that no one else could." He shook his head. "I figure you'll find a way. I don't know how and don't want to."

I wish I had that much confidence in what I could do. "I'll have to think about it."

"Think quickly," he said. "The chief is about out of work."

He turned and grabbed the door handle and then turned back to me. "You didn't get that from me." He didn't wait for a response.

# CHAPTER 52

I stared at the front door. I couldn't tell what surprised me more, having had a civil conversation with Detective Brad Burton or being handed a document that might give me the upper hand on our illustrious mayor.

I had always done my best thinking while seated on the ocean end of the Folly Pier. I needed that advantage, so I left the comfortable, and peaceful, confines of my cottage and headed three blocks to the landmark. It was early for many vacationers to be on the beach, but there were already several people optimistically watching their fishing poles propped against the pier's railing. I nodded to a couple of familiar faces along the way and then climbed the steps to the second level of the pier. The sun was beginning to leave its mark on the temperature, and I knew that in a couple of hours it would be unbearable.

I was the only person on the second level, and I took out the paper Burton had bestowed upon me. The document was heavy with words but light in provable content. The author, whose name was neither on the paper nor disclosed by Burton, said little more than what the detective had shared. It was woefully inadequate to prove anything, but was it strong enough to carry weight in the court of public opinion? I imagined the document plastered on the front page of the newspaper and wondered if it would garner enough anger with voters to affect how the mayor ran the city. Lally had sold his software company to a publicly traded company. Could the revelations stir enough interest for the Securities and Exchange Commission to initiate an investigation?

Even if they didn't, would they be enough to give the company a black eye and possibly affect its stock price? Either way, how would that affect the pompous mayor? How would he react to knowing that some of his upstanding—read, wealthy—citizens thought he was responsible for the death of the person who wrote the note? It couldn't prove that the mayor pushed the author to suicide. But Lally couldn't prove that he hadn't.

The pier failed to work its magic. Answers to what I should do with the document were elusive, and my mind drifted back to the conversation with Burton about the murders. He had listened, but to be honest, I knew I hadn't shared anything that would significantly help him with his investigation. Alexander had ties to two of the victims. Burton didn't say if he already knew that. A competent detective would have figured that out in time, but I still wasn't ready to elevate Burton to that level. Melinda's speculation about Damian and my theory about Anne's husband were even weaker. Either man could be the killer. I didn't know what Anne's husband looked like, but Damian was the right size, and the long, dark hair could have been a wig. He could have talked with each of the victims—"could" being the operative word. No one had tied him to any of them, and no one, not even the most car identification–challenged individual, would mistake a "little Jap car" for a Ford Crown Vic. I also didn't know how Anne's husband would have learned the details of why they were on Folly and realized that no one would notice they were missing. And I was still wondering about the alibi for O'Hara and whether the killer was even a male.

After an hour switching back and forth between thinking about the killings and how to use the document against the mayor, I concluded that I was as productive as the five fishermen who leaned against the railing on the pier and stared mindlessly at their extraordinarily unsuccessful fishing rods. I wouldn't solve either dilemma sitting here, so I slowly walked back toward the parking lot. Instead of going home, I walked by Folly Curls to see what Damian drove. It wasn't that I doubted Melinda. To be honest, I didn't know what else to do. The two-block walk out of my way was wasted. The only vehicle in the lot was an older Buick LeSabre. A silver and red bicycle was propped against the side of the small salon. This would be a good chance to talk to Anne about the victims without Damian being around. If she hadn't seen them, I couldn't figure how Damian would have talked with them.

Anne looked up from trimming a teenage girl's hair. "Hi," said Anne. "I'll be with you in a minute. I'm almost done."

I didn't want to start talking about murder in front of the young customer, so I sat in the chair under the window and started flipping through a six-month-old issue of *Glamour*. I was shocked to see that not a single one of the male models resembled me in physique or hair style—or, more accurately, lack of hair style. Where was *AARP: The Magazine* when I needed it?

Anne interrupted my daydreaming when she said she was ready for me. The teen had pedaled away on her bike.

I put the magazine back on the table and introduced myself.

"I know," she said.

I didn't ask how. "Actually," I said. "I wanted to ask if you had ever seen the women who've been killed." I opened the flyer that Charles had been showing around and started to show it to Anne. I knew that Charles had already been here with it, but I thought it was a good way to broach the subject. I was again struck by how much the shop owner looked like two of the dead women.

She wiped the shears with a towel and neatly arranged the tools of her trade on the table by her chair. "Charles Fowler has already asked me about them," she said without looking up.

"Oh," I said, "sorry." I shrugged. "So you haven't seen them?"

She took a broom from the corner and swept the floor around her chair. She still didn't make eye contact, but said, "I've been out a lot over the last few weeks. Umm, been to a stylists' conference out of state, done some hair at nursing homes on James Island. It's possible they could have been in. I didn't see them."

*Having an affair was quite time consuming*, I thought. "Think some of your other stylists would know? Doesn't Charles's aunt have her hair done by what's-his-name?" I looked toward the partition separating Anne's chair from Damian's.

"Damian," said the helpful shop owner. "Yeah, Melinda does, and I know Charles asked Damian about the women."

"Isn't there another lady here?" I asked.

"Yes, Carrie," said Anne. She stared at the side of my head. "She's off today, and Damian's out for a couple of hours. Sure you don't want a haircut?"

I smiled. "Not today."

"Sorry I can't help," she said and looked at her watch as if I was taking too much of her time. We were the only two in the salon, so I didn't feel guilty about keeping her from work.

"Charles's number is on the bottom of the handout if you think of anything," I said and placed my copy of the flyer on the table on top of the out-of-date issue of *Glamour*.

"No problem," she said.

I faked a smile, thought about how much I hated "no problem," the phrase du jour, and stepped out into the heat of the day. Perhaps I could have learned less at Folly Curls—I wasn't certain how.

# CHAPTER 53

The gallery was closer than the house, so I used the computer there to search the local paper's archives for a bio on the mayor. I skimmed the article to find the company he had founded and wasn't surprised that it had been named Lally Unlimited. He sold it to IGS, Inc., a company I hadn't heard of. According to its website, it was a large, international corporation specializing in software solutions for "problems big and small." Its revenue approached nine hundred million dollars last year, so I suspected it didn't spend much time on the solutions for small problems. Lally Unlimited, which was now named LU, was one of thirteen companies under the IGS umbrella. Lally was vice chair of the board of IGS, Inc. I didn't know about the company's software solutions, but their solution to company names appeared to be using acronyms. Only two of their thirteen companies had actual words in their names.

I searched news stories from around the time of the suicide that mentioned Lally. No luck. I then looked for more recent articles mentioning Lally and IGS, Inc., and found three. The most recent, dated in June, talked about how he was expected to be named chairman of the board at October's annual meeting.

I turned the computer off, sat back in the chair, looked at the ceiling, and wondered—wondered how the revelations in the letter combined with the writer's suicide would affect his chances of ascending to the board chairmanship. Provable or not, wouldn't the potential scandal slow down, or possibly even halt, his rise to fame, more fortune, and, in his case, a huge dose of ego serum?

I reminded myself how Mayor Lally had treated me, how he had forced Chief Newman off the force, how he'd used his clout to harass me, and how he and his buddy Officer O'Hara had discounted Samuel's story, which eventually resulted in two attempts on Charles's life.

I pounded my fist on the table, cursed to the empty room, and walked to the front of the gallery to look out the window toward city hall. There was only one way to see how the letter would affect Lally, and there was no better time to find out. I scanned the document and made three copies. I hid one behind the microwave, put one in a file folder and labeled it "Lally," put the original in an envelope and addressed it to myself, and folded the remaining copy and put it in my pocket. I briskly walked toward city hall, gathering my courage along the way.

Lally's office was on the second floor, opened directly into the corridor, and overlooked Center Street. The door was open a crack, and I heard his voice and saw him on the phone. I waited for him to hang up. I knocked and pushed the door open. He looked up from his desk. His head jerked back. I was equally surprised to be there but didn't let it show.

I didn't wait to be invited in and walked across the room and stood a foot from his desk. He took a deep breath; his fists were clenched. "How may I help you, Mr. Landrum?"

I moved two binders off the chair in front of the desk and sat. "Mayor," I said, "I have something I think you'll be interested in."

"Only if it's your one-way ticket out of town," he said.

"Sorry," I said. "It's more about you than me."

He looked over my shoulder toward the door like he hoped someone would appear and throw me out. Apparently there wasn't anyone there, and he turned toward me. The look in his eyes expressed anything but warmth. "Then get on with it. I'm busy."

I took the document out of my pocket and unfolded it before flipping it across his desk. He pushed a stack of file folders aside and picked up the paper. He put on black-framed reading glasses that had been on the desk and slowly started to read.

He stared at the paper for a minute or so and looked at me over the top of his glasses. "Where did you get this?" he said.

I shrugged. "Doesn't matter." I moved my hands below the lip of the desk so he couldn't see them shake.

He looked back at the paper for another minute without saying anything. He then turned it face down on the desk, yanked his reading glasses off, and slammed them down on the letter. That told me that the document was accurate.

He stared at me. "There're only a couple of people who … who … never mind. It sure as hell does matter where you got it. Who, dammit?"

I returned his stare. "That's not important," I said. "I have it, and it's accurate."

"You can't prove one iota of it," he interrupted.

"Don't have to," I said.

"What's that mean?" he asked.

"Simple," I said. "All I have to do is get this in the right hands and the damage will be done."

"Who?" he said.

I didn't know whether he was that stupid or just he hoped that I was. "How about the newspaper?" I said. "And then maybe the members of your council? Oh yeah, how about the board of directors at IGS, Inc.?" I smiled. "Is that enough for starters?"

"You little shit," he said. "You think you're man enough to get in a pissing contest with me?"

I assumed that his term of endearment and question were rhetorical, so I remained silent.

He pushed away from his desk and stood. He walked around the desk and past me to the door. He slammed it closed and then walked back to the desk and turned to the window facing Center Street. I remained seated and waited for round two.

He continued to stare out the window but said, "What do you want?"

"I haven't decided," I said as noncommittally as possible. I was getting way too much satisfaction out of seeing him squirm.

He paused and then said, "Newman to keep his job?"

"My understanding is that you don't have enough support to fire him, and I've heard that he's lost interest in resigning." That might have

"Oh, you came back for that haircut," she said as I walked through the door. She then saw Charles. She stopped folding towels and got a strange look on her face. "What's going on?"

"What do you mean?" I asked.

"What do I mean?" she said, looked at Charles, and sighed. "First, your aunt comes in and leaves just as quickly. Damian watches her out the window and then rushes back to his chair like the building's on fire. He grabs his tools and charges out the door like a bat out of hell. Doesn't say bye or anything." She stopped and looked at the door like she was reliving his departure.

"There's more, isn't there?" I said.

"Yes. Not five minutes after Damian left, a rumpled detective walks in like he owns the place and starts asking questions about Damian."

Burton had taken me seriously. "What kind of questions?"

"Like how long had he worked here? What kind of car did he drive?"

"Was that Damian's Ford here earlier?" asked Charles.

"No," said Anne. "It's his sister's. His Honda's in the shop again. Damian borrows his sister's car when his is being worked on. She has two."

"What else did the detective ask?" I said.

"Wanted Damian's address and if I knew his sister's address or name. I told him where Damian lived and found his sister's information. It was on his application."

"What happened then?" I asked.

"Nothing. The detective thanked me and left. What's going on?"

"The police want to ask him some questions," I said. "It's nothing to worry about."

I asked her for his home address and the information on his sister. Her hands shook as she handed me his application. I copied down the addresses.

Anne rubbed her eyes and then looked at me. "Does it have something to do with those poor women?"

"It might," I said.

"Damn," she mumbled.

I agreed.

# Chapter 55

Charles and I rushed back to Melinda's. Anne had said that Damian took all his tools, which meant that he didn't plan to return. He knew Charles had scoured the island for information on the women and that Melinda had acted suspicious earlier. When he saw her checking out his car, he knew it was simply a matter of time before we put everything together. His days on Folly were numbered, and he knew it.

I doubted he would go after Melinda, since she hadn't seen him with any of the women and all she knew was that his sister's car looked like the suspicious vehicle. Regardless, we had to make sure she was safe. Charles ran in, and I waited in the car. He quickly returned and said she was safely tucked in and had her door double locked.

"Now what?" said Charles.

"Let's go by his apartment. If Burton's there, we'll keep going. I'm afraid Damian may have already skipped town."

Damian lived in a first-floor apartment in a two-story house on East Huron. The house, located three blocks from town and two blocks from the marsh, was owned by an elderly widow in an assisted-living home on James Island. Anne said that Damian loved the cheap rent and privacy.

Damian's house was the fourth of five two-story frame houses on a slight rise on the left side of the street. Three of the houses had had extensive renovation work, and the other two, including Damian's, looked like they hadn't seen a can of paint or a lawnmower since the Vietnam War. Weeds, decorative grasses, and wilted flowers covered the front and one side yard. A gravel drive with patches of weeds covered the bulk of the other side yard. The only vehicle we saw was a rusty orange bicycle with a missing front wheel.

"Now what?" said Charles for the second time in five minutes.

I saw what Damian meant by liking the privacy. The house to the right had a faded *For Rent* sign in the yard, and it didn't look like the sign had been successful. And with his landlord in a nursing home, he would have had the run of the place. A bomb could have gone off in his living room and I doubted anyone would have heard it. The same went for a scream. It would have made a perfect haunted house. A knot tightened in my stomach.

"Burton probably drove by and didn't see a car," I said. "He would then have headed to the sister's house. Let's look around."

I parked two houses down the street. I didn't want to be in the drive if Damian came home. Four wooden steps led to the front porch. Two were broken, and the other two creaked as we carefully made our way to the front door. I didn't expect an answer but knocked anyway. I then walked to the window that overlooked the porch. It was covered by a thin, lacy drape. Through a two-inch gap on the left side, I could see a Victorian-style couch and chair in the living room. A layer of dust on the floor looked like it hadn't been disturbed in months.

"Let's go around back," I said as we walked down the steps. The handrail was as shaky as the steps. The door to Damian's apartment was on the right side of the house about five feet from the drive. Two large bushes on the left side of the door blocked its view of the street and the house next door. The door had a two-by-three-foot window that was covered on the inside with plywood. That was strange since the windows were in good repair. Several layers of paint had peeled off the door, but there was a new, brass lockset. That was odd.

I leaned close to the door and heard the muted sounds of a television. I held my breath and turned the knob. It didn't budge. It was times like these that I wished for Larry, the reformed cat burglar. Charles had walked around behind the house, returned, and waved for me to follow.

The deep backyard was more private than the side yards. Four massive live oaks and a row of overgrown shrubs shielded the property line. Weeds and plants of all shapes and sizes had haphazardly filled in every vacant spot. An old cast-iron bathtub was on its side next to a small, wooden storage building, and rusting tools were on the ground beside the building. I barely saw the roof of the houses on the next street over. Trees cast eerie shadows on the yard and the rear of the house.

Two small windows were on the lower level. One had been covered with plywood like the door. The other window was smaller, a little higher, and frosted. I assumed it was in the bathroom. Charles held his finger to his lips and then pointed to the window with the plywood. I put my ear to the window and barely heard the television. I clearly heard what sounded like the low, whimpering sounds of an animal—or a person.

My heart pounded. I didn't know how well the plywood was secured and if it was possible to get past it. The bathroom window was our best chance to get in. I grabbed a tire iron from a pile of junk near the storage building and pointed to two concrete blocks that leaned against the house. Charles helped me move the blocks under the bathroom window.

I stepped on the blocks, covered my face with my left arm, and swung the tire iron at the window. The glass broke into thousands of pieces. I raked the iron around the edges of the frame to break off any sharp pieces sticking out. The noise from the television was louder, and so were the pained sounds coming from somewhere in the house. They were human.

Charles pushed me up through the window. It was above the toilet, and I managed to crawl through and get enough leverage on the toilet's water tank to get in without falling. I hesitated and looked around the nearly dark room for a light switch. I heard Charles whisper for me to give him a hand. I helped him through before I turned on the light. An empty cologne bottle was on the vanity.

I grabbed the tire iron. I felt confident that Damian was gone but was still hypercautious. The whimpering voice was louder and then uttered, "Help."

Charles walked to the small living area and turned the television off. I looked around to get my bearings and see where the voice came from. The apartment was small, so it didn't take long to spot the three-quarter-height door at the back of a tiny bedroom. It had an industrial-looking latch on the door and a padlock through the latch. The lock wasn't fastened, but it held the hasp in place. I looked around to make sure no one was there and then removed the lock and unlatched the door.

I took a deep breath and slowly pulled the door. The room was windowless and almost completely dark. I saw movement on the far wall and reached around the corner for a light switch. I flicked it on. What was in front of me could have been out of a horror movie.

# CHAPTER 56

A woman strained to stand on her tiptoes, her back pressed against a concrete block wall. She was in her twenties and had on green shorts and a gray, sweat-stained Nike T-shirt. She was barefoot. An inch-thick rope was attached to the low ceiling and looped around her neck. The rope was unyielding, and the slightest movement downward would have choked her to death. Her arms were restrained by smaller ropes anchored in the wall. She could only move her arms a few inches from the wall. Her face was blood red, and her arms shook uncontrollably. Tears ran down her cheeks.

I yelled for Charles to find a knife and then hurried to her. I assured her that everything would be okay as I lifted her sagging body to loosen the tightening noose. The front of her T-shirt was wet from tears.

She mumbled, "Thank you."

Charles arrived with a steak knife. He looked around, grabbed a wicker chair that was beside an army surplus cot on the other side of the room, and moved it close to the woman. The chair was rickety, and he carefully balanced himself on it to reach the overhead restraint. It seemed like an eternity before he cut through the noose. She fell into my arms. Charles then sawed his way through the ropes holding her arms.

We carried her to the twin bed in the small bedroom adjacent to her room of horrors.

"Who are you?" she asked.

She was hoarse, and I barely understood her. I told her who we were and why we had come to the apartment. Then I asked her to rest a minute while I called the police. Charles went to get her water, and I called 911.

She took a sip, thanked Charles, rubbed her blood-red neck, and then took a larger sip. She said she was Erica Lane, was from Wisconsin, and had recently separated from her husband. She had read about Folly Beach in a magazine and thought it would be a good place to escape her past. She had cleaned out her bank account and arrived a week ago. Her story was strikingly similar to those of the three murdered women.

"How did you run into Damian?" I asked.

She finished the glass of water and asked if she could have more. Charles nodded and took her glass to the kitchen for a refill.

She blinked a couple of times. "In college I won a couple of beauty contests. When I got married, my husband thought it was wasteful to regularly get my hair fixed. We lived on a small family farm, and most of the days we worked outside." She took a deep breath and slowly exhaled. "The first thing I wanted to do when I got here was to spoil myself—get a facial, a manicure, and a pedicure and have my hair styled." She paused. "It sounds self-centered and like I'm a spoiled brat."

"Not at all," said Charles as he returned with her water.

I smiled and said, "Go on."

She slowly sat on the side of the bed and put her arms on the mattress to steady herself. She kept looking at the entry door. I reassured her that Damian was gone. She finally continued, "I stayed the first two nights at the Tides until I found an apartment. I was wandering around town the third day here and saw Folly Curls." She shook her head. "Then I made a terrible mistake." She hesitated and then blinked. A tear rolled down her cheek. "I went in."

"And met Damian?" said Charles.

She looked at Charles and then down at the filthy, beige rug. "Yeah," she said. "He was the only one there. Said the owner was out having fun. He laughed when he said it. I don't know why. Anyway, I told him I would like to make an appointment to get my hair done. He pointed to his chair. 'Why not now?' he said. I was surprised and said okay."

"Hang on a second," interrupted Charles. "I'm going to open the door so the police can find us."

Erica took another sip, and then Charles returned. "Okay," he said.

She shook her head. "He was so nice. He wanted to know about my trip. Who I was with, where I was staying." She shook her head again. "I just put my head back, let him start working on my hair, and spilled my guts." She sighed. "What an idiot I was. What an idiot!"

I reached over and patted her knee. "No, you weren't. You didn't do anything wrong."

"Then what happened?" asked Charles.

"He seemed like such a nice guy at first. To tell you the truth, I thought he was gay."

"Why?" asked Charles.

"Nothing specific. He acted feminine, you know, like a gay beauty pageant director I had in college." She giggled. "Found out pretty quickly that I was wrong about Damian. His hand started lingering on my shoulder, even rubbed my back." She reached back and ran her left hand along her lower neck. He was also taking way too long with the haircut. I felt uncomfortable and wanted to get out of there."

I heard a siren in the distance. "How did you end up here?" I asked. We would be politely pushed out of the way once the police and EMTs arrived, and I wanted to hear her story first.

"He finished my hair and then stood between me and the door. He smiled at me. He still had the shears in his hand, and then the bastard had the nerve to ask me out." She paused. "I made up a story about having a dog in my apartment and needed to get back to feed it. He stared at me. His smile had disappeared. He said, 'Erica, Erica, you know that's a big, fat lie. If you had a dog you would have told me when you were babbling on about your life.'"

The siren reached the front of the house and stopped wailing. "Then what happened?"

"He glared at me—it was scary. He said we were going to take a ride and then go to one of the finest bars in Charleston for a drink. He still had those long scissors in his hand. He wasn't much larger than me, but I was afraid. I thought if we went to a bar, I could say I had to go to the restroom and then get help. There'd be others around. He wouldn't hurt me in front of them." She shook her head. "That's what I thought."

"Police! Anyone there?"

I recognized Cindy's voice and asked Charles to meet her. I heard a second vehicle slide to a halt in front of the house. Erica's hands had finally stopped shaking, and her breathing was steady. I heard Charles tell Cindy that everything was okay and that she might want to check the rest of the house to see if anyone was there. He was stalling. Cindy said something to the second officer who had arrived and then told Charles that an ambulance was on the way.

"What happened then?" I prompted.

"The bastard put his arm around my waist and pulled me close. The scissors were still in his other hand. He walked me out to his car and opened the passenger door and asked me to get in. I was too scared not to." She shook her head. "That was a big mistake, I know. But there wasn't anyone around. I didn't know what to do. He steered with his left hand and kept a death grip on my wrist with his other hand. He's strong."

"Did he bring you here?"

"Uh-huh."

"When?"

She hesitated. "Maybe four days ago. I'm not sure. I was in that room most of the time. No windows, so I couldn't tell if it was light or dark."

"Were you tied up all the time?"

"No, just one other time until today. But the doors were padlocked, and I couldn't get out." She looked back toward the room where she had been bound. "The first time he didn't put the rope around my neck, but he tied my hands. I must have been there for seven or eight hours—it seemed longer."

"Did he hurt you?"

"No, but I thought he was going to. He alternated between rage and telling me how much he enjoyed having me here. He said I'd really like him once I got to know him." She paused and looked at the ceiling. "He's crazy."

Cindy was on her radio in the living room. I didn't have much longer to talk to Erica.

"What happened today?" I asked.

"I'm not sure. I was in the room and heard him pull into the drive. Then he slammed the front door. I heard stuff being thrown around and him cussing."

"What was he saying?"

"I couldn't understand, but he sure was mad." She hesitated. "I was so afraid."

"What happened next?"

"He unlatched the door to my room and then flung it open. I saw a suitcase outside the door. I was standing here by the cot. He grabbed me around the waist and yanked me over to the wall and looped the rope around my wrists. Kept mumbling something about a damned green-haired old lady and a kid. I didn't know what he was talking about, but I knew something was wrong. He was jittery, all hyper-like." She closed her eyes, and her shoulders shuddered. "That's when he left the room and returned with that rope … I was so scared."

"It's okay," I said. "He's gone."

"He … put the rope around my neck and then attached the other end to that hook in the ceiling. He pulled it so tight that I had to stand on tiptoes to keep from getting strangled." She nervously rubbed her neck.

Cindy peeked around the corner. She glanced at the ropes attached to the wall and the ceiling and then over to Erica. "Are you okay?"

"I am now," she said.

Officer O'Hara was the next through the door. "We'll take it from here, Mr. Landrum," he said. I wondered if he would arrest me for breaking in.

I didn't argue, knowing that Cindy would fill me in on anything I missed. I patted Erica on the back and told her that she was in good hands. I heard an ambulance pull in front of the house and stood to leave.

Erica grabbed my hand and pulled me back. "Before he left, he looked at me struggling against the ropes. He said, 'Guess we won't have that date.' He then laughed like it was hilarious. That man's crazy."

Two EMTs rushed into the room. One knelt down beside Erica and started asking her questions. I motioned for Cindy to follow me to the living room. Officer O'Hara followed on her heels. "What happened?" asked Cindy. "How did you find her?"

I looked around the room. "Just a sec," I said, and walked into the larger bedroom and looked around. The closet door was open, and the only thing in it was an empty coat hanger. Dirty socks were in the corner, and the bed was unmade. Damian was gone.

I walked back to the living room, where Cindy looked through the drawer in a small table by the ratty couch. Officer O'Hara stood in the doorway as the EMTs checked out Erica. Charles was seated on the couch. "Cindy," I said, "you're standing in the apartment of the man who murdered the three women. If it hadn't been for Charles and me, you'd have one more body."

I then shared everything that had happened in the last couple of hours. I told her that Detective Burton was looking for Damian and that, most likely, he had gone to Damian's sister's house on James Island. I told her about the borrowed Crown Vic. O'Hara took notes. To his credit, he kept his mouth shut.

"We need to get her statement, if she's up to it, before they transport her to the hospital," said Cindy. "Hang around."

The air-conditioning was off, and the apartment was stifling. Charles and I walked out to the backyard. He asked me what Erica had said while he was out of the room, and I began to tell him. Then it computed about what she had told me Damian said about a "green-haired old lady and a kid."

I grabbed Charles's arm. "Let's get to Melinda's."

# CHAPTER 57

Her apartment was fewer than six blocks from Damian's, but the drive took forever. Traffic was heavy, and more pedestrians clogged the street than usual. I told Charles what Damian had said about the green-haired old lady and Charles said for me to smack the horn and stomp on the gas.

There were four vacant parking spaces in front of Melinda's building, so I grabbed the one closest to the front door. I didn't see a Crown Vic, but there were several hidden drives where he could have parked.

Charles was out the door before the car stopped moving. I called for him to wait. He didn't need to confront Damian alone. The corridor was eerily quiet. The only sound I heard was the squeaking floor boards as we ran to Melinda's apartment. Charles stopped in front of the door, looked at me, and shrugged. I made a knocking motion with my hand. He looked at the door and then back at me and whispered, "that's the best plan you have?"

I nodded, and he moved his cane to his left hand and knocked with his right. There was no answer. He put his ear to the door and closed his eyes. He then turned to me and shook his head. I whispered for him to knock harder. He did, but the results were no better. Finally, he smacked the door twice with his cane and said, "Aunt M., are you there?"

The door flung open. Charles lost his balance and tumbled backward. I ducked like I was afraid some projectile was headed toward my head. Melinda stood in the doorway with a two-foot-tall, iron table lamp in her hand. Its cord snaked behind her.

"Thank God," she said. "Thank God." She sat the lamp on the floor in the hall and threw her arms around Charles and buried her face in his chest.

"It's okay," he said. "It's okay."

I picked up the lamp and ushered them into the apartment. I closed and locked the door. She slowly moved away from Charles and then lowered herself onto the couch. There were now five beer cans on the table.

"He was here," she said. "Damned Damian was here."

"Like in here?" asked Charles and pointed to the floor.

She pointed to the door. "Out there. He knocked and knocked. I was so scared."

"How'd you know it was him?" I asked.

"Didn't at first. But whoever was making such a racket at the door wasn't a Bible salesman. He pounded and pounded. I had the door locked and wasn't about to open it. Damn, I was scared."

"If you didn't open the door, how'd you know it was him?" asked Charles.

"He pounded about four times, and then I heard him curse. I recognized his voice. He then left. I heard the floor creaking on his way out. And then I heard the heavy front door close."

"Aunt M., you didn't go out there?" asked Charles.

"Yes, sir, I did. I rounded up my courage and peeked out the door. The hall was empty, so I walked out to the front door. I didn't get too close to the door, but I could see out those side windows enough to see him in that big old car. He figured I wasn't home."

"Aunt M.," said Charles as he shook his head, "you shouldn't have done that."

"I'm old and dying. What could he do to me?"

Charles put his arm around Melinda and squeezed. That's when she began to cry.

I went in the kitchen and brought her a bottle of water and then sat in the only chair in the room. Charles told her about Erica and how her clue had saved the young woman's life. Melinda wiped away her tears and smiled when Charles repeated how Melinda was the only reason Erica was alive.

My pulse was on the path to normal, and I rehashed what Erica had said. I remembered her comment not only about the green-haired old lady but also about the kid. It had to be Samuel—the only person who had actually seen Damian abduct one of the women.

I stood and looked at Charles. "Call Heather and see if she's close by and could stay with Melinda while we run an errand?"

He looked at me like I was out of my gourd. "Errand?"

"Umm, yeah," I said. I didn't want to alarm Melinda more, but I had a sinking feeling about Samuel. We needed to find him. Charles didn't know what I was thinking, but my expression told him it was important. He looked at my pocket, and I took out my cell phone and handed it to him. He punched in Heather's number. She answered on the second ring and told him she was on her way home and only a block away. She'd be here in seconds.

I paced the floor until she arrived and thanked her for staying with Melinda. She said, "No problem. We'll sit around and talk about Chucky when he was a toddler." She then giggled.

To her credit, so did Melinda.

*     *     *

Traffic had thinned some, and we made it to Samuel's street in less than a minute.

"Oh no," said Charles as he pointed to the right side of the road. We were a block from Samuel's modest home. There were two houses, two vacant lots, and one other house before Samuel's. A gravel drive separated the two vacant, overgrown lots. A black Ford Crown Vic was backed into the drive. A porch light across the street was the only reason we saw the Ford. It could have belonged to anyone, but I knew better.

I slowed as we passed the car but didn't stop. Lights were on in Samuel's living room. Someone was home.

"Now what?" Charles asked as I parked on the street a half block from the house.

If Damian was as erratic and hyper as Erica had described, we didn't have time to think. He would have killed Melinda if she'd answered the door, and she hadn't seen him abduct anyone. Samuel was in grave danger, and we couldn't wait for the police.

"We'll figure it out as we go," I said and then opened the door.

Charles got out and carried his cane over his shoulder like a bat. It was one of the few times I wished I had a weapon more substantial than my arthritic hands.

"Let's call the police?" asked Charles. We were in front of Samuel's house.

"No time," I said.

Two windows faced the street. The illuminated living room was on the left. The dining room window on the right was dark. The living room window treatment was sheers rather than drapes, and I saw movement from the room. I stood to the side of the window and stooped low enough to see under the fabric.

Samuel was in the upholstered chair that faced the sofa that I'd sat on when I had visited his dad. His arms were twisted in an awkward position, apparently bound behind the chair. He sat rigid, and his head was tilted to the left. His eyes were closed; his hair was matted down with sweat.

Damian's back was to me, and he paced back and forth in front of the teen. His black wig was crooked on his head, and he brandished long, black hair shears like a sword. I couldn't hear everything he was saying, but he was yelling. I made out, "Why … open … big mouth?" and something about minding your own business. He then turned away from Samuel and yelled to no one in particular, "All I wanted … be nice to me. What was so hard about that?" Samuel opened his eyes and watched him pace. Damian had lost it.

I leaned close to Charles and whispered for him to go around back. I said that when he heard me making a ruckus, he needed to get in the house any way he could. "Don't dally," I suggested—strongly.

I gave Charles a couple of minutes to figure out how he would get in and then pounded on the front door. "Hey, Damian!" I yelled. "Come here." I pounded again and again. I hoped it was enough noise to mask Charles's breaking in, but I figured if I was any louder, everyone on the island would be stepping outside wondering who was going crazy.

The door swung open, and Damian glared at me. Who was crazier, Damian or me? The look in his glassy eyes answered that question. He looked toward the street and stepped back out of my range. "Get in here," he said through clenched teeth. He then rushed back to the chair where Samuel sat and pointed the shears at the trembling teen.

I was afraid that he would lash out and stab Samuel. I put my hands in front of me and said as calmly as I could. "It's okay, Damian. I just want to talk."

The heat slapped me in the face as I stepped into the room.

He put the shears at Samuel's throat. "Shut the door," he said.

I looked at him and reached back and pushed the door closed. I leaned against the doorframe, as far away from Damian as I could get. I needed to calm him down before he hurt Samuel. The air conditioner roared but clearly was not providing cool air. Maybe the noise from the worthless machine combined with the ruckus I had made at the front door had masked the sounds of Charles breaking in.

Damian faced me but held his arm back with the shears pointed at Samuel's face. "Talk?" he growled. "You must be kidding. Talk about what?"

I lowered my head. Hopefully he would see it as an acknowledgment of his dominance. "What did those women do? I know you're a good guy. Melinda thinks the world of you. Those women must have been terribly cruel." I nodded like I fully understood that he had to do something. "They must have been horrible."

He moved the shears from Samuel's face and pointed it at the door. "Horrible? Yeah. Came in the shop, wanted to frou-frou their hair, flirted with me. I knew they wanted me. That Gildehous lady asked me to show her the island. She wanted to check out the bars. Even had me put a red streak in her hair—what does that tell you?"

I had no clue but nodded. The more he talked the safer Samuel would be—I hoped.

"I didn't mean to kill her, you know." The knife was back in Samuel's face.

Sweat rolled down my cheeks. My polo shirt stuck to my body. "What happened?" I asked.

"We were in my sister's car. I was showing her the county park out at the end of the island. The sun was going down behind us. She turned to look at the sunset, and I put my arm around her shoulder. Just put my arm around her shoulder. That's all."

"What did she do?"

"She screamed bloody murder!" he yelled. He then turned and slashed Samuel's right ear.

# CHAPTER 58

Samuel howled and turned his head away from the blades. Blood streamed down his cheek. I took two steps forward and calculated whether I could get to the slasher before he took the shears to Samuel again.

Damian turned back toward me. He took a deep breath and then said. "I had to shut her up, didn't I?"

He appeared to have forgotten Samuel and acted like we were having a normal conversation. It was anything but.

"What happened then?"

"All I did was squeeze her neck. Wanted to stop her yelling." He looked down at the floor and at the shears in his hand. "She stopped screaming," he whispered. "She stopped."

"You buried her out where they were rebuilding that pier to the marsh?" I said.

He laughed. "Yeah. What was I supposed to do with her?" His laughter stopped as quickly as it had started. "No one was supposed to find her. Nobody even knew she was here. Nobody would miss her."

Blood continued to run down the side of Samuel's face and neck and mixed with perspiration. His breathing was labored, but his eyes were alert.

"What about Nicole Sallee?" I asked.

He shook his head. "Such a sweet girl, so smart. She was a model, you know. She loved me working on her hair—came in twice the first week she was here. I asked her out. She didn't know anyone. She said yes and wanted to see Folly from the ocean after dark. I had to steal a boat, but it was worth it." He glanced at the ceiling and then back at me. "I thought it was."

"Didn't turn out that way?" I said.

Where was Charles?

"How was I to know that she couldn't swim—how?" He waved the shears at me but quickly returned them to Samuel. He was less than a foot from my friend's throat. "All I did was reach out to kiss her. She pushed me. I had to stop her from making too much noise. We weren't that far from shore. I shoved her. Her foot caught on the seat. She hit her head on the side and she fell out." He slowly shook his head. "Maybe I should have tried harder to find her. It was dark, you know. It was pitch dark; no moon, no stars ... no Nicole." He stared at me, waiting for a sympathetic response.

I saw movement from the kitchen but didn't want to look.

"I understand," I said. "What about Corman-Eades?"

He smiled. "She was a spry one, yes, she was. Bopped into the shop telling me about all the beauty pageants she'd won, how she'd run to Folly to 'find herself,' whatever that meant. I followed her to the beach and saw her swimming out where the dolphins were feeding. She was beautiful. I waited for her to get out and asked her if she wanted to get a drink."

I was getting used to his mood swings and wasn't surprised when he gritted his teeth and then said. "She laughed at me, so I grabbed her and forced her into the car." He hesitated and quickly turned to Samuel. "And this damned kid saw me. I didn't see him, but when your buddy, Charles, started telling everyone on the island about it, I knew who it was.

Damian stepped closer to Samuel and lifted the shears over his head. He stopped and abruptly turned toward the kitchen and saw Charles. Instead of going after him, he lunged at Samuel.

I bolted toward Damian and grabbed his arm before the deadly shears slashed Samuel.

Damian reached around with his free arm and hit my head. I stumbled on Samuel's leg, and the two of us fell away from the chair. Damian pushed off the floor and tried to stand. I rammed my foot into his left ankle. He screamed and rolled away.

Charles had pushed Samuel's chair out of the way as Damian and I were rolling around on the floor. I grabbed a small wooden side table and shoved its leg into Damian's stomach. I had given it my best shot, but the nearly four-decade age difference was in his favor. He stood, picked up the shears, and started toward the door.

I was ten feet away when he reached for the knob. I used the couch to pull myself upright and then charged after him. Not one of my brighter moves.

Damian had the door half-open, but instead of running out and easily winning a footrace, he turned and pointed his shears at me. Pure evil was in his eyes. Charles saw what had happened and came at Damian from the side. All the years I had known Charles, he had never seriously explained why he carried the wooden cane. He swung it at Damian's hand, and I promised myself that I'd never ask him again.

The cane hit Damian just above his wrist. He howled, and the black shears flew in the air. He turned back toward the door and started to run. Too late. I was close enough to get my arms around his middle and slammed him against the wall. This time I had leverage. He struggled but couldn't break away. Charles grabbed his left arm and twisted it behind his back, and the two of us dragged him back into the living room and hurled him down on the couch.

Charles then untied the rope holding Samuel's hands. Samuel's legs were wobbly, but he managed to stand. I asked him to call 911, and Charles got the rope and started tying Damian's hands behind his back. I heard Samuel on the phone. He had trouble giving the address but got it right on the third try.

Damian pushed himself up from the couch, but Charles tapped him on the head and said, "Don't even think about it." The killer's wig had fallen off and was on the floor.

I took my phone from my pocket and called Detective Burton. I gave him an abbreviated version of what had occurred and directions to Samuel's. He said he'd be right over.

It seemed like the entire Folly Beach police department arrived in minutes. Cindy and Officer O'Hara were the first through the door but were closely followed by Brian Newman and an officer I didn't know. O'Hara slapped handcuffs on Damian and removed the rope that had been holding his hands. Cindy read him his rights.

I flopped down in the chair that Samuel had been held captive in. Samuel sat at the kitchen table a few feet away. The bleeding had already stopped, but I asked Brian to call the EMTs to check him out. Samuel said he'd better call his dad at the Pig. Melinda would be worried, and I handed Charles the phone so he could call her.

By now, the small living room was full. When Detective Burton arrived, he looked around and said to no one, "Am I late to the party?"

I was beginning to like the grumpy detective—almost. Burton pointed to me, Charles, and Chief Newman and asked us join Samuel in the kitchen. He told Officer O'Hara to go ahead and take Damian into custody. Cindy said she would wait in the living room for Samuel's dad and straighten things up. I looked back at the room. It looked like a tornado had stopped by for cocktails.

Samuel told the detective how he had been home watching television when someone knocked. He had talked to his friend, Jason, earlier and expected him to stop by to work on a school project. He assumed it was Jason and said, "I nearly pissed in my pants when I saw that hairdresser standing there." He said Damian pushed his way in, called Samuel a couple of names that he wasn't going to repeat, and took the scissors from his pocket and stuck them in Samuel's face.

Samuel started shaking again. Where was the ambulance? He then said that the hairdresser accused him of causing all this trouble and said he would have to eliminate the problem. "I thought he was going to stab me to death right there and then. Instead, he had a rope and tied me to the chair." He looked at Burton and then at me. "I don't know why he didn't kill me—except that he said the others were accidents and that he wasn't a cold-blooded killer."

*He would have fooled me*, I thought.

Burton asked Samuel a few more questions before Samuel's dad burst into the room, looked around the table, and asked what happened. I told him that his son had been courageous and had helped the police solve the string of murders. Samuel said that his ear had a little cut on it and an ambulance was on the way to check him out.

His dad pulled a chair up to the table and carefully removed the kitchen towel that Charles had wrapped around Samuel's head. He inspected the gash and gave a sigh of relief. I told him that if Samuel hadn't brought the abduction to my attention, we never would have caught the killer. Samuel beamed from ear to gashed ear.

# CHAPTER 59

Emergency vehicles lined the street in front of Samuel's house along with two television news vans, a radio station's small SUV, and a reporter from Charleston's daily paper driving a faded Toyota Corolla. Newspaper readership was definitely on the decline.

Chief Newman, who had a strong aversion to the media, was forced to make a statement to get them to leave. He stood in Samuel's front yard, illuminated by the artificial television lights, and told the gathering reporters that Damian Sharp, a resident of Folly Beach, had been taken into custody for the murders of the three women. He conveniently failed to mention the woman we found in Damian's apartment.

The chief was asked how the police had identified the suspect, and he said something about observant citizens and threw the rest of the credit to the police work of Detective Brad Burton. Charles and I had sneaked out of the house through the back door and stood behind the newspaper reporter. It was cooler outside than in the stifling house. The EMTs had arrived and said that Samuel's slashed ear wouldn't require a trip to the hospital. We left him with his dad and Detective Burton. When Newman credited Burton, Charles elbowed me and said, "Did you hear that?"

He knew that I hadn't gone deaf, so I simply nodded. I figured that Brian didn't want to get Samuel's involvement any more attention than was necessary, and he knew that we didn't want to have Charles's or my name mentioned. The mayor already had it in for us.

For the first time, I realized that sweat was pouring from every pore in my body. Brian was still saying something, but all I could think of was my ex-wife. Despite what everyone had told me, I knew there must have been something I could have done to save her. Perhaps saving Damian's next victim, and my young friend Samuel, could soothe some of the burning in my stomach and pain in my heart over what had happened and what could have been—perhaps. It was then that I also realized that there was little difference between the tastes of perspiration and tears as they both rolled down my cheeks.

Charles glanced over at me and then quickly turned his head away but patted my shoulder. I will be forever grateful for that kind gesture.

The chief finally told the gathering that there wouldn't be additional statements until tomorrow, so the television crews cut their lights and started packing their equipment. Other members of the media headed back to their vehicles, and the predictable gathering of locals standing around the adjacent yards and in the street scattered.

I took a couple of deep breaths, gave a silent prayer, and then asked Charles if he was ready to go. He nodded. We drove to Melinda's apartment and spent the next half hour telling her and Heather what had happened. Melinda's collection of empty beer cans had increased by one, so I wasn't sure if she would remember our conversation later. But at the moment she was clearly relieved.

Heather said, "Oh, Chucky, my hero," at least five times during our recounting of the events. All I wanted to do was go home, take a hot shower, and sleep for two days—or maybe a month.

# CHAPTER 60

A week after Damian Sharp had been officially charged with the murder of three women and the abduction of another, Folly Beach began to return to normal—or in the eyes of outsiders, return to abnormal. After all, it's not every day that the tiny island unveiled a serial killer.

Melinda, Heather, and, for some reason, Chester Carr had decided to throw a "Killer Catchin' Party" to honor Samuel, Charles, and me. To show how generous they were, they determined that the bash should take place in Landrum Gallery and be financed by the gallery's owner. Melinda was so enthusiastic about the event that I had no choice but to say, "Great idea. I'd love to pay."

Karen and Brian were the only people I had invited. I didn't know how many others the organizers had invited, but Melinda had borrowed my cell phone to access my contact list. Fortunately, I didn't have many contacts. She told me I'd better buy plenty of libations and enough food to feed thousands. I had hoped she was teasing.

Chester had lobbied to decorate the gallery with red, white, and blue streamers and two dozen balloons. Melinda reminded him that three women had been killed and didn't think that the gallery should look like a Fourth of July celebration. He conceded, and they agreed on four tasteful flower arrangements that I could pay for. I was relieved that they didn't think we needed two hot air balloons and a flyover by the Blue Angels.

Charles, Melinda, and Heather arrived a half hour before the party was to begin. Charles and Heather offered to help set everything up, and

Melinda wanted to make sure we had enough booze. Thankfully, Cal had agreed to furnish the beverages from his bar at cost provided that I didn't turn him in to the Department of Revenue and Taxation.

Melinda came through the door with a big smile, a bounce in her step, and a head unencumbered by a wig. I smiled and said, "Great look."

"It worked for Demi Moore in *G. I. Jane*," she said as she rubbed her head. "Figure it can't hurt me."

"It looks great," added Charles.

"Good," she said. "'Cause I threw out my wig. That damned Damian—excuse my language—touched it. Yuck." She frowned and just as quickly smiled. "Besides, Chester thinks it's sexy."

That silenced the rest of us.

Dude was the first nonorganizer to arrive. "This be party central?"

Charles assured the aging hippy that he was in the right place and offered him a drink.

"Why else be here?" said Dude. He then grinned and said, "Just be kiddin'. Wouldn't miss el basho."

He took a beer from Charles and then walked over to Melinda and kissed her head. "Cool," he said.

"Think it's sexy?" said Melinda.

"Boss," said Dude.

He sipped the beer and turned to me. "Hear the news?"

I've always found that to be a difficult question to answer and simply asked him what news.

"Your fave, Mayor Lally, be skedaddling."

Charles was on his way across the room to get drinks for Cindy and Larry, who had just arrived. "Whoa, what?" he said and came to an abrupt halt. He told them to get their own beer and rushed over to Dude and me.

"Lally's mom-by-law be ill. She's in big-wave state, and he's moving there."

"Resigning as mayor?" said Charles.

Dude gave a thumbs-up.

*What a coincidence*, I thought. Now we really had something to celebrate.

Cindy and Larry overheard part of Dude's butchered news flash and joined our small group. She asked where he had heard it and he said, "Here and there." She asked when he would be leaving and he said he wasn't sure but that it would be soon. I was feeling better by the minute.

Karen was next to arrive, with her dad in tow. She came over and kissed me on the cheek. Then she hugged Melinda and kissed her head. Brian nodded to each of us and then headed to the makeshift bar. Charles followed him and said, "Is it true?"

I identified with Brian when he said, "You're going to have to narrow that down a bit."

Charles impatiently shook his head. "That jackass quit?"

Brian laughed. "If you mean my boss, Folly's duly-elected mayor, yes."

Charles gave his best faux frown. "That's too bad."

"Yes, it is," replied Brian.

I could tell he was lying from ten feet away.

"He has to move to California to be close to his mother-in-law. She's terribly ill."

"That's what I heard," said Charles.

"I don't think he can help her much," said Brian. He hesitated and took a sip of white wine and shook his head. "According to his data sheet, his wife's parents are both dead."

Charles rubbed his chin. "Must have forgot."

"Probably," said Brian. He then walked over to me. "The sheriff's office sent me an e-mail and said that they have enough evidence to send Damian Sharp away for about nine lifetimes. He's not a cat, so you won't have to worry about seeing him around here again."

I sent him over to repeat that to our guest of honor, Samuel, who had arrived with his father. The chief said that it would be a pleasure.

Four people I didn't know entered, looked around the room, and then headed to the food and drinks. They were followed by Chester, who spotted Melinda and planted a big, sloppy kiss on her lips. Apparently the top of her head wasn't as appealing to him as it was to others. She smiled and gave him a lingering hug. She seemed livelier than I had ever seen her. I had no idea how much time she had with us, but we were going to make the most of each minute.

Charles inched up to me, looked over at Melinda and Chester, and whispered, "As Thomas Jefferson once said, 'The art of life is the art of avoiding pain.'"

I started to agree, but he quickly moved to the front door to greet three others who had arrived—three more strangers.

"Nice party you're throwing in your honor," said Karen. She gave me a hug and another kiss on the cheek. "Got a message for you," she continued. "Saw Detective Burton yesterday."

"Sorry to hear that," I said.

"It's my job," she said. "He huffed, puffed, cursed, and then said for me to tell you thanks."

"Will wonders never cease?" I said.

She smiled. "He also said that you're not as big a troublemaking asshole as he thought you were."

The room was packed. I counted a dozen strangers. Charles said no when I asked if he had invited them.

"Where did they come from?" I asked.

He looked around the room. "Could have something to do with the big sign my dear, sweet Aunt M. put outside."

I zigzagged my way to the front door and stepped outside. In front of the window was a brick with five helium-filled balloons attached and a handwritten sign on poster board that read: "Free booze, food, and a sexy bald chick. Come on in!"

I wiped the sweat off the back of my neck and smiled. There have been hotter summers on Folly Beach, but I'd never experienced one. I love it here.